Praise for
Furbidden Fatality

"If you like cats, dogs, and entertaining mysteries, you're going to love *Furbidden Fatality*."
—Donna Andrews, *New York Times* bestselling author of *The Falcon Always Wings Twice* and *The Gift of the Magpie*

"*Furbidden Fatality* has everything a cozy mystery reader is looking for—a clever heroine, a puzzling mystery, and a collection of adorable animals. Deborah Blake writes with passion and charm. She's a new mystery writer to watch."
—Dorothy St. James, author of *The Broken Spine*

"Clever, engaging, and filled with lovable (and furry) sidekicks, *Furbidden Fatality* is an A+ debut in what is sure to be a must-read series by Deborah Blake."
—National bestselling author Laura Bradford

"*Furbidden Fatality* has all the cute cat and dog cameos you'd want in a fun pet cozy. Animal sanctuary owner Kari Stuart teams up with a knowing kitty and several pet-loving friends to collar the culprit in this fast read."
—Jennifer J. Chow, author of *Mimi Lee Reads Between the Lines*

Catskills Pet Rescue Mysteries

FURBIDDEN FATALITY
DOGGONE DEADLY
CLAWS FOR SUSPICION

Claws for Suspicion

 A Catskills Pet Rescue Mystery

DEBORAH BLAKE

BERKLEY PRIME CRIME
New York

BERKLEY PRIME CRIME
Published by Berkley
An imprint of Penguin Random House LLC
penguinrandomhouse.com

Copyright © 2022 by Deborah Blake
Penguin Random House supports copyright. Copyright fuels creativity, encourages
diverse voices, promotes free speech, and creates a vibrant culture. Thank you for buying
an authorized edition of this book and for complying with copyright laws by not
reproducing, scanning, or distributing any part of it in any form without permission.
You are supporting writers and allowing Penguin Random House to continue to
publish books for every reader.

BERKLEY and the BERKLEY & B colophon are registered trademarks and
BERKLEY PRIME CRIME is a trademark of Penguin Random House LLC.

ISBN: 9780593201541

First Edition: May 2022

Printed in the United States of America
1   3   5   7   9   10   8   6   4   2

Book design by Gaelyn Galbreath

To all the folks at Super Heroes in Ripped Jeans, the rescue that inspired the one in this story. These folks do amazing work without the benefit of anyone who won the lottery. Founder and real-life superhero Terra Butler started this incredible organization, and single-handedly saved tiny Diana when the kitten was horribly ill while I was fostering her. Then hardly laughed at me at all when I told her that Diana was going to be a foster fail and stay with me (apparently they both already knew that, even if I didn't). My cat Harry Dresden was fostered by the lovely Kristin Kulow, and she was incredibly patient with me when I was adopting him in the midst of losing my treasured Magic and Mystic. And a special HUGE shout-out to board VP and teacher Lisa Meschutt, who fell in love with the first book in this series, gave copies to all the English teachers at the local middle school to see if they thought it was appropriate for that age, and then got a grant (big thanks to Lisa Manning!) so they could buy copies for every single fifth, sixth, seventh, and eighth grade student, using the local independent bookstore to do so. It was one of the most rewarding moments in my entire career, and I can't say how much it meant to me. If you want to support this organization, you can find them online at superheroesirj.org. Or support your own local shelters. They are all doing heroes' work.

🐈 One

Kari Stuart gazed around her kingdom and smiled with satisfaction. Okay, it wasn't really a kingdom, it was an animal shelter, and a small golden retriever puppy had just piddled in one corner of it, but still, it had come a long way from the run-down, nearly defunct rescue she had taken over a few months ago.

From her position behind her desk at the back of the room, Kari could see the usual low-keyed hum of activity you might expect on a relatively quiet Wednesday in early October. Over by the new top-of-the-line wood-framed cages against the wall, her friend and head volunteer, Sara, was showing a young couple some kittens, and trying to persuade them that two would be better than one. From the looks on their beaming faces as they cuddled a pair of little tiger-striped siblings, Kari suspected Sara had been her usual convincing self.

Of course, after more than forty years teaching English to ninth graders, the feisty seventy-two-year-old could get almost anyone to do what she suggested. Kari called Sara her secret weapon. Only the turquoise streak in Sara's gray hair hinted that she might not be the mild-mannered retiree she appeared to be. She had been working at the shelter long before Kari bought it, under its previous owner Daisy, and had stubbornly refused to give up on either the place or their few remaining misfit animals.

Bryanna Jenkins, another dedicated volunteer (now a part-time employee when not attending vet technician classes at the two-year college in neighboring Perryville), was over in the corner cleaning up after the puppy she'd been handing over to its new owners.

Bryn had dealt with plenty of puddles in her time at the shelter, so she was completely unfazed by the mess, laughing and joking with the middle-aged man and his excited teen daughter as they finished filling out the final paperwork. Bryn's dark hair was pulled back into many tiny braids, all of them tucked neatly under a rainbow colored bandana to keep them out of the way, and the bright red Serenity Sanctuary tee shirt she wore looked good with her light brown skin.

She and Kari hadn't hit it off right away when Kari took over, but these days they mostly got along just fine. The younger woman was learning to trust Kari's genuine desire to improve the shelter, and it didn't hurt that Bryn got along so well with Kari's best friend Suz, the local dog groomer.

The main room glowed in the sunlight that poured in from the large windows, showing off the gleaming new linoleum floors and the soft blue paint on the walls. The L-shaped oak desk at the front had comfortable ergonomic stools for the volunteers who greeted visitors, as well as neat stacks of applications and information sheets. On the corkboard behind the desk, there were pictures of that month's featured dogs and cats, along with helpful descriptions like, "Gets along with other dogs and cats. Rides well in cars, but could use additional leash training," along with the basics like age and breed. One adorable hound dog with innocent looking brown eyes had a note that said, "Very sweet. Will eat your shoes."

Kari couldn't help beaming with pride as she took it all in. She knew some people—most people, maybe— thought she was crazy when she used a large chunk of her unexpected lottery winnings to buy and refurbish the sanctuary. But they had desperately needed help, and she had needed to find a purpose in her life. So far at least, she had no regrets at all.

The pen she'd been using suddenly rolled across the desk and onto the floor with a sharp click, jarring Kari out of her reverie.

"Queenie," she scolded. "How many times do I have to tell you that my pens are not your toys?"

The little black kitten perched on top of the pile of bills Kari had been attempting to pay ignored this reminder with the ease of long practice, yawning up at Kari and showing off a pink tongue and sharp white teeth. At seven months old, Queen Nefertiti, or Queenie as she was known, was small for her age, and likely to stay that way, according to Kari's vet. Probably a combination of heredity and her rough start in life as a stray.

In fact, Queenie was directly responsible for Kari buying the sanctuary. When she'd rescued the kitten at about three months old, Kari had discovered to her dismay that all the local shelters were at capacity and beyond. So she'd bought the sanctuary, and ended up keeping the kitten. Or more accurately, the kitten had kept her.

Queenie more than made up for her diminutive size with her stubborn determination to get her own way, and a slightly uncanny ability to know everything that was going on. She insisted on going in to work with Kari every day, rather than staying in the farmhouse on the property with Kari's other two cats, Westley and Robert, and her mixed-breed dog Fred. The kitten was as much a fixture around the sanctuary as Tripod, the friendly three-legged yellow tom cat who had been around so long he was practically their mascot.

"I need to get to that paperwork," Kari said to Queenie, who seemed unimpressed by this fact. "Now stop throwing my pens on the floor." Kari tucked her long brown hair behind one ear as she bent down to retrieve the writing implement. Naturally, the pen had rolled well underneath the desk, so she had to duck down and stretch her arm out to reach it.

As her fingertips touched the smooth barrel, she heard the brassy sound of the bell that signaled the front door opening, and footsteps approaching her desk.

A pleasant tenor voice said, "Hi honey, I'm home."

Kari straightened up so fast she smashed her head against the bottom of the desk. For a moment she saw stars, and her eyes watered from the impact. She supposed it was too much to hope for that she had given herself a concussion and hallucinated hearing that familiar voice. Unfortunately, she didn't think she could be that lucky.

Holding her head, she sat up slowly and looked across the expanse of paperwork and wood. A tall, attractive man with professionally cut dark brown hair, twinkling brown eyes, and broad smile stood there, holding a small bouquet of red roses.

He was impeccably dressed in a black suit that had clearly been chosen to show off his still slim and muscular body, and at forty, only a few silver hairs were visible amid the brown. No doubt women thought it made him look distinguished. That and a few tiny wrinkles around his eyes were the only thing about him that had changed since Kari had last seen him, in court when their divorce was finalized four years ago.

"Hello, Charlie," she said in a calm voice. "Long time no see. You look good. Don't let the door hit you on the way out." She pointed at the front entrance with a finger she was pleased to see wasn't trembling at all. Her stomach, on the other hand, was doing somersaults, as if it had suddenly been taken over by a conga line of drunken mice.

Across the room, Sara's keen ears had clearly picked up on Kari's unaccustomed rudeness and the former teacher raised one gray eyebrow in her direction. Kari just shook her head and focused on Charlie, who didn't seem remotely put off by her less-than-enthusiastic welcome.

"Now is that any way to greet your long-lost husband?" Charlie asked cheerfully. "Look, I brought you roses." He plopped them down on the desk, scattering the neat piles of paperwork in the process. "What a cute kitten, is it yours?" He reached out one hand to pet Queenie, who hissed at him.

Out of the corner of her eye, Kari could see Sara's other eyebrow go up, since normally the kitten was friendly with everyone she met, whether human or furry.

"You tell him, Queenie," Kari said, standing up so she wouldn't get a crick in her neck. At five foot six, she was still a lot shorter than Charlie's six foot two, but at least she wasn't at quite as much of a disadvantage. "And yes, she's mine. You, on the other hand, are not, and I'd just as soon you stayed lost. So if you don't mind, please take your flowers and get out. We don't have anything to say to each other."

"Oh, you'd be surprised," Charlie said, looking around. "Nice place you've got here," he said, not sounding like he really meant it. "I couldn't believe it when I heard from someone that you'd bought an animal shelter in this backwater town in the Catskills. What on earth possessed you?"

Kari tried to figure out who he could have heard the news from. She hadn't stayed in touch with any of their mutual friends, who had mostly been his friends and business associates anyway. His mother had hated Kari from the first Thanksgiving dinner, and Kari hadn't spoken to her since she'd left. Suz was about the only friend who had been around during their three short years of marriage, and she had despised Charlie from day one and begged Kari not to marry him. It definitely hadn't been her.

Oh well, it didn't matter how he'd found out. He was here now, and unless something drastic had changed in the ensuing four years, that meant he wanted something. The sooner she discovered what it was, the sooner she could say, "**No**," and send him on his merry way.

"Believe it or not," Kari said, "I wanted to do something meaningful with my life. Helping animals who would otherwise have fallen through the cracks seemed like a good way to do that. And Lakeview is hardly a backwater town. We have a thriving tourist trade, especially now during leaf peeper season."

She picked up Queenie, who looked like she was considering attacking the roses. Kari would have been happy to let her, but not until after they'd been checked for thorns. Any gift from Charlie was likely to smell sweet and have hidden prickles. "Besides, the commute is short."

Charlie shook his head, giving her the kind of indulgent look you might bestow on a cute but not very bright child. "You always did have a soft spot for critters, didn't you?" he said with a chuckle. "Wouldn't it have been easier to just adopt a few? I doubt there's much money in the shelter business."

Queenie gave a quiet growl and Kari did her best not to do the same. Charlie had never liked animals—he thought they were messy and smelled and took too much work. One of the many reoccurring arguments during their marriage was about whether or not to have pets.

Kari never did win that one. Practically the first thing she'd done once she'd finally settled into her own apartment was to go out and get a dog. Feline brothers Westley and Robert had followed not too much after.

"Nope," she said. "No money in it at all. So if that's what you're here for, you might as well take your flowers and leave. In fact, no matter what you're here for, I can assure you, you're barking up the wrong tree." She nodded in the direction of the puppy, who was now attempting to gnaw on his new owner's sneakers. "Pun intended. I have no interest in anything you might have to say."

"Oh, I think you'll find you do," Charlie said. He perched familiarly on the corner of her desk and smiled up at her. "I have kind of a surprise for you."

Kari hated surprises. In her experience, they were very rarely of the pleasant variety.

"My birthday's not until April," she said. "And I'm

not likely to celebrate our anniversary unless it is by burning you in effigy. So whatever it is, I don't want it."

"You may want to rethink that anniversary thing," Charlie said, a hint of smugness in his smooth tone. "Because it turns out, we're still married."

Kari's legs turned to jelly and she sank into her chair before they gave out on her. This had to be a bad joke, right?

"What the heck are you talking about, Charlie Smith?" she asked. "We stood in a courtroom together and a judge accepted the terms of the divorce. Which if you'll recall, were mostly in your favor. There is no way we are still married."

"The divorce wasn't official until we both signed the paperwork and mailed it back in to the county clerk's office," Charlie said. "And apparently you never did that. I checked, and there is no record of our divorce being finalized and officially filed. We're married, all right."

Kari swallowed hard around the lump in her throat. Of course she had sent in the papers. Hadn't she? It was four years ago, and once everything was done with, she'd tried to put it as far behind her as possible.

The kitten jumped out of her arms and nudged at a piece of paper, as if trying to make a point. Over the last few months, Kari had figured out not to ignore her hints.

"Charlie," Kari said in a carefully neutral tone, "Why would you have checked on that, after all this time? Are you planning on getting remarried?" She had been his second wife, twenty-two to his thirty-three at the time, and he'd never been one to be without a woman. Or a few women.

He threw back his head and laughed, making everyone in the place turn around for a moment and stare. His laugh always seemed genuinely charming, just like the rest of him. "Not at the moment," he said. "And it turns out that's a good thing, since I'm already hitched to you."

He straightened the crease on his perfectly pressed pants. "No, I decided to double check with my lawyer when I heard your good news. Just in case I was entitled to something. He was the one who found out the paperwork had never been properly filed."

Kari's heart sank into her sneakers. She was pretty sure she knew which good news Charlie meant. "The good news about my buying the sanctuary?" she said.

"Don't be silly, Dumpling," he responded, using the nickname she'd always hated. It sounded affectionate, but it had been his subtle dig at the extra ten pounds she constantly seemed to be battling. Charlie specialized in the art of the understated put-down. Too bad it had taken her so long to figure out how damaging that was. "I mean your good luck, winning all that money in the lottery. Congratulations, by the way. Well done."

"Thank you," she said. "Ironically, I bought the ticket when I stopped at the convenience store on the way home from work so I could pick up cat litter. So if you think about it, if we had been together, I never would have won at all. And you do realize that the payout isn't nearly as big as the original prize. After taxes, and with the penalties for taking it all at once, there was only about five million dollars."

"A respectable sum," he said. "My lawyer says that since we're still legally married, I'm entitled to half."

"That's ridiculous!" Kari said, trying not to panic. "We haven't even seen each other in four years. We are supposed to be divorced. Besides, I've already sunk a lot of my winnings into buying and rehabbing the sanctuary."

"No problem," Charlie said with a smirk. "I'll take that. The land isn't worth much, but I'm sure I can do something with it."

Kari stood up again, aware that their discussion was now the center of attention from everyone in the room. She didn't have the energy to care. "Let me say this very clearly, so there is no confusion," she said through clenched teeth. "You will get this sanctuary over my dead body." She glared at him. "Or if necessary, yours."

Charlie just laughed at her and rose from his perch. "My same old feisty little Dumpling, I see. I'll go now and give you a little time to adjust to the idea. I'm sure you'll see reason in the end."

He blew her a kiss and strolled out the door, leaving both Kari's desk and her peace of mind a lot more disturbed than when he'd arrived.

⌁ Two

Sara hustled the young couple through their adoption paperwork in record time, and Bryn got the new puppy owners out through the door right behind them. As soon as the place was empty, they moved in on Kari like great white sharks on a drowning surfer.

She was sitting at her desk, staring blankly at the stack of bills while Queenie played with a stray rose petal. The rest of the flowers were upside down in the trash can next to her. Kari wished the rest of her problem could be disposed of as easily.

"Do you want to tell us what that was all about?" Sara asked, pushing a strand of turquoise hair out of her face. It was clearly a rhetorical question, much like when she had asked the same basic thing years ago after finding Kari and Suz standing in front of a locker with a screaming cheerleader locked inside. (Hey, Missy Carlyle had been making fun of Suz's height and flat chest. There was no way Kari was going to put up with that. The three days in detention were well worth it.)

"Yeah," Bryn said eagerly. "Who was that guy? He was seriously tall, dark, and handsome. Way too old for me, and you know, the wrong gender, but you should definitely hit that."

"You weren't paying attention," Sara said with a wry twist of the lips. "From what I could hear, she already did. And it didn't go well."

Bryn tilted her head, causing her braids to sway gently back and forth. A few of the tiny beads she'd woven into them clicked together musically. "Ex-boyfriend?" she said.

"Ex-husband," Kari replied, giving up on the bills and putting them to the side in a neat pile for later. "Or so I thought until five minutes ago. We may have a problem."

"I'll get coffee and those chocolate muffins Bryn picked up on her way in," Sara said decisively. "This sounds like it is too complicated to discuss hovering over your desk. And definitely an occasion that calls for chocolate."

She marched off in the direction of the small kitchenette at the back of the shelter, which now actually had a tiny section dedicated to human needs, in addition to the stacks of canned cat and dog food, bins of dry chow, and the various bowls and dishes that went with them.

"If you're just going to throw these out, can I have them?" Bryn asked, plucking the roses out of the garbage. They were only slightly battered from their abuse, a condition Kari felt a certain sympathy with. "My aunt loves roses."

Since Bryn's aunt Izzy was both the town librarian and one of Kari's favorite people, she figured that was as good a place for them as any. "Sure," Kari said, getting up and going over to the front counter. She filed the adoption paperwork under "pending" before sitting down on one of the stools.

They would phone the couple's vet and check to make sure that any animals they already owned were up to date on their shots and checkups, as well as calling whatever references they had listed. As soon as everything came back okay, another set of kittens would be going to a new, loving home. Usually this was a guaranteed hit of happiness, but Kari wasn't quite up to appreciating it at the moment.

Once the three of them had gathered around the counter, Sara fixed Kari with a piercing blue-eyed gaze. "So, are you going to explain why an ex-husband we never heard of before has suddenly shown up at the shelter, and how exactly he is going to be a problem?"

Kari sighed and took a sip of coffee. "You never heard of him because I happily left that part of my life behind me when I moved back to Lakeview. And the problem is that he says our divorce was never finalized due to some kind of technicality, and he is entitled to half of my lottery winnings."

"What?" Bryn said. Her mouth dropped open. "But, that can't be right, can it?"

Sara looked thoughtful, a crease forming between her eyebrows as she considered Kari's statement. "The first part of his claim should be pretty easy to prove. Or disprove. You must have a copy of the official divorce decree." Sara had been happily married to her husband Dave for over forty-five years, but she tended to know all sorts of random facts.

"I'm not sure I do," Kari said unhappily. "I don't remember seeing it, anyway, although that would have been four years ago. Things were a little crazy for a while after I left Charlie. I moved around from one friend's house to another for about six months, sleeping on people's couches with everything I owned packed into the back of my old Toyota."

She still thought of that car fondly, even though she'd finally given in and bought herself a newer model with her lottery winnings, one with a hatchback that was large enough to haul animals or supplies around in if necessary. It was a lovely shiny blue and she almost liked it as much as its rusty, duct-taped-together predecessor.

"How did you end up in Lakeview?" Bryn asked.

"I actually grew up here. And Suz was here," Kari said. "We've been best friends since grade school, and once I was sure Charlie wasn't going to come after me, she convinced me to move back." She shrugged. "It's ironic, really. When I graduated from high school, I couldn't wait to go to college and get out of this town. Now I can't think of anyplace I'd rather be."

Sara put down the muffin she'd been nibbling on. "What do you mean, once you were sure he wasn't going to come after you? Was he abusive? Should we be concerned?" She pulled out her cell phone as if she was going to call one of the many useful people in her speed dial—a cop, maybe, or possibly a lawyer. It wouldn't have surprised Kari if there was a hit man in there, too.

Kari waved her down. "He wasn't abusive in the conventional sense, if that's what you mean. Charlie never hit me, or did anything obviously cruel. He was just controlling, and emotionally manipulative. It wasn't so much that he wanted me back as that he didn't like losing. He only consented to the divorce after I agreed to walk away from the house and everything in it I hadn't owned before the marriage."

Both women looked indignant on her behalf, but Kari just shrugged again. "Hey, he was the one earning most of the money, and he owned the house before we got married. I wanted out a lot more than I wanted to hang on to any stuff. Most of it wasn't my style anyway. I even let him be the injured party, to salve his ego. So I didn't *really* think he'd try and find me afterward. But after three years of feeling progressively more powerless, it took me a while before I could relax and stop looking over my shoulder."

"That sounds rough," Bryn said.

"It wasn't that bad," Kari said, not quite honestly. "But it did mean that I was so focused on surviving, I didn't really think about things like paperwork. And honestly, I moved around so much, some of my mail never did catch up with me." She bit her lip. "I suppose it's possible that I missed something important."

"Well, you'll just have to look and see if you can find it," Sara said in a decisive tone. "What about your safe deposit box?"

Kari laughed so hard she startled the kitten as she was trying to get a little black paw onto a crumb of muffin. "Safe deposit box? Up until the time I won the lottery, the most valuable thing I owned was a twelve-year-old car and a sterling silver locket handed down from my grandmother. I don't have a safe deposit box. I have a file labeled 'Important Papers' stuck somewhere at the back of my secondhand metal filing cabinet, in between 'Health-care Bills' and 'Insurance.'"

Sara pursed her lips and snagged the last muffin before either of the others could grab it. "Well, I guess you'd better go look in that file then. Because if you can't find your divorce papers, we might have to consider that your ex is telling the truth. And if he is, the shelter could be in a world of trouble."

As soon as the shelter closed at five, Kari helped Bryn, Sara, and the other workers do the evening cleanup and feeding. All the cat cages had to be thoroughly wiped down and disinfected twice a day and the litter changed in the boxes. The large feline room, which housed the mature cats that weren't sick, pregnant, or nursing kittens, was cleaned every morning, but the boxes still had to be scooped, and all the food and water bowls throughout the shelter were swapped out with fresh water and food.

One of the things that had stunned Kari the most when she'd first taken over the sanctuary was how much time and effort was spent keeping everything clean and sanitary. Endless sinks full of dishes needed to be washed, and the clothes washer and dryer were in constant use since each cage and kennel had blankets or towels or cozy beds, all of which had to be changed daily. And that had been when there were only a few dogs and cats still left in residence.

Now that they were open again and taking in new animals, paid workers and volunteers alike were kept busy with the day-to-day tasks involved in running a shelter. Kari didn't know what they'd do without the people who volunteered their time to walk the dogs and socialize with the cats.

She was itching to go looking for that paperwork, but

it was important to her that she pitched in and helped out with all the jobs, no matter how dirty or tedious. She didn't want people to see her as just some woman who had gotten lucky with the lottery and bought herself an unusual hobby.

Kari's heart and soul were completely invested in the shelter, and she wanted everyone to know it. Besides, she didn't really mind the work. After working a series of dead-end jobs, even changing litter boxes was strangely fulfilling, when the cats who used those boxes were depending on her.

Finally, everything was done for the night. Everyone was tucked away where he or she belonged, except for the few original shelter cats like Tripod and One-Eyed Jack, who had lost one eye to an infection as a baby. They had the run of the place at night, with their choice of cat trees and beds in the main room.

Kari scooped up the kitten and turned off the last of the lights before hitting the switch for the alarm. There hadn't been one originally, but after some trouble back when she bought the place, she'd put in a state-of-the-art system. Frankly, she was more likely to set it off herself than anything else, but it was still reassuring to know it was there.

Dusk was falling as she made her way down the path that led to the small farmhouse that came with the sanctuary. Daisy, the previous owner, had moved out not long after Kari bought the place, and once they had both been cleared of the local dog warden's murder, had headed off to a new life out of state.

The house wasn't much to look at, with battered pine floors that tended to slant so that anything you dropped rolled into the corners, and a decorating scheme that dated back to the seventies, but after years living in a crappy apartment, it seemed like heaven to Kari. A place of her own, where she could have as many animals as she wanted and no one could tell her what to do? Bliss. Now that the major renovations on the shelter were done, she had a whole list of improvements she intended to make to the farmhouse. It had mostly been a matter of finding the time and energy to deal with it. Now, of course, there might be a bigger problem.

Kari took a moment to let Fred, a dog of dubious parentage named in honor of Mister Rogers because he (the dog, not the public television star) had a tendency to eat sweaters as a puppy, out to do his business in the yard. Then she fed him, Westley, and Robert in the kitchen, and gave Queenie her kitten food in the other room. Kari glanced longingly at the refrigerator, thinking about dinner for herself, but she was too nervous to try and eat anything until she'd taken a look for that divorce decree.

She headed straight for the old gray metal filing cabinet, yanking hard on the drawers, since they had an inclination to stick. There was nothing really official looking in the important papers folder, other than the title for her new car, and the reams of legalese that came with buying a house and the property it came on. Biting her lip, she considered that perhaps it was time to get that safe deposit box after all.

In desperation, she looked through every single file, in case the paper had gotten stuck in the wrong place accidentally. Nothing. Then she went up to the attic and dragged down a box of miscellaneous paper stuff she'd added to over the years—old birthday cards, a few letters her mother had written to her when she'd gone away to camp as a kid, interesting recipes she'd ripped out of magazines with the delusion she'd eventually try making them, silly drawings Suz used to send to cheer her up. But no divorce decree.

Drat.

Kari shoved it all back into the box in no particular order and wiped a dusty hand across her face, then pushed the box away from her with a sigh.

"Just because we didn't find it right off doesn't mean it doesn't exist," she told Queenie, as the kitten sat licking a dainty paw while supervising from the arm of the sofa. "It probably just got lost in the mail. I'm sure there's an official copy filed away somewhere, uh, official. I'll just have to find out where that is and call them."

Queenie gave a quiet meow as if in agreement, then suddenly sat up and stared at the front door, the meow transitioning into a low-pitched growl.

Kari looked from the kitten to the door. "Oh, come on," she said. "Not again." All she wanted was some dinner and a glass of wine, and a couple of hours to unwind and process the events of the day. Something told her that wasn't going to happen anytime soon.

Three

Sure enough, when she opened the door, Charlie Smith's unwelcome visage gazed back at her. Kari seriously considered slamming the door in his face until he lifted one hand, showing off the obviously expensive bottle of merlot he'd brought with him.

"Peace offering," he said with a small smile, then pulled the other hand out from behind his back to reveal a plastic takeout bag that emitted tantalizing smells. "I brought kung pao chicken, too. I hope that's still one of your favorites."

Kari was going to say something snarky, but her stomach chose that moment to growl loudly and she decided that she might as well eat the food and be snarky afterward. No point in wasting good Chinese when you haven't had dinner. Queenie, who was standing at her feet, sniffed the air and flounced away, ten percent fur and ninety percent attitude, as usual.

"I don't think your cat likes me," Charlie said, sauntering in and placing the bag on the counter. "And did you know you have a smudge of dirt across your nose?"

No doubt from going through paperwork trying to prove he belonged anywhere other than there, Kari thought to herself, rubbing at her nose. She pulled a couple of plates out of the cupboard, pretty handmade pottery from one of the shops in town, and grabbed two pairs of chopsticks out of the drawer, along with some spoons for serving and mismatched glasses for the wine.

"Have a seat," she said in a grudging tone, and pointed at the card table at the edge of the kitchen. She'd disguised it with a pretty cloth, but she had plans to replace it with a real dining set any day now. Most of the time she was perfectly happy with her old thrift store furniture, but she could just guess what it looked like to more critical eyes.

Charlie glanced around, not disguising his curiosity. The ancient farmhouse was quite a contrast to the spacious modern suburban home they'd shared together on Long Island. That residence had been outfitted with every convenience and professionally decorated within an inch of its life. It had about as much personality as a Tupperware container.

Kari's house, on the other hand, had a cast iron wood stove with a glass front so you could watch the flames, wide pine boards scuffed and darkened by time and all the feet that had trod them through the years, and beams overhead hewn from local trees long before she'd been born. She loved every rustic inch of the place, but hadn't had time to do much to it since she'd moved in, beyond having her brother Mickey repaint and fix a few things when he'd visited during the summer.

"It's, uh, quaint," Charlie said. The downstairs was

essentially one big space, so from where he sat in the dining area at the edge of the kitchen, he could see the kitchen, living room, and the door to the downstairs bathroom, which was tucked under the stairs to the second floor.

"Thank you," Kari said. "I like it. There are some improvements I plan to make, and I still need to get around to replacing the old furniture I brought with me from the apartment I lived in before this, but it suits me just fine." She handed Charlie a corkscrew for the wine and slid into her chair, serving herself some rice and fragrant kung pao before sliding the containers in his direction. If he was waiting for her to serve him, he was going to get very hungry.

Charlie poured the wine and looked down at the chopsticks next to his plate with dismay. "You know I hate using these things," he said.

"Really? I hadn't remembered," Kari said, a smile tugging at her lips. As usual, as soon as there was food on her plate, Fred magically appeared, hovering by the table in case there was a sudden need to clean up anything that might fall on the floor.

Charlie jumped as a cold nose touched his leg. "You have a dog," he said, sounding almost accusing. "I thought it was just that kitten." The kitten in question was sitting in her favorite spot on Kari's shoulder, having jumped up there when Kari took her seat. Apparently her need to supervise everything had overruled her dislike of Charlie. "And you know, it's not really sanitary to have her this close to the food."

"She's neater than you are," Kari said in a mild tone. "And I have two older cats too, Westley and Robert." She waved her chopsticks in the direction of the stairs, where the yellow cats stared down through the banister, obviously uncertain as to whether or not they wanted to brave the room with its unexpected visitor despite the temptation of food.

"Three cats and a dog," Charlie said, struggling to get a piece of chicken into his mouth and finally managing it. "You don't need an animal shelter; you're running one in your house." He shook his head. "I've never understood your fixation with pets."

"You never understood a lot of things about me, Charlie," Kari said. "That's part of why we ended up divorced."

"Except we didn't," Charlie said. He nodded in the direction of the file cabinet, still hanging open from her search, and the box of papers sitting on the sofa. "I'm assuming you looked for the official divorce decree and didn't find it. I told you, it was never filed. You can check with the county clerk's office back in Suffolk. There's no record of it."

Kari swallowed hard around a piece of food that suddenly seemed to have been turned into rock and took a swig of wine before she answered him. "It doesn't matter," she said finally. "If they can't find the correct papers, we'll just fill them out again and file them for sure. How big a deal could it be?"

A gleam lit Charlie's brown eyes, although the cunning look he was going for was undercut for a second as his next bite went flying off the ends of his chopsticks and through the air. Fred snapped it up before it could hit the floor.

"Stupid things," Charlie muttered, tossing the chopsticks down next to his plate before locking eyes with Kari across the table. "You're missing the point, Kari.

Things have changed since we originally agreed to the terms of our divorce. You won a lot of money. A *lot* of money. Enough to share."

Kari shook her head in exasperation. "Charlie, you make a very good living as a property developer and investment advisor. The last time I checked, you had plenty of money. You don't need mine."

Across the room, the two yellow cats decided the tension was too much for them and slunk back upstairs. She wished she could join them. There probably weren't too many dust bunnies under the bed. Maybe she could hide there until Charlie left town again.

Charlie's face never lost its pleasant expression, but the muscles around his eyes and mouth tightened minutely. "I wish that were true, Dumpling. But the last couple of years have been . . . challenging. My investments lost a lot of money when the stock market took its last big downturn, and some of my clients no longer have faith in me. I bought my house at the height of the property boom and it's worth less than the mortgage I've got on it. Things are a little iffy right now and I could use an infusion of cash to kick-start some new deals. Half of your winnings could make a huge difference."

Kari could feel her stomach knotting up around what little food she'd eaten. "I'm sorry to hear that, Charlie," she said. "But I told you, I already put about half of it in this property and the sanctuary. If you took the other half, I'd have nothing left. I'm not going back to living hand to mouth again, and I need the cushion in case things go wrong at the shelter."

"You don't need to worry about that," Charlie said, giving her his smoothest smile and reaching across the table to take her hand. She promptly took it back again.

She'd fallen for his charm once. There was no way she was doing it again.

"And why would that be?" she asked suspiciously. The kitten on her shoulder let out a tiny growl. Kari wasn't sure if Queenie was picking up on Kari's tension or voicing a feline opinion of her own.

"Like I said earlier, I'll just take the property." White teeth gleamed at her. "I have some great plans for the land. Stick with me, and you could even end up with more money than you started with. A lot more."

Kari clenched her jaw. "You might not have noticed, but this property is already being used for a shelter. It isn't as though I can just pick that up and put it someplace else. Even if I could, why the heck would I? I love it here."

"Here? In this run-down old house?" Charlie waved a dismissive hand around. "In this backwater town? There are more trees here than people. Ugh." He must have picked up on her growing ire because he switched gears again. "I mean, the lake is nice and all, but if you came back home with me, you would have all the luxuries you were used to. And if you are really determined to do something with animals, you could start some little rescue thing there, I'm sure."

"Come back home with you?" Kari pushed back from the table, toppling her wine glass and sending merlot cascading across the space in Charlie's direction. "What on earth are you talking about? I'm not going anywhere with you. Have you lost your mind?"

Charlie jumped up from his own seat, brushing at his pants with a napkin where a few minute drops of wine might have hit the expensive fabric. He backed up a couple of steps and narrowed his eyes. "In fact, I have not," he said calmly. "You might want to consider taking a nicer tone with me. I was fairly easy on you the first time you asked for a divorce. This time around I could make things a lot more difficult if I choose to."

"We haven't been together for years, Charlie," Kari said. "You're not entitled to any of my lottery winnings, much less half." She tossed her napkin down onto the table, mostly stemming the flow of liquid.

He gave her his shark's smile, the one he used on business rivals, opponents on the golf course, and her. The one that said, *you think you're okay, but you're swimming in* my *ocean.* "A judge might disagree with that, Kari. Fickle people, judges. You never know which way they're going to go. And legal battles can be expensive and drag on for a long, long time. Time in which you won't be able to spend any more of that money, just in case the judge decides that half of it belongs to me."

The lump in Kari's stomach seemed to double in size and weight. He wasn't wrong about either of those things. The law wasn't always fair, and if they really were still legally married, it was possible a judge might decide that since Charlie had mostly supported her during the years they were together, he was entitled to something. Even half.

She remembered one time when Suz got sued by a grooming client who had come to pick up her dog when Suz was out on a coffee run. The woman had stepped over a standing dryer on the way in, then tripped on it on her way out and broken her arm. Suz had wanted to fight the lawsuit, but her lawyer said that the judge could rule that leaving her door unlocked while she was gone was criminal carelessness, and her insurance company had insisted she settle out of court rather than risk a larger settlement. It wasn't fair, but that was that.

Kari didn't think a judge would side with Charlie, but she couldn't be sure. And clearly that was what he was counting on. She had no idea if he was right or not, but just like when they were married, she knew he wouldn't hesitate to make her miserable in order to get things his own way.

"I'll tell you what," he said, straightening his tie and glaring at Fred, who was licking wine droplets off Charlie's highly polished shoes. "I'll give you a couple of days to think things over. I'm going to be sticking around town, so we'll talk about it again soon."

Oh, swell. "I'm not giving you the sanctuary," Kari said as firmly as she could manage, in the hopes that he would take her seriously for a change. "I'm really not."

"I don't think you're going to have a choice, Dumpling," Charlie said as he went out the door. "Do try and be sensible for a change."

"Grrrrr," Kari said, grinding her teeth together. Queenie, still clinging to her spot of Kari's shoulder, leaned up and nuzzled her cheek.

"Thanks for the support, baby," Kari said, gently removing the kitten and putting her on the floor before throwing the remains of dinner into the garbage. She'd lost her appetite. Besides, she was pretty sure anything Charlie had touched had cooties. She almost threw out the wine as well, but after a moment's serious consideration, decided that would be taking a good idea just a bit too far. Instead, she cleaned up the mess from her overturned glass and refilled it. After all, alcohol killed germs. Everyone knew that.

"I can't believe that man is back and trying to take my life away from me," Kari said to the kitten. "Again. This is my worst nightmare."

Queenie meowed loudly, showing off a set of sharp fangs.

"You're right," Kari agreed, taking a long pull on her glass. "We're definitely not going to let him get away with it." She slumped down onto the couch, where the kitten jumped into her lap and curled up, purring. "I'm just not sure exactly how the heck we're going to stop him."

Kari gazed across the table of her favorite booth at the Lakeview Diner at Suz, who was glowering, and Sara, whose brow was furrowed in thought. Suz's short spiky lavender hair was standing even more on end from her running her hands through it, and her green eyes were narrowed as she no doubt plotted various ways to dispose of Kari's ex without leaving a telltale stain.

The diner was quiet, since it was early on a Thursday morning, and most of the tourists who had come to town to enjoy the changing autumn leaves hadn't wandered in yet. A quartet of elderly men played an amicable game of pinochle at one table over cooling cups of coffee, and a tired-looking trucker was tucking into a gigantic plate of eggs, home fries, and sausage at the long counter as if it were his last meal.

Scattered local folks had waved hello to Kari as she'd walked in to join her friends. Not only was she well known from the shelter and to those who had been around when she had been growing up in town, but she'd also spent a couple of years working at the diner as a waitress before she bought that fluke winning ticket. Cookie, the head waitress whose bouffant blond hair and amiable roundness fit in well with the diner's retro décor of red leatherette booths and matching stools, sometimes forgot that Kari no longer worked there and absentmindedly asked her to fetch a cup of coffee for a customer. Kari usually did it.

The air was scented with the twin aphrodisiacal aromas of coffee and frying fat, but even the plate of fluffy blueberry pancakes with extra crispy bacon in front of her couldn't lift Kari's spirits. Suz reached out and snagged a piece of bacon, crunching on it with her straight white teeth.

"You should eat that before someone else does," she commented. "You need to keep your strength up so we can kick Charlie Smith's butt into next week."

"She needs," Sara said in a stern tone familiar to three generations of students, "to get a lawyer." She took a bite of her own omelet and added less adamantly, "And to eat those pancakes before I grab one for myself. My waistline could do without it."

Suz, who was six feet tall and pretty much straight up and down, gave them both a smug look and reached out for another piece of bacon. Kari smacked her fingers with the fork in her right hand, then used it to actually pick up some food. It was too good to waste, even if her stomach was still in a knot. She hadn't gotten much sleep, either.

"I haven't had a great experience with lawyers," she said to Sara. "I'm pretty sure the one Charlie and I used for our divorce took advantage of how much I wanted out of the marriage to get Charlie a better deal."

"Wait, you and your ex used the same lawyer?" Sara's jaw dropped. "What were you thinking?"

Kari shrugged. "Charlie said that since our divorce was more or less amicable and we agreed on all the terms, it didn't make sense to spend money on two law-yers. And honestly, I didn't have much money of my own at that point, since I'd just been working part time as a secretary at Charlie's office, so it seemed like a reason-able approach."

"I told her she was an idiot," Suz said around a mouthful of waffles. "Repeatedly."

"She did," Kari agreed. "And in hindsight, she wasn't wrong. But I was worn down and desperate." She signed and drank some coffee. "Either way, I don't love the idea of dragging this whole thing into court all over again. But you're right too, and if you know of a good lawyer, I should probably at least find out how much trouble I could be in and what my options are."

Sara scrolled through her phone contacts and scrib-bled a name and number down on a napkin. "Carmen Rodriquez. She was one of my star pupils about fifteen years ago. Now she's got her own law firm—small, but she specializes in helping women. Give her a call and tell her I sent you."

"Okay," Kari said, tucking the napkin into her purse. She wasn't sure if she would actually use it. The thought of talking to another divorce lawyer made her squirm. "But I don't really know what to tell her. It's kind of embarrassing to admit I'm not even sure if I'm divorced or not."

"You're going to call the county clerk where the pa-pers should be registered, right?" Sara said.

"As soon as they open," Kari said, giving up and pushing her plate to the middle of the table so the other two could pick at it. "Maybe they'll tell me Charlie is lying, and everything is filed away just the way it's supposed to be." She tried to sound upbeat and hopeful, but her tone sounded less than convincing, even to her own ears.

"I hope so too," Suz said. "But if not, I think you should play along."

"Play along!" Kari shrieked, then lowered her voice as people turned around and stared in her direction. "Play along? Are you crazy? I don't even want to be in the same room with the man."

"I don't blame you," Suz said. "I'm not thrilled about the idea either. But since you won't let me run him over with my car, it's the only other choice. If he thinks you're not going to fight him on this, he might give you a better idea of what he is up to, and whether or not he's really going to try and get half of your winnings, or if he is just trying to put pressure on you in the hope that you'll cave and give him something smaller."

"I suppose that makes sense," Kari said reluctantly. "But he won't believe it if I suddenly cave in."

"She's not suggesting that," Sara said. "Simply go along as if you might possibly consider some kind of compromise. Keep the lines of communication open."

"But do *not* let him actually talk you into anything," Suz said with a fierce look.

"Absolutely not," Kari said.

But inside, she wasn't sure it was going to be that easy.

Four

"You're sure you can't find them?" Kari said to the very nice woman on the other end of the phone. "Maybe you should look again."

The faintest hint of a sigh wafted over the ether. "I did already check twice, Ms. Stuart. Both on the computer and in our paper files. I can't find a copy of any divorce decree with your name on it. There is an earlier decree for Charlie Smith, but you said that was from his previous wife, correct?"

"Yes," Kari said despondently. At least that one was legal, so she wasn't a bigamist. It was something, she supposed.

"Could it be under Kari Smith?" the woman, who had given her name as Maria, asked.

"It shouldn't be," Kari said. "I never changed my name when I got married. Why, did you find one for a Kari Smith?"

"Uh, no," Maria said. "Sorry. I just wondered."

"Oh," Kari said. "Drat."

"You're sure you were married in Suffolk County and still living there when you were divorced?" Maria asked. "Maybe you're calling the wrong place."

"Unfortunately, I am sure," Kari said. "But thank you for being so patient."

"There's probably some kind of reasonable explanation," Maria said helpfully. "Paperwork gets misplaced all the time."

"In both the computer *and* the paper filing cabinets?" Somehow Kari didn't think that was likely.

"Well, not usually, no," Maria said, her voice tinged with sympathy. "If we can't find it in one place, it usually turns up in the other. But I'll tell you what. I'm not the one who normally handles this stuff. The woman who does is out on vacation for a few days. Why don't you give me your phone number and I'll ask her to take a look when she gets back in. Maybe she'll be able to think of something I haven't."

Kari thanked Maria and gave her the information, although it didn't seem likely that the files would magically reappear just because someone else was searching for them. Then she ended the call and stared at the kitten glumly.

"If it turns out Charlie is right and we're still married, I'm in a load of trouble, Queenie," she said. "I guess I'd better call that lawyer Sara told me about."

Queenie reached out one black paw and patted Kari's arm, then turned and hissed in the direction of the front door.

"Oh, come on," Kari said. "You've got to be kidding me." She really wasn't ready to have another confrontation with her ex. "No, no, no."

But sure enough, there was a knock on the door and

when she opened it, there was Charlie, looking as dapper as ever and holding a flower arrangement three times larger than the one he'd brought yesterday and presented in a crystal vase.

"I thought you were going to give me some time to think about things," Kari said. "It hasn't even been twenty-four hours."

"Hello to you too, Kari," Charlie said cheerfully. "Look, I brought you more flowers. I don't want to fight. Can we just sit and talk for a few minutes?"

Kari suppressed a sigh and tried to smile back. She reminded herself of what Suz had said at breakfast about playing along. After her recent phone call, it was even more important to find out exactly what Charlie was up to.

"Why don't we sit over there?" she suggested, pointing at the picnic table they'd placed under an oak tree for the staff and volunteers to use on their breaks. "I can't talk long though, because I'm supposed to be helping with the cleaning."

She headed over to the table, the kitten prancing along at her heels, and Charlie shrugged and followed her. Maybe, she thought, he'd realize how much work she'd put into the shelter, although of course he hadn't seen it before its new coat of perfect white paint, black-trimmed windows, and all the flowers and shrubs they'd planted to make it look so inviting. Even the sign, with its fancy scrollwork letters that spelled out *Serenity Sanctuary* was new. The multicolored leaves of fall only made the place look prettier.

"Why are you helping with the cleaning?" Charlie said, completely ignoring the picturesque scene in front of them. "I thought you owned the place."

Kari rolled her eyes. "I do. I also work here. Everyone pitches in to do what's needed. Am I supposed to just sit around and watch them?" She held up one hand as he started to speak. "Never mind. It was a rhetorical question." Charlie had never been one for the dirty jobs.

"Look, Dumpling," Charlie started to say. The kitten growled at him and he started again. "Uh, Kari." He stared at Queenie, who stared right back. "You know, I don't think that cat of yours likes me."

"Really? She gets along so well with most people." Kari smothered a laugh. "You were saying?"

"Right. I don't want to fight with you," he said again. "I assume that by now you've had a chance to check with the county clerk back home and you've found out that I'm telling the truth about us still being married."

There wasn't much point in lying about it. "They told me they'd keep looking," Kari said. "But yes, for the moment it does seem that the paperwork has somehow been misplaced."

"Or not filed in the first place," Charlie said. "But maybe that will turn out to be a good thing." He gave her that smile again, the one that said *just do what I say and everything will work out just fine*. In her experience, that smile was almost always a precursor to disaster.

"I don't see how," she said. "We're supposed to be divorced. For four years. That's longer than our marriage lasted. We'll just have to do it all over again. Refile the paperwork, whatever."

"Let's not be hasty," Charlie said, nudging the huge mass of overpriced hothouse flowers in her direction as if to remind her that he could be nice when he put his mind to it. It mostly only reminded Kari that he had never really known her, but she figured this probably wasn't the time to bring that up. Personally, she'd always thought cut flowers were a waste of money. She'd much rather have something that lasted longer and used less chemicals. In her current mood, a cactus might do it.

"What are you talking about, Charlie?"

"It isn't as though our marriage was all bad," Charlie said. "We had some good times, didn't we? The wedding was beautiful."

Kari stared at him with her mouth open. "Are we remembering the same wedding?" she asked. "My father showed up halfway through the reception, got drunk, and fell into the chocolate fountain. My brother slept with not one but *two* of my bridesmaids, who then got into a fistfight outside the venue. And I'm pretty sure it rained."

Charlie smothered a laugh behind one hand. "I'd forgotten about the bridesmaids. That was actually pretty funny. Your maid of honor had to break it up by dumping a pitcher of cold water over their heads. Sally, right? Tall odd woman with bright blue hair."

"Suz," Kari said, not surprised that he hadn't bothered to remember the name of her best friend. They had never gotten along, and when Kari had gone back to visit Lakeview, Charlie had always found some work excuse as a reason not to join her. "And her hair is lavender now. She's still tall, though." And odd, but Kari liked odd, so that was kind of a selling point in her book.

Charlie rolled his eyes. "So the wedding wasn't perfect. At least the honeymoon was nice, right? Who wouldn't love Hawaii? All those gorgeous beaches and drinks with umbrellas. We had a great time."

"Hawaii was your first honeymoon, Charlie," Kari said, clenching her hands so she wouldn't scream. "You took Sylvia to the gorgeous beaches. Me you took to the freezing mountains of Gstaad." She shivered, just thinking about it. The Swiss Alps had been beautiful, but *cold*. "You said you wanted our destination to be a surprise. It definitely was."

"Hey, how was I supposed to know you didn't ski?" Charlie said indignantly. He waved one hand around to indicate the rolling hills surrounding the space where they sat. "Who grows up in the Catskills and doesn't learn how to ski? There are ski resorts everywhere up here."

"People who don't like the cold, that's who," Kari responded. "My idea of a winter sport involves hot chocolate, a book, and a nice warm fire." The kitten meowed at her and she added, "And a cat, of course." Luckily, she'd had all of those (except the cat) at the ski resort they'd stayed at, and she'd spent most of their honeymoon reading while Charlie was out skiing. And she had to admit, the food had been good. Nothing but four stars for Charlie Smith.

"Well, never mind all that," he said. "That was the past. We've both changed since then. I know I wasn't the most attentive husband, always busy making deals, but I've got some big plans now, and if they work out, I'd be sitting pretty. *We'd* be sitting pretty. We should forget about getting divorced and give it another try. Things would be different this time, you'll see. We could even take another honeymoon, any place you want. You've never been to the south of France, right?" He gave her that charming smile that used to make her heart beat faster.

Thankfully, she seemed to be immune these days.

"What big plans?" Kari asked. "I thought you said the investment business wasn't going so well."

Charlie sat up straighter, eyes sparkling with the slightly manic energy he always got when he thought he was on to something special. In the beginning, she'd been impressed and excited too, but she'd found out the hard way that when deals turned sour, so did his mood.

"Have you ever heard of glamping?" he said.

Kari blinked. "Glamping? You mean that thing where people pay ridiculous amounts of money to go 'camping' but with all kinds of luxuries and creature comforts?" Personally, she thought the whole concept was absurd. If you wanted to stay in a fancy hotel, stay in a fancy hotel. If you wanted to camp out, then roughing it was half the fun. "What on earth does any of this have to do with glamping?" Did people "glamp" in the south of France?

"When I was looking into where you were, I saw some articles about this place, and I realized it would be just perfect," Charlie said. "It's an easy drive from New York City, Long Island, and New Jersey. There's a pretty lake right down the road, a quaint little town with cute shops, and it's not so popular that everyone is already coming here. And the area is quite lovely, if you like that kind of thing." He made an involuntary face, showing what he thought of the pleasures of rural life.

"Wait a minute," Kari said. "You want to build some kind of glamping facility in Lakeview?" The other shoe was starting to drop, and she didn't think she was going to like where it landed.

"Not in Lakeview," Charlie said, waving his arm around again. "Here. On this property. Like I said, it is perfect. All we have to do is build a few luxury cabins, put up some of those fancy tents with all the amenities, turn this building into a main office and mini-store, and we're good to go."

He was practically jumping up and down on the uncomfortable wooden bench, he was so excited. "I've already got a glamping developer interested. Really interested. Like, ready to sign on the dotted line as soon as he checks the place out for himself. Only this time, I'd be a partner. You and I could share the proceeds from the sale and keep making money from the resort, too. Add in the rest of your lottery winnings, and we'd be set for life."

"Let me get this straight," Kari said through gritted teeth. "You want to turn *my* shelter into a glamorous campground for the wealthy elite?"

"Exactly!" Charlie said. "Since we're still married, this would solve all our problems."

Kari had a feeling her problems were only just beginning. The first one was figuring out how to restrain herself from killing him on the spot.

Sara tapped one finger on her chin as she pondered Kari's story. The other hand idly stroked Queenie's belly as the spoiled kitten sprawled across the counter at the front of the room. As soon as Charlie drove away, Kari had stomped inside the sanctuary to update Sara, Bryn, and Jim, who had just come in from walking the dogs and was now sitting on a stool, gaping at her with disbelief.

Jim was another one of the stalwart volunteers left over from the earlier incarnation of the sanctuary. He preferred to work in the back with the dogs, away from the public. Most people only noticed the abundant tattoos and metal band tee shirts, but over the months she'd been there, Kari had come to appreciate his unswerving loyalty and support.

"You have got to be kidding me," Jim said, absently swiping at a wet spot on his jeans, no doubt caused by Floppy, a large and affectionate mastiff they joked should have been named Drooly instead. After spending the morning taking care of the dogs, Jim gave off a faint odor made up of wet fur, cleaning liquid, and the inevitable eau de poop. Kari had been there long enough, she barely noticed it anymore.

"I wish I were," she said.

"After all the work we've put in to turn this place around, your ex-husband wants to come in and turn it into some kind of fancy pseudo-camping resort for snotty rich people who are too lazy to sleep on the ground?" Jim made a low growling noise at the back of his throat that sounded remarkably like one of his charges. "That's, that's," he sputtered to a stop, clearly lost for words.

"It's actually quite brilliant," Sara said, a thoughtful look on her face as she snuck Queenie a treat.

"What?" Jim almost fell off his stool. "You agree with him?"

"Of course not," Sara said, gazing at him reproachfully. "I've worked just as hard as anyone else to take the Serenity Sanctuary from a run-down semi-abandoned shelter to the state-of-the-art well-run rescue it is now." She took a moment to let her eyes wander around the room with its shining clean floors and bright paint job.

"But that doesn't mean he isn't onto a good idea," she

continued. "Glamping is huge right now. There's a lot of money in it, and Kari's husband was right about all the reasons why this area would work well for attracting the kind of people who would be willing to pay for that kind of vacation."

"Ex-husband," Kari corrected her automatically. "No matter what the paperwork or lack thereof says."

"You're not going to let him have the shelter, are you?" Bryn said, her brows knit together in concern.

"Of course I'm not," Kari said. The kitten chimed in with a loud meow, as if in agreement. "This place means as much to me as it does to the rest of you."

Maybe more, since before she'd been led there by finding Queenie, Kari had been floundering around, trying to find some purpose in her life. The sanctuary had given her that, plus a place to finally call home. No ex-husband showing up like the Ghost of Christmas Past was going to take that away from her.

"If I have to, I'll go to court and fight to convince a judge that he doesn't deserve a penny of my lottery winnings," she said.

"That could go either way," Sara reminded her. "If you get a judge who is hard-core family values or misogynistic—and there are plenty of those—it's always possible that he could rule that since you and Charlie are still legally married, Charlie is entitled to half your winnings. You might not have a choice."

Bryn's eyes filled and Jim slumped down even further on his stool. But Kari just shook her head. "First of all, that's a worst-case scenario. I could also get a judge who would say that since Charlie hasn't even spoken to me in four years, and we legitimately believed that the divorce had gone through, he shouldn't get anything. Or some kind of lesser sum that wouldn't be that hard to come up with."

She rapped her fist on the counter. "Either way, I'm not giving this place up. I still have about half the money in the bank. If it comes down to it, I'll give him that before I sign over the sanctuary."

Bryn's mouth dropped open. "But that would leave you with nearly nothing."

Kari shrugged, resigned to the possibility now, no matter what she'd said to Charlie. "I've had nothing before. And at least I don't have a mortgage or rent payments, and we've done most of the major improvements on the shelter already. We'd manage. But hopefully it won't come to that. I've still got to talk to that lawyer whose number Sara gave me, but I'm thinking I might try offering him a smaller amount of cash just to go away."

"That's a good plan," Sara said. But she didn't sound very happy. "I'm just concerned that Charlie has got it into his head that he can make a lot more money from this glamping scheme than any amount of cash you might be able to give him. Plus he could get control of the rest of your winnings by staying married to you. From what you've said, it doesn't sound as though he is a man who gives up easily once he decides he wants something."

Kari remembered the aggressive way he'd wooed her, taking advantage of her grief over having just lost her mother to cancer, not to mention her relative youth and inexperience. Arguing with Charlie was a little bit like having a confrontation with a bulldozer—it paid no attention to whatever was in its way, and just kept pushing and pushing until the objections were removed.

"That's true," she said, crossing her arms over her chest. "But I'm not the person I was when he married me. I don't give up so easily either." She smiled at them. "Besides, I've got all of you, and Suz, and Queenie on my side. The man hasn't got a chance."

Sara opened her mouth, either to agree or say something cautionary, when the door to the shelter opened and a woman came in. She was pretty in a kind of faded way, with too-bright lipstick and blond-streaked hair that didn't really suit her pale complexion. Her clothes looked as if they'd been bought for someone twenty years younger and ten pounds lighter, and she wobbled a bit as she walked over to the front desk, as if she were wearing heels slightly higher than what she was used to.

Sara stood up to greet her, since she was technically on front desk duty, and Jim beat a rapid retreat through the door at the back of the room that led to the canine area. He preferred not to interact with the public if at all possible. A quiet man, he was much more comfortable with dogs than he was with most people.

"Good afternoon," Sara said. "Welcome to the Serenity Sanctuary. Is there anything I can help you with?"

"I, uh, I want to adopt a dog," the woman said. She gazed around the room, her eyes narrowing as they fell on Kari. "Are you the woman who bought this place after she won the lottery?"

Kari blinked. "Yes, I am. Nice to meet you. We have lots of great dogs here right now. Were you looking for something large or small, or doesn't it matter?" She walked over to join Sara.

"What?" the woman shook her head, as if she had been thinking about something else. "Oh, uh, a smaller one I guess. Maybe a puppy? My son would really like a puppy. You're older than I thought you'd be."

Kari shot a sideways look at Sara, as if to ask if she had any idea what was going on. Sara just raised one gray eyebrow and shrugged.

"I, er, sorry?" Kari said, not sure how to respond to the comment. "Did you want a male or a female? Was there a particular breed you had in mind?" She pointed at the board behind the front desk that featured photos of all their adoptable pets. There were plenty of larger dogs, since pit bulls and some of the other big breeds tended to be harder to adopt out, but there were currently about a dozen she could safely refer to as small. Small-adjacent, anyway.

"Not that we have many purebreds, but we have a couple of beagles, and a poodle mix, plus a few puppies whose mother was a dachshund, although no one has any idea what the heck the father was." They were still cute, though. "Or you could consider a cat instead, if you didn't have your heart set on a dog. Some people find them less work, although it really depends on what you're looking for."

Interested feline faces were already peering out of some of the stacked cages that lined the far wall, maybe hoping to convince this stranger that kittens were far cuter than dogs, although other occupants still slept or played and ignored the newcomer.

"Have you run this place for long?" the woman asked.

"Not really," Kari said. "I bought it from the original founder earlier this year."

"I see," the woman said. "It seems like an awful lot to handle by yourself. Do you have a boyfriend who helps you?"

Kari was beginning to think this woman was just curious, not seriously interested in adoption. She'd had a few of
those, but that had been back in the beginning. She couldn't
think of any reason why a reporter would be sniffing
around now. Maybe the woman was simply nosy.

"We've got some really sweet dogs that are a little
older," Kari said, ignoring the last question. "They make
great additions to the household because they aren't as
high energy as puppies. All our animals are neutered
and come with their shots and up-to-date flea and tick
treatments."

"Okay," the woman said, but she didn't look very excited as Sara walked her up and down the wall of pictures.

After a few minutes, they walked back to the front
desk, Sara rolling her eyes at the other two behind the
woman's back.

"Would you like to fill out our adoption paperwork?"
Sara asked, pulling a sheet of paper out of a folder and
putting it on the desktop. "All our prospective adopters
have to be checked out before we allow them to take
home an animal. We'll need several references and the
name of your vet if you currently have other pets. Doing
it ahead of time means you're ready to go if you find a
dog you fall in love with."

"Oh, uh, no, that's okay," the woman said, her eyes
darting from Sara to Kari and back again, but not meeting the gaze of either. "I'm thinking of buying a house
in the area, but right now I'm staying in a B and B." She
stared at the huge vase of flowers on the front desk
where Kari had plopped them down after coming inside.
"Nice flowers. Somebody must really like someone who
works here."

"How were you planning to adopt a dog if you're staying in a B and B?" Bryn asked, a slight edge to her voice. Kari could tell she was irritated that the woman had wasted their time, when there was so much work to get done.

"I was just thinking of getting one later," the woman said. She made a show of looking at her watch. "Oh, dear, is that the time? I must get going. Thank you for showing me the pictures. I'll be back soon." Then she scurried out the door, still wobbling a little as she crossed the floor.

"That was odd," Kari said.

"People," Bryn said in a disgusted tone. "Some of them don't have the common sense God gave a flea." She shook her head, making the tiny beads in her braids click together. "Speaking of which, those new cats that came in as rescues yesterday definitely have fleas. I'm going to go give them a bath and then a flea treatment." She walked toward the door that led to the larger feline room and the small space just off of it where sick cats and new intakes were quarantined until they were cleared to go back with the others.

"Great," Kari said. "Angus, I mean Doctor McCoy, will be in later to check them out." She blushed a little, since she was still getting used to the idea that she and the attractive veterinarian were dating. They'd been taking things slowly, but it was clear that there was a mutual attraction there.

"How do you think he's going to react when he finds out your not-so-ex is in town?" Sara asked. "Or have you told him already?"

Kari swallowed hard. To be honest, she'd been so focused on trying to find the missing paperwork and dealing with Charlie himself, it hadn't even occurred to her that having him show up might put a serious crimp into her budding relationship with Angus. But she'd definitely have to say something to him about it.

"Crap," she said.

"So that would be a no," Sara said with a smirk. "That should be an interesting conversation."

"I'd rather give a cat a flea bath," Kari muttered. Or clean the dog yard. Or any of a number of other dirty jobs. This was definitely not a discussion she was looking forward to.

🐈 Five

_____

As it turned out, Angus had been running late and they hadn't had much time to discuss the issue. He'd just blinked and said, "Well, that's an unexpected wrinkle. Why don't we get together for lunch tomorrow and you can tell me all about it."

Now as Kari gazed across the table at his pleasant face with its open expression topped by a tousled mop of slightly shaggy red hair, she realized again how much she liked Doctor Angus McCoy. It wasn't just that he was cute (although he was) and good at his job. Mostly he was just so different from the other men she'd known, her ex especially. She'd never heard Angus raise his voice, and the only time she'd ever seen him get angry was when animals were being abused.

Now, instead of being upset or suspicious, he listened to her story of the return of the prodigal husband with a slight smile that brought out a flash of a dimple at the corner of his lips, and shook his head ruefully.

"Wow," he said. "That must have been quite the shock, having him show up like that."

They'd decided to have lunch at the diner, since neither of them had a lot of time, and the food there was both delicious and fast. In fact, she could already see Cookie hustling across the floor with a coffee pot and two cups on a tray. Today's bouffant hairdo was adorned with a jaunty yellow bow, and yellow sneakers matched her old-style waitress uniform, over which she'd tied a white half apron embroidered with her name.

"Shock is one word for it," Kari said to Angus, while trying to figure out what that delicious aroma wafting from the direction of the kitchen was. "I would have been perfectly happy to go the rest of my life without ever seeing Charlie Smith again. I can't believe he's back and trying to take the sanctuary away from me."

"That's not going to happen," Angus said in a confident tone, reaching over to give her hand a squeeze.

"How can you be so sure?" Kari said. Her own doubt was manifesting itself in tight neck muscles and an impending headache.

He smiled at her. "Because I've met you," Angus said.

Against her will, she found herself smiling back. His faith in her was refreshing. She'd never been in a relationship with someone who believed in her so much. It was a wonderful feeling. She just hoped it was justified.

"Hi, you two!" Cookie said cheerfully, putting down cups and pouring all in one smooth motion. She knew her regulars well enough to know when she didn't have to bother to ask if someone wanted coffee. "What can I get for you today?"

There were menus on the table, but Kari didn't even

look at them. "Is that Yuri's famous Reuben I'm smelling?" she asked.

The scent of warm corned beef, sauerkraut, and melting Swiss cheese was unmistakable. Yuri was one of the three short order cooks who worked at the Lakeview Diner. Originally from Russia by way of New York City, Yuri's accent was almost as thick as his sandwiches, most of which could rival the best delis in the City.

Cookie nodded, copious amounts of hair spray ensuring that not one strand fell out of place. "It is. Today he is making it with half corned beef and half pastrami, extra Russian dressing, and coleslaw on the side." She pulled an order pad out of her apron along with a pen. "I assume one of them has your name on it?"

"You'd better believe it," Kari said. All that yummy goodness between two buttered slices of rye bread hot off the grill was going to go a long way toward improving her outlook.

"I'll take the same thing," Angus said. "I've never had one, but I've heard enough rumors about their excellence that I wouldn't want to miss out."

Cookie strolled over to the kitchen to put in their order, stopping along the way to top off a few cups. But then, to Kari's surprise, she came right back.

"Please tell me he hasn't run out already," Kari said in a plaintive voice.

Cookie snorted. "What, and cause a riot before we're halfway through the Friday lunch service? No, I just thought I'd better tell you there was some guy in here earlier asking all sorts of questions about the sanctuary. Like, not about the animals, but weird stuff, like how far it was from the lake."

"Yeah," Tina, a pert brunette who worked in the county clerk's office, leaned over from the table next to them, where she had been unabashedly listening in. If you ate in the diner, you could expect your business to be everyone else's business. It was part of its charm. Sort of.

"Cookie told me about it when I came in. I'm pretty sure that same guy stopped by the office earlier and asked to look at the land survey maps. He was checking out the acreage, among other things. I couldn't exactly say no, since all those maps are open to the public. You're not planning on selling, are you?" Tina's hazel eyes were concerned. She'd been in just last week with her twelve-year-old son to look into getting a new dog to replace their elderly schnauzer who had died the year before.

"Definitely not," Kari said through clenched teeth. "Was this man tall, dark, and good looking, really well dressed, and really, really charming?"

Cookie frowned. "What? No, the guy I talked to had very light blond hair, gorgeous blue eyes, and glasses."

"Yeah, that sounds like the one I saw too," Tina said.

"Huh." Kari scratched her head, baffled. It definitely hadn't been Charlie, but then who had it been?

A sudden movement caught her eye, and she thought for a second that she saw the strange woman who had been in looking at puppies the day before, sitting at a corner booth not too far from their table. But the angle of the booth and the fact that whoever was sitting there had the huge menu held up in front of her face—it had just twitched violently, which was what had grabbed Kari's attention—meant she couldn't be sure. Anyway, the woman had said she was staying in town, so it wouldn't be that unusual for her to be at the diner at the same time Kari was, although Kari could have sworn the woman had been staring at her, before pulling the menu up in a hurry.

"Odd," she said to Angus, as Cookie hurried off to pick up their food and Tina went back to eating her own lunch. "I think that woman in the corner was at the sanctuary yesterday. There's something shifty about her."

Angus turned around briefly to look, but then they were both distracted by the arrival of their Reubens, which smelled like heaven on a plate and tasted even better.

"Oh, man," Angus moaned around a large mouthful. "This may be the best sandwich I've ever eaten." Bits of sauerkraut rained down onto his plate. Luckily, Kari had already warned him that the huge overstuffed sandwiches were incredibly messy to eat, so they both had napkins spread on their laps.

For the next fifteen minutes, they concentrated on the food, only stopping occasionally to chat about something benign or say hello to people they knew as they came into the diner. Cookie came over once to refill their coffee cups, give them the beneficent smile of a woman who knows she's in for a very large tip, and bear their compliments to the cook.

Finally, Kari put down the last ragged edge of toast with a sigh. There were a few bites left, but there was no way she was going to be able to cram them in. She was definitely going to have a small dinner tonight. If she ate at all. One of Yuri's Reubens could probably hold you for a week. On the Russian Steppes. In the middle of winter.

She was starting to feel as though maybe things weren't as bad as she'd thought they were when a familiar voice said, "You've got Thousand Island dressing on your shirt."

Oh, come on. There was the scrap of metal legs against the floor as Charlie dragged a chair up to the table and sat down uninvited.

"Hi there," he said pleasantly, holding one hand out to Angus. "I'm Charlie Smith, Kari's husband. I don't think we've met."

Angus looked down at his own hand, currently covered in the drippy remains from his own sandwich, and hurriedly wiped it off on his napkin before reaching out to shake. Kari fought back a snicker as she watched the ever meticulous Charlie hold back a wince.

"Hello," Angus said in a neutral voice. "Kari mentioned you were in town."

"And did she happen to mention that we are still married?" Charlie asked with a slight edge. "We have big plans together. I just wanted to make sure you were clear on where things stand." He placed one hand on Kari's shoulder in a proprietary manner and she shook it off.

"Oh, shut up, Charlie," she said, more than a little irritated by his nerve. "We do *not* have big plans together," she said, turning to Angus. "Charlie has big plans that are still under discussion. A discussion that will not be taking place here, now, in this diner."

She turned back to Charlie. "I'm finishing up lunch with a friend. If you want to talk to me, it can wait until I'm back at the shelter."

"We're married, Kari," Charlie said in a mild but implacable tone. "I'm thinking that means I can join you for lunch with your 'friend' if I want to." He made air quotes as he said the word.

"I'm thinking that Kari said she doesn't want you here," Angus said in response, pushing back from the table and standing up. "I suggest you respect her wishes and leave. Immediately."

"I'm sure Kari is fine with my staying," Charlie said, wrapping strong fingers a little too firmly around her wrist. "Aren't you, Dumpling?"

"Ow," Kari said. "Let go."

"You heard her," Angus said, clenching his fists. "Let her go right now."

"Or what?" Charlie said with a sneer, standing up without releasing Kari's wrist. "You're going to make me?"

"I'll be happy to," Angus said, and shoved Charlie in the chest, hard enough that he had to drop her wrist in order to keep his balance.

"Oh, you're going to be sorry you did that," Charlie said. "How about we step outside?"

Kari gritted her teeth. "Gentlemen," she said in a low voice, well aware that the entire diner was now staring in their direction. "I am not a bone for you to fight over like two stray dogs."

She pointed at the chair opposite her and said to Angus, "You. Please sit down so we can finish our lunch like civilized people." Then she turned to Charlie. "And you, go back to wherever you're staying. I will call you later and arrange a time for us to get together and talk." She lowered her voice even further. "Someplace where we have a slightly smaller audience."

Angus opened his mouth to protest but something in her expression must have told him that wasn't a good idea, and he subsided meekly into his chair instead.

Charlie smirked at him, but then shrugged, saying, "Fine, fine. Whatever. I need to go find someplace decent to eat anyway." He stared meaningfully at Kari. "I'll be waiting for your call."

He stalked out of the diner as Cookie came over and put their lunch bill on the table. "You okay, honey?" she asked, her plump face screwed up in concern. "That looked kind of unpleasant. Was that the ex?"

Kari didn't even pretend to be surprised that Cookie knew her ex-husband was in town. This entire episode would be common knowledge by evening among those who kept abreast of the local gossip.

"It was. And I'm fine, although I'm sorry about the fuss. I hope we didn't ruin anyone's lunch."

Cookie winked at her. "I expect they appreciated the free show," she said.

Kari reached into her purse and pulled out money for the sandwiches plus a large tip. Once you've worked as a waitress and found out how hard it was, you over-tipped for the rest of your life. Angus made a move toward his wallet but she shook her head at him.

"I apologize for the interruption," she said. "Up until then, it was a perfectly lovely meal."

"Not your fault," Angus said. "But you should tell that guy to get lost once and for all. From what you said, you don't have any interest in having him in your life, and he's clearly a jerk. Agreeing to talk to him is just going to encourage him."

As if anything short of a brick wall with razor wire and guard dogs could *dis*courage Charlie. Heck, even that would probably just slow him down. Kari shook her head. "I don't want to do that until I get more information on what he's up to. I need to know if he is really going to go after the sanctuary, or if he is just trying to pressure me into giving him some money."

"I don't like it," Angus said. His expression was distinctly unhappy, and that dimple she was so fond of was nowhere to be seen. "I don't trust him."

"Oh, neither do I," Kari assured him. "Not for a minute."

The woman who had been sitting in the back booth got up to leave, hustling by their table as fast as she could. Dark glasses and a large floppy hat made it hard for Kari to decide if it was the same person who had come into the shelter the day before or not.

Angus got up too, and said a little abruptly, "I should be getting back to work. Thanks for lunch. I'll talk to you soon."

Kari watched him go with a sinking feeling in her stomach that had a lot less to do with too much corned beef and a whole lot to do with the worry that her old relationship had just put a big crimp in what had been a promising new relationship.

At the end of a long afternoon spent wrestling with paperwork and then helping to do the evening feeding and cleaning, Kari was still edgy and anxious. She worked off some of that excess energy (and the huge sandwich from lunch) by taking a few of the bigger dogs out for walks on the pathways they'd created out back. Once she'd been pulled around the half mile circle by Rufus, who was half Bernese mountain dog and half Shetland pony ("Very sweet, good with children, needs additional leash training"), Kari finally figured she'd done enough for the day.

She checked in with Sara, who was finishing one last load of laundry and said she would be happy to lock up when that was done, then walked down the short pathway that led to the house. It felt good to shut the door behind her and toss her tote bag on the table next to it.

It was wonderful to come home to a place that was hers, and not a crappy apartment in a bad neighborhood, or a sterile perfect house in a good neighborhood. The little farmhouse was maybe a little worn around the edges and could use some fixing up, but it was the first place she'd ever really felt safe. There was no way on earth she was going to let Charlie Smith take that away from her.

In the meanwhile, though, she had more pressing issues. Queenie was staring at her from atop the counter, giving Kari a look that most likely translated to, "I can't believe you left me here all afternoon while you were out doing fun and interesting things without me. I will never forgive you." The other two cats and Fred the dog just tried to look pitiful and starving, Robert going so far as to nudge his empty food bowl across the floor, in case she had forgotten what it was there for.

"You, young lady, are not allowed on that counter," Kari said, scooping the black kitten up with one hand and plopping her down with the others. "What's more, you know that perfectly well. As for the rest of you, yes, I know it is dinner time. I promise, you're not going to fade away from hunger in the next five minutes."

Kari used to feel self-conscious about talking to her animals as if they were people and could understand every word that she said. Then she discovered everyone at the shelter did the same thing with the cats and dogs (and occasional ferrets and rabbits and once a gigantic snake that only Bryn had the guts to deal with) there, and Suz had a strange tendency to sing to her bunch in Spanish, so Kari figured she wasn't as odd as she'd thought.

Gourmet dry food was measured into various bowls and topped with a small amount of canned tuna deliciousness for the cats and some warm water for Fred, and the bowls put into their designated positions. The kitten and her bowl went into the other room until everyone else was done and Kari finally got to pour herself a glass of wine from the bottle of white zinfandel she'd opened earlier. It was Friday night and it had been a *long* week. She definitely deserved a drink.

She subsided onto the couch with a sign, lulled by the peaceful sounds of crunching and Westley's surprisingly loud "I'm so happy I have food" purr. Westley and his brother were both the same orange color with slightly lighter stripes, but Robert's stripes were more prominent, and Westley was substantially larger at twenty pounds to Robert's more normal fifteen. On top of being so big, Westley had extra toes on all his feet, so his paws looked gigantic. Kari thought it was adorable. Fortunately, he was a gentle giant, and never threw his weight around.

Once everyone had eaten, and Fred was snoring quietly on the braided rag rug in front of the currently unlit wood stove, Kari seriously considered making herself some dinner, too. But between her huge lunch and unsettled state of mind, she really wasn't hungry.

"I suppose I should just get this over with," she said

to Queenie, who had curled up in Kari's lap and was diligently cleaning each paw in case a crumb of food had accidentally sullied the black fur there.

The kitten gazed up at her and blinked, then licked Kari's hand before going back to her own grooming.

"Thanks," Kari said. "I appreciate the support."

She picked up her phone and punched in the numbers for Charlie's cell phone. He'd made sure she had it, of course.

Kari had kind of been hoping for voicemail, but sadly, her once-and-future-ex picked up on the first ring.

"Kari, I've been expecting your call." He made it sound as though she should have called hours ago, although they'd only just seen each other at the diner earlier that day.

"I had things to do," Kari said, purposely not mentioning that she'd chosen walking a one hundred and eighty-five pound mammoth and picking up his poop afterward over talking to her ex-husband. "Anyway, I'm calling you now. I thought we should set up some kind of meeting to discuss matters further."

"Absolutely," Charlie said. "How about dinner tomorrow. I heard there was a fairly decent French restaurant a few towns away."

Kari rolled her eyes, even though he couldn't see her. The restaurant he was talking about was overpriced and badly lit, with a chef who had more pretensions than actual skill. And it was a fifty-minute drive from Lakeview. There was no way Kari was going to spend an extra fifty minutes in a car with Charlie, one hundred and forty if you counted both directions. Having to eat dinner with him was bad enough.

"There are plenty of good restaurants right here in

town, Charlie," she said. "You like Indian, right? We have a great Indian place. But I can't do tomorrow. I already have other plans."

"With your 'friend' the veterinarian?" Charlie said in a disapproving tone.

"With Angus, Suz, and half the town," Kari said, refusing to rise to the bait. On her lap, the kitten let out a tiny growl and Kari patted her absentmindedly. "It's the yearly Oktoberfest celebration at the Lakeview Lagerhaus Brewery. It's a lot of fun and pretty much everyone goes. They serve food from local vendors, and samples of their special seasonal ales, and there is live music. Plus their beer is absolutely fabulous."

"I find that difficult to believe," Charlie said with a sniff. He was as much of a beer snob as he was a food snob. "Local microbreweries are usually highly overrated. It's probably all watery pale ales with no body or flavor."

"You're right," Kari said. "It's not your kind of thing at all. Crowds of people you don't know, music you'd hate, and beer that no one with any taste would drink. If I were you, I'd avoid it like the plague." The last thing she wanted was for him to turn up at one of her favorite events of the year and spoil her enjoyment of it. Or pick another fight with Angus, who was still meeting her there as far as she knew.

"How about Sunday night?" she said. "It's just one more day."

"You know I don't like to be kept waiting," Charlie said, then apparently caught himself and added, "Although of course you're worth it, Dumpling."

Kari had to bite back a laugh. He was still trying to be charming, and struggling not to just order her around.

It was obviously painful for him, which made it almost funny. Almost.

"Well, you could try exploring the town," she suggested. "It's really very nice. We get tons of tourists at this time of year who come specifically to see the beauty of the changing leaves. There are also some wonderful orchards with a wide variety of apples and cider, and Saturday's farmer's market features those, along with regional cheeses and fresh vegetables."

"It sounds positively charming," Charlie said in a dry voice. Although he did add, more cheerfully, "I'll bet that would be a selling point for the glamping center. Hang on while I make a note of it."

Kari hung, if by that you meant grinding your teeth and making faces at a kitten.

"Got it," Charlie said. "I knew you'd be a big help."

"Great," Kari said. *Not.* "Well, I guess I'll talk to you Sunday then."

"Hang on," Charlie said. "There's something else you can help me with."

"Oh, goodie," Kari said, taking a large sip of wine. "What is it? You want to adopt a dog? I have some very nice ones who are extremely tolerant of most people."

Charlie sputtered at her. "Don't be ridiculous, Kari. You know perfectly well I don't want to adopt a dog. No, what I need is a book."

"Excuse me?" Kari said. "You want to borrow a book? On anything in particular?"

A sigh wafted over the phone in her direction, as if he couldn't believe she was being so obtuse. "I doubt you would have anything I'd want to borrow, Dumpling. I'm just saying that if I am going to be stuck in this town for longer than I'd expected, I'm going to need something to read. Maybe a nice juicy thriller, with lots of dead bodies.

"I could download something on my phone, of course, but you know I don't like to read in digital formats because they strain my eyes. So I wondered if you could recommend a good bookstore anywhere within driving distance."

Ah. This she could do. "I can recommend one in walking distance of where you're staying, actually," Kari said, putting down her wine glass so she could pet the kitten. "There's a great bookshop right on Main Street called Paging All Readers. It's owned by my friend Paige Adams. Paige with an 'a' and an 'i.' She moved to town and opened the store about a year ago and hosts a book club I go to every month. I'm sure you'll find something you like there."

She wasn't surprised he wanted something to read— their love of books was one of the few things they'd had in common when they met. Their tastes had been vastly different, though, with her preferring light fantasies and romance and Charlie leaning toward hard science fiction with lots of space battles or grim detective novels with graphic violence and a high body count.

"What is it with this town and all the stupid cute business names?" Charlie grumbled. "It's just annoying."

"Well, you don't have to stay here, Charlie," Kari said, holding on to her dwindling patience by a thread. "No one is making you."

"Don't be so sensitive, Dumpling," Charlie said. "It's a perfectly nice town, if you like this kind of thing. But it's not as though we could possibly live here once we're back together. If you really like it so much, maybe we could get a chic little cabin and use it for weekend getaways. I'm sure I'll want to visit periodically to check on the business anyway."

Kari ground her teeth some more. This was typical Charlie—completely ignoring the fact that she had built an entire new life which she loved, and that she hadn't agreed to get back together with him. Quite the contrary.

"Charlie," she started to say, but as usual, he just plowed right over her.

"You see?" he said. "I've got it all planned out. You'll come back home and live with me. After all, when we sell off the rescue, you won't have a job, so you won't have any reason to stay here. And with that and your lottery winnings, it isn't as though you need a job anyway. You can become a lady of leisure. Maybe start a nice book club for the other wives in the neighborhood."

Kari remembered those snotty elitist women quite well, and thought she'd rather clean up Rufus's poop every hour on the hour than have a book club with them.

"I don't think so, Charlie," she said. "We can discuss all this when we have dinner on Sunday, okay? You can tell me all about your plans then. And maybe we can talk about some possible compromises."

"Compromises about what?" Charlie asked. "Oh, never mind. Fine, we'll talk on Sunday. I have things to deal with before then anyway." And also as usual, he hung up without wasting time on frivolous goodbyes.

"Swell," Kari said, but she was talking to dead air.

She tossed the phone down on the table in front of her and picked her wine glass back up.

"I don't think I like the way this is going," she said to

Queenie, who gazed up at her with wide green eyes. "I sure hope I can convince him that I have no intention of leaving either the sanctuary or Lakeview without him threatening to drag me into court." Kari sighed. "The problem is, Charlie Smith never listened to me before. I don't know how I'm going to get him to do it now."

Six

Kari spent more time getting ready to go out that evening than she usually would. For one thing, Oktoberfest was one of the highlights of Lakeview's social calendar for the year. Such as it was. For another, she wanted to make an effort to look nice for Angus. She hadn't seen him since yesterday's disastrous lunch, although they'd talked briefly this morning to arrange when they were going to meet up at the brewery.

She wasn't sure if the conversation had been more stilted than usual or if she'd just imagined it because she was worried that Charlie's presence was putting a crimp in her budding relationship with Angus. They'd only had a minute to chat, since she had been in the middle of the cage cleaning routine at the shelter, and Angus was heading out to lead a nature walk he did every other Saturday for the tourists.

It turned out that on top of being a veterinarian, Angus was something of a foraging enthusiast, so the town's tourism board had roped him into giving a guided informational walk through a section of the local woods. Kari had gone on one last month and it had turned out to be surprisingly interesting. Angus was entertaining and knowledgeable, and she had been impressed to find out how many edible plants you could discover on a short stroll outside of town.

One of the things she liked about him so much was that he didn't just have one focus in life (like making money, no matter what it took), but was in fact remarkably multifaceted. He got excited by so many different things, and that made him even more fascinating to be with.

But the nature walk meant he hadn't come in to the shelter, as he sometimes did on Saturdays, which left Kari feeling uncharacteristically nervous about their date tonight. She'd put on a little more makeup than she typically wore—a subtle rosy blush, eye shadow in graduating shades of brown and bronze, some eyeliner, and even a touch of mascara. She'd finished off with her favorite lipstick, but now she was standing in front of her closet looking at her wardrobe selection with increasing despair.

"Let's face it, Queenie," she said to the kitten, who had been supervising as she so often did. "I seriously need to go clothes shopping one of these days." Kari hated clothes shopping, which is probably why the closet didn't offer many choices for an event where most people got a little more dressed up than usual.

Her work attire mostly consisted of jeans and tee shirts, short-sleeved for the warmer weather and long-sleeved for when it got cooler. Sadly, her nonwork clothes were pretty much the same, only with fewer suspicious stains on them. There was a wide array of comfortable fleeces and sweatshirts, but nothing that jumped out as appropriate for the occasion or the temperature, which was likely to dip into the low fifties as the evening went on. When Kari left her old house with Charlie and the lifestyle that went with it, she'd left most of her fancy clothes behind, too. She might have actually set a few of them on fire in the backyard. But she wasn't admitting to that, because it would have been petty.

Queenie peered into the closet, first to the left and then to the right. She backed out, a dust ball decorating the top of her head, and meowed at Kari decisively.

"What are you up to?" Kari asked, but she yanked a few hangers toward the middle so she could see better in the direction the kitten was indicating. "Hey, I forgot that was there!" She pulled out a calf-length knit dress with a draped cowl neckline in a rich wine color that went well with her dark hair, and made the most of her (some might say overly) curvy figure. There was a matching lightweight sweater in black with gold and wine colored leaves that looked as though they were drifting down through the air. She'd bought it for a class reunion a few years ago that she'd decided not to attend after all, and then just stuck it back in the closet.

A few minutes later, she slid her feet into a pair of comfortable low-heeled boots that, along with the tights she'd put on for warmth, made for a pretty snazzy ensemble, if she did say so herself. Kari hoped that Angus would agree. Either way, she'd made the effort, and that was what mattered. (Okay, it mattered what he thought, but no modern self-actualized woman was going to say that, even to herself in the privacy of her own bedroom.)

After a brief argument with Queenie at the door, which resulted in one very disgruntled kitten staring at her from the window as Kari got into her car, Cinderella was on her way to the ball. Or in this case, the Okto-berfest.

When she got there, the Lakeview Lagerhaus looked very festive indeed. Located a couple of miles outside of town on the shore of Heron Lake, the brewery was lit up in the waning autumn dusk with rows of standing torches and strands of solar globes hung along the cast iron fences that surrounded it. A long wooden building with large windows, the brewery seemed to glow with a welcoming light. From somewhere out of the night an owl hooted, as if welcoming her to the party.

Inside, she could see some visitors taking a tour around the giant shiny silver metal vats used to make the beer, but most people were outside. Some were standing around raised circular tables on the large wooden patio, chatting and eating and meeting up with old friends. Others gathered in clumps on the lawn where there were portable fire pits with benches to sit on.

Speaking of which, Kari spotted Suz's tall, slim fig-ure waving at her from a spot across the crowded space. Kari made her way over to where Suz was standing, one arm draped around a smiling Bryn. The two of them were on their first official date, and it was hard to say which one of them was happier. Suz wore a woven tunic top in her favorite purple, with simple black cotton pants. The row of studs that ran up the edge of her left ear were amethyst tonight, and her spiky lavender hair sported gold tips for the occasion.

Bryn had on a short royal blue dress that set off her dark skin, and had matching beads woven into her tiny braids, which hung to her shoulders when they weren't pulled back for work. Three bangle bracelets clinked together on one wrist and a matching ankle bracelet set off her slim legs. Together, she and Suz were definitely eye-catching. But Kari only had eyes for the man standing next to them, his red hair tidy for a change.

"You look great," she said as she walked up to him. "I don't think I've ever seen you dressed up before." Angus was wearing a casual suit jacket over dress jeans, and a button-down shirt in the exact same blue as his eyes. She'd always thought he was cute in his regular clothes and the scrubs he wore to work, but this took him to a whole new level. Butterflies suddenly swarmed in her stomach, and she got a feeling like champagne bubbles in her veins that she'd never had before.

From the look on his face, she was having the same effect on him. Thank goodness.

"I've never seen you with your hair down, either," Angus said. "I hadn't realized it was so long." It was true, her hair nearly reached the middle of her back, but since it was always pulled back in a ponytail or a braid, it was hard to tell. "And curly." He hooked one finger into a ringlet and tugged playfully. "I like it."

He gave her a smile that sent tingles down to her toes. "You look great. Not that you don't always." He made a show of peering into the small purse she'd slung over her shoulder. "No kitten tonight?"

Kari laughed. "No, I thought Queenie should probably skip this one, although we did have quite the discussion about it. Somehow I didn't think a small cat, large crowds, and a lot of alcohol would be a good mix."

"She is underage," Angus said. "And speaking of alcohol, you don't have a beer." He lifted his own disposable cup (the brewery used biodegradable compostable cold cups), which was still nearly filled to the brim. "Do you want me to go grab you one?"

"No, you stay here," she said. "I'm going to hit the food table too, and I'll meet you all back here." She headed off to the tables at the other end of the patio, relieved to see that Angus was acting just the same as usual toward her, despite the unexpected arrival of her ex in town. Maybe things were just fine after all.

Tempting aromas arose from the long tables holding various nibbles, including many featuring local products. Kari loaded up a paper plate with a variety of hot and cold offerings, including a spicy cheese puff made with the house ale she'd had before and knew she loved. There were mushrooms stuffed with crabmeat, tiny meatballs with fancy toothpicks stuck in them, and the usual crudités. Then she moved on to the line in front of the liquid refreshments. Although the brewery offered nonalcoholic choices like cider and coffee, it was their beers that were the most popular, and for good reason.

Later they would have waiters circulating with tasting samples of the three special seasonal beers the brewmaster had created for release at the event, but for now they were pouring six of their most popular standard stock. Kari debated for a moment between a Belgian-style white and a heartier dark ale, but really, it was a foregone conclusion, since the dark ale was her favorite and perfect for a cool autumn evening outside.

"That one's my usual choice too," a voice said by her elbow.

"Izzy!" Kari said, happy to see her friend. She wore her hair in a short Afro and tended toward bright cheerful colors that matched her outgoing personality. The kids who went to her story hours at the library adored her. Kari did, too. "Did you see Bryn? She's over there with Suz and Angus." Kari tried to point without spilling her beer. "Do you want to come join us?"

"I'm actually hanging out with a couple of my friends," Izzy said. She was about twenty years older than Kari, so they didn't always run in exactly the same circles. "But I'm glad to see that you and Angus are here together. I heard there was quite the fuss at the diner yesterday. Is it true your ex-husband is in town?"

Kari scowled. "Alas, yes, although I'm hoping he will leave soon. Would you believe he is trying to get me to sign the Serenity Sanctuary property over to him? Apparently there was a glitch in our divorce and we're still technically married. He's insisting that means I owe him half my lottery winnings."

"Is that why Angus punched him?" Izzy asked, her round open face filled with good-natured curiosity.

"Oh for the love of . . . is that what they're saying?" Kari shook her head. Gossip always grew by leaps and bounds if you didn't head it off fast enough. "Angus didn't punch him. There wasn't even really a fuss. Charlie grabbed my wrist and wouldn't let go, and Angus shoved him. Not even that hard. It wasn't a big deal."

"Oh, that's good," Izzy said. She didn't quite look Kari in the eyes. "To be honest, I was a little worried when I saw him out to lunch with someone else earlier today."

Kari's heart skipped a beat and she told herself to get a grip. After all, Angus could have been to lunch with a friend, and just not mentioned it. And it wasn't as though they'd gotten to the point where they'd discussed whether or not they were seeing other people. Heck, they'd barely started seeing each other.

"Oh?" she said, in what she hoped was a casual tone. "Anyone I'd know?"

Izzy shook her head. "No one I recognized, so she's probably not local." She took a bite of what looked like a mini Brie pastry and pointed over Kari's shoulder. "She's here though. Over there by the fountain. The blonde."

Kari turned around and followed Izzy's gaze to the decorative fountain just past the edge of the patio. "Hey, I know that woman. Well, I don't *know* her, know her, but she came into the shelter the other day and said she was interested in adopting a dog. I think I saw her at the diner when I was having lunch with Angus, too."

The woman in question was standing in front of a tall, dark-haired man. Their rigid postures and the blonde's jabbing finger made it clear that whatever the two were discussing, it wasn't a casual or pleasant conversation. Unfortunately, they were too far away for Kari to overhear what they were saying. But she had to wonder about two things.

One, why was this mysterious woman arguing with Kari's ex-husband?

And two, why had Angus had lunch with her?

That's interesting," Kari said to Izzy, turning slightly away so it wouldn't look as though she was staring. "That man she's with right now is my ex-husband, Charlie."

Izzy's brown eyes widened. "You're kidding me. Whoever she is, she sure gets around."

Kari shrugged. "It might just be a coincidence. It's a small town, after all. But I don't know what he's doing here. I did my best to convince him that this wasn't his kind of event."

"Well, it *is* the biggest thing going on in the area tonight," Izzy said. "Maybe he just got curious."

Or maybe he'd come to put more pressure on her, in his usual subtle way. But Kari was determined not to let her ex ruin her evening. At least if he was talking to that blonde, whoever she was, he wasn't bothering Kari.

"I'd better get back to the gang," she said to Izzy, placing a small heap of jalapeño poppers on her plate, because she knew Angus loved them. "Are you sure you don't want to join us?"

Izzy winked at her. "I don't want to cramp Bryn's style," she said. "Nobody wants their aunt the librarian hanging around on their date."

Kari laughed and walked off, trying not to slosh beer on her good outfit. By the time she returned to where Angus, Suz, and Bryn were standing around one of the high tables, they'd been joined by Sara and her husband Dave who had retired from his job as a mathematics professor at the nearby college and spent most of his days golfing when the weather allowed, and talking about golf when it didn't. Sara had said more than once that coming in to volunteer at the sanctuary was probably saving their marriage, although it was clear from the way they looked at each other that they were still as in love as they'd always been.

Kari didn't know if she would ever find that kind of relationship with anyone, but she finally felt as though perhaps she was ready to try. As long as her past didn't keep coming back to haunt her. At least she scored some points with the poppers, which Angus pounced on as soon as she put her plate down. The brewery made them extra spicy, with some secret addition to the breading on the outside. They were a little much for her palate, but she knew from the one time they'd come here for lunch at the brewery's café that Angus really liked them.

"Ah, there you are," Charlie said, materializing from out of the growing darkness about ten minutes later. "I've been looking all over for you."

Angus gazed at him wordlessly before turning to Kari. She raised a hand before he could say anything. "No, I didn't invite him," she said, then raised an eyebrow as the blond woman walked up and stood next to Charlie.

"Hello, Charlie," Kari said in a resigned tone. "I wasn't expecting to see you here. Are you going to introduce us to your friend?"

"What?" Charlie looked startled when he swung around to find the woman right behind him. "Uh, she's not a friend. We're just staying at the same B and B and happened to bump into each other. Tanya, right?"

The woman nodded, giving Kari a tight smile. "Yes, hello. I think we met when I came to the shelter the other day. And I met Angus this morning when I took his nature walk. I don't really know anyone else in town, so I thought I'd stop by and say hello."

"I hope you enjoyed it," Angus said. "Nice to see you again."

Sure. Something about this wasn't sitting quite right with Kari, but she didn't know what it was. Too bad she hadn't brought the kitten with her—Queenie probably could have given her a hint. Like about why Angus wasn't mentioning that he'd had lunch with the woman after the nature walk. Perhaps he didn't want to embarrass the woman, who already looked uncomfortable intruding on their group. Or maybe he didn't want to try and explain it to Kari in front of other people.

Kari had just finished introducing Charlie to those who hadn't met him ("My ex-husband Charlie, he won't be staying") when a stranger walked up to the table to stand on Charlie's other side and clap him on the back in a familiar manner. The man was on the short side, with wide shoulders, neatly clipped whitish-blond hair, and very blue eyes behind black plastic rimmed glasses. He was wearing a suit that was slightly too good for the occasion paired with sneakers bearing the name of a sports legend and tied with fluorescent orange laces. Kari knew she'd never seen him before, but something about him seemed familiar.

"James!" Charlie exclaimed, exchanging a firm handshake with the other man. "Everyone, this is James Torrance. He's a business acquaintance of mine. He's an investor and developer who specializes in high-end glamping resorts." He turned to Kari. "James is interested in our property for one of his next projects. He's had a lot of success with these kinds of ventures."

Kari ground her teeth. No wonder the guy rang a bell—he must have been the one who had been asking about the shelter and checking out the acreage at the clerk's office. Could this evening get any better? "It's not *our* property, Charlie," she said in a low tone, not wanting to start a fight in front of all her friends. "It's my property."

He flapped a hand in her direction. "Yes, yes, technicalities."

His attention swung away from her toward a young waitress who was approaching their group, a large tray carefully balanced on one palm. "Oh, look. Those must be the specialty samples." He quickly emptied the cup already in his hand. "It turns out the Lakeview Lagerhaus has some really great reviews online, and the beer is much better than I expected. This should be quite interesting. I do love a good exotic ale."

Angus had apparently decided to just put up with Charlie's unwanted presence by trying to ignore him. "This year's seasonal specialties sound pretty good," he said to everyone else. "There's Merlot Medley, a Belgian ale aged in merlot wine casks that is supposed to have subtle sweet undertones, and the Lakeview Lady, a white wheat beer."

The waitress laughed as she got to them. "Hey, Dr. McCoy, it sounds like you're doing my job for me." She held the tray out in front of her and pointed at one grouping of glasses. "These are the Merlot Medleys, the ones to the right are the Lakeview Lady, and over here we have 'Orange is the New Black,' a pumpkin-spiced stout. Feel free to help yourself to one of each."

Most of them reached for the first two. Only Charlie looked excited by the stout. Kari made a face. He had always liked odd flavors, the stronger the better. Tanya took one of them too, but just sniffed it, and made a face. "Ugh. This smells like old gym socks," she said. "It must be something only a connoisseur would enjoy. I suspect my palate isn't sophisticated enough to appreciate it. Not that it matters."

She swiveled to watch the waitress walk away and then turned back around and put the small sample down next to Charlie's cup of the same thing. "I don't actually drink beer. I just took it to be polite, so you can have this."

"Luckily, I do have a sophisticated palate," Charlie said with the hint of a sneer. "So thank you."

Tanya flushed, the heightened color only barely visible in the lights scattered around the lawn, and ducked her head. "I think I'll go back to the snack table. Nice meeting all of you."

Charlie didn't even bother to say goodbye, although Kari thought he looked slightly relieved when the woman walked away. Maybe she had been bothering him at the bed-and-breakfast. Charlie usually liked it when women flirted with him because of his dark good looks, but he did prefer to be the pursuer and not the pursued.

"Mmmm," Angus said, trying the Merlot Medley. "This is great. You can actually catch a hint of the wine flavor, but it somehow doesn't clash with the beer."

"A veterinarian and a beer expert. Fabulous," Charlie said in a sarcastic tone. He reached his hand across the table and snagged one of the jalapeño poppers off the plate in front of Kari, one of his typical subtle possessive gestures. It used to drive her nuts when he ate more food off of her plate than he did his own. "You don't mind, do you, Dumpling? I didn't get a chance to grab any food yet."

"I wouldn't eat that if I were you, Charlie," Kari said.

"Oh, don't be selfish," he said, and stuffed the whole thing into his mouth, chewing rapidly. Within a few seconds, his face turned red and he started making choking noises.

"Gah! Hot!" he said, washing it down with the entire contents of his small "Orange is the New Black" sample cup. Charlie glared at Kari accusingly as he gasped for air. "You know I hate spicy things. Why didn't you stop me?" He looked for the cup Tanya had left behind, then drank that one, too.

"I did actually tell you not to eat it," Kari said, trying not to laugh. Next to her she could feel Angus's shoulders shaking with suppressed mirth, and past him Suz was out-and-out giggling. Bryn tried to shush her, but her full lips were turned up at the corners. Only James Torrance looked vaguely sympathetic.

"Want some of my Lakeview Lady?" he asked, holding out the cup. "I haven't touched it yet."

"I don't think so," Charlie said, scowling around the table at everyone else. "I'm going to need something a lot larger than those tiny samples to wash the taste of that thing out of my mouth. And some edible food, too." He turned to head to the end of the patio where both those things could be found, muttering under his breath about rude people.

"Hold up," James said, following him. "I'll come with you. When you've gotten your stuff, I have some people I want to introduce you to. Possible investors. Might as well work the party, eh?"

The tension level around the table sank by a measurable level as the company went back to being their own little group, and Sara raised her glass in the air.

"To spicy food," she said in a cheerful tone. "Savior of the evening."

They all lifted their glasses and drank, Kari as cheerfully as everyone else. She still had some unanswered questions, but if she was lucky, James would keep Charlie distracted for the rest of the evening and she could enjoy the company of her friends and the crisp autumn night.

She smiled up at Angus and offered him her plate. "Popper?" she said. "I hear they're very tasty."

He grinned back at her, white teeth gleaming in the torchlight. "I think they might be my new favorite food," he said, putting one arm around her. Kari relaxed into the warmth of his embrace and thought to herself that they might just be her favorite, too.

Seven

To Kari's immense relief, Charlie did in fact stay away for most of the rest of the Oktoberfest celebration. He cornered her right before she left to remind her that she'd promised to have dinner with him the next day, but she managed to convince him to come to brunch instead.

He'd always liked her Sunday brunches when they were married, and she thought it might put him in a more receptive frame of mind. Not to mention that he was less likely to view brunch as romantic, and revisiting her decidedly less-than-luxurious house might remind him that despite the lottery win, she wasn't exactly rolling in money.

So she popped in to the shelter briefly to check on everything, then cooked a bacon and cheddar quiche, some blueberry muffins, and added a plate of sliced up melons and strawberries while a fresh pot of coffee brewed. The kitchen smelled delicious.

The animals seemed to agree, as they all miraculously appeared from wherever they'd been napping. Fred graciously accepted a half a slice of bacon before going back to curl up on his bed in the corner of the living room, and the cats each got a tiny piece of cheese. Queenie jumped up on the table and tried to help herself to a slice of strawberry, since she had an inexplicable fondness for most fruit, but Kari scooped her up and placed her on the couch.

"Try and behave, will you please?" she scolded the kitten. "This is going to be difficult enough to get through without having to listen to lectures about how unsanitary cats are."

She'd made some effort with her appearance, more to prevent his habitual criticism than because she really cared what Charlie thought. Fresh jeans, a long-sleeved scoop-necked dark blue tee shirt with an innocuous picture of an arching oak tree under a full moon, and a pair of sneakers that had not, as far as she knew, walked through any dog poop. This was pretty much as dressy as she got at home, and it was going to have to be good enough. She pulled her hair back into a ponytail and figured she was as ready as she'd ever be.

A brisk knock on the door made her jump, but she forced herself to put a smile on her face when she went to open it.

"Hello," she said, then stopped short as she took in Charlie's appearance, which was less than usually polished. He must have stayed later at the party than she had. His eyes were bloodshot and his skin looked pale and sweaty. "Oh dear. You don't look too good. Come in and I'll get you a cup of coffee."

Charlie gave her what was supposed to be a charming

smile but ended up resembling a grimace instead. "Thanks. Could I have tea instead? My stomach is a little upset this morning. Earl Grey, if you have it."

Kari went to the cupboard as her ex sank into a seat at the table. "Sure," she said. "Although I think you'll have to settle for English Breakfast. I'm sorry you're not feeling well. Do you want to do this another time?" She hoped not—she'd just as soon get it over with, and she still wanted to get a better idea of how open he might be to taking a smaller payoff and going away for good.

"No, no, I'll be fine," he said as she handed him the mug and then poured herself some coffee. "I've been looking forward to our chat." He glanced at the food and swallowed hard. "But perhaps I'll just nibble. I'm not very hungry."

"It's not like you to drink too much," Kari said, putting a plate in front of him so he could help himself to whatever he wanted and then sitting down opposite him. Queenie immediately jumped on her lap, and Charlie didn't even make a rude comment. He really must be feeling rough.

"I didn't drink too much!" Charlie sputtered. "I know how to pace myself. There must have been something wrong with the food they served. I should have known better than to eat off a buffet at some small-town brewery."

Kari raised an eyebrow. "I ate the food and I feel fine. And I saw Bryn at the shelter this morning and she looked the same as always. If fact, I haven't heard anything about anyone else getting sick."

"Well, I've always had a delicate stomach," Charlie said. "Now, can we stop talking about my digestive system and focus on more important matters, like our plans for the future?"

"Okay," Kari said. "How about we start with the fact that I'm not giving up the shelter or this house."

"But we agreed," Charlie said, pulling out a handkerchief and patting his forehead.

"You agreed," Kari reminded him. "I told you I didn't want to move. Do you have a counteroffer?"

"Uh, a counteroffer," Charlie said slowly. "Uh, sure. A counteroffer." He stopped short, as if confused. Kari thought his eyes looked spacey. Could he be on something? That didn't seem like the Charlie she knew, but it had been a while.

"Charlie?" she said.

"Hold that thought," he said, pushing back from the table. "Where did you say the bathroom was?"

Kari pointed him in the right direction, then sat for a while until he came back, looking, if anything, more pale than before.

"I'm sorry," he said. "I think I am going to have to do this another day after all. I'm going to go back to the bed-and-breakfast and lie down." He shook his head. "Oktoberfest in Lakeview. I should have known better."

Kari walked him to the door and watched him drive off, relieved to see that he seemed well enough to stay on the road. She went back inside and wrapped up the mostly untouched food, nibbling on a muffin instead of sitting down at the table by herself.

"That was odd," she said to Queenie, absently plucking out a blueberry and giving it to the kitten, who chewed on it happily. "I hope he doesn't have a stomach bug or something." She shuddered at the thought of catching such a thing herself. They really were miserable.

"I almost feel sorry for him," she said. Queenie tilted her head, either in question at the statement or in hopes of getting another berry. "I said almost. After all, he came here to get my money, so there's only so much sympathy I can have." She picked up the kitten and kissed her on the nose. "And no more fruit for you. The last thing we need is someone else around here with an upset tummy."

A few hours later, Kari was outside raking the fallen leaves when she thought she heard the phone ringing inside the house. She ran in to grab it from the table by the door, thinking maybe it was Suz, wanting to give her the lowdown on how last night's date had gone. Kari hadn't felt comfortable asking Bryn, since they didn't have that kind of relationship, but the younger woman had seemed unusually cheerful, going so far as to sing along with the radio as she cleaned the litter boxes, so Kari had hoped that was a good sign.

But the number on the phone wasn't a familiar one. She answered it anyway, since sometimes people called her directly about animal issues, instead of calling the shelter.

"Hello," she said.

"Is this Kari Stuart?" a slightly breathless female voice asked. "Charlie Smith's wife?"

"Ex-wife," Kari said automatically. "If you're looking for him, he's staying at the Lakeside Landing Bed and Breakfast."

"Oh, yes," the woman said. "This is Charlyn Carter. I own the Lakeside Landing. I didn't realize you and Mr.

Smith were divorced. When he checked in, he told me you were his wife. Anyway, I'm sorry, but I didn't know who else to call, and I thought you should know."

"Know what?" Kari said, starting to get worried. Had Charlie had an accident on his way back from her house? She checked her watch. It was nearly three and he'd left around eleven thirty. Surely if that had been the case, someone would have called her sooner.

"I'm afraid Mr. Smith has fallen seriously ill," Charlyn said. "I had to call an ambulance to take him to the emergency room, and the EMTs said they would probably be admitting him. He really didn't look at all well."

"Oh," Kari said. "He seemed a little off when he was here earlier, but I thought it was just a bug or too much beer at the Oktoberfest last night."

"I think it was something more than that," the landlady said, her voice low and concerned. "I asked if they thought it was his heart—my late husband died of a heart attack, and it didn't come on with the symptoms you'd normally think of—but of course, they couldn't tell me anything because I'm not related to him. That's why I thought I'd better call you."

Crap. "I see," Kari said. "Well, thank you for letting me know. I appreciate it." Not really, but she couldn't tell the poor woman that by informing Kari of Charlie's condition, that put her in the position of having to decide whether or not to go to the hospital to see him, which was really the last thing she wanted to do with her day.

After she hung up the phone, having assured Charlyn that she would keep the woman posted, Kari paced back and forth in her small living room. She doubted there was really anything all that serious wrong with Charlie. He hadn't been kidding about having a delicate digestive system, and he tended to be overly dramatic whenever it acted up. He probably did have a stomach bug, or had gotten a mild case of food poisoning. But on the other hand, what if it was something bad? The only other person Charlie knew in town was his developer friend, James, and Kari couldn't see the hospital letting a business acquaintance have any information on a patient.

"Drat," she said to Queenie, who was watching her movements with avid interest. "I'm going to have to go, aren't I?"

The kitten scampered over to the front door, standing near the tote bag Kari sometimes used to take the adventurous feline on outings. To be honest, Kari would have felt a lot better if she could have brought the little black cat along, but somehow she thought the hospital personnel would frown on that.

"Not this time, baby," Kari said, tossing her phone into the bag and slinging it over her shoulder. "But I'll tell you all about it when I get home."

Two hours later, Kari was still sitting in the waiting area of the emergency room at the Perryville General Hospital, waiting for a doctor to come and brief her. It was a small facility, and apparently there was only one doctor and a physician's assistant working, and neither one had made it out yet.

The receptionist behind the sliding glass of the emergency room check-in desk had told Kari someone would come update her eventually, although after the third time she'd asked, the woman had shoved her red bifocals back up her nose, sniffed loudly, and said that there was no way of telling how long that would take. The "AND STOP ASKING" was implied.

The place looked like every emergency room Kari had ever been in. Rows of easy-to-clean plastic seats molded to fit no human bottom ever created, a few tables stacked with bedraggled magazines and children's books, and the receptionist's desk at the far end, near the door that led to the forbidden territory of the cubicles with their sliding curtains and hard metal tables.

Kari tried to concentrate on one of the ancient copies of *People Magazine* on the table next to her, but she really didn't care who was best dressed at the Oscars in 2007. Heck, she hadn't even cared in 2007. The truth was, she'd hated hospitals since her mother had died of cancer and had spent the last miserable weeks of her life in one, and Kari was beginning to think that coming here had been a bad idea.

So far she'd seen a tall gangly college-aged kid with an obviously broken arm come in with two buddies wearing fraternity sweatshirts and slightly guilty expressions— probably a dare gone wrong—and a small towheaded boy who'd somehow manage to fit a half a dozen peanuts up his nose. The beleaguered look on his mother's face and the familiar way she was greeted by the receptionist made Kari think this wasn't his first visit for something along the same lines.

The only actual emergency had been a heart-attack victim who arrived by ambulance about twenty minutes ago, its sirens blaring and making her jump in the uncomfortable hard plastic seat. The ambulance's occupant had been brought in through a rear entrance and two women who were presumably the man's wife and grown daughter had come in not long after. The wife had been hustled through to the back and the daughter, a woman in her thirties with dirty blond hair in a messy ponytail and worn jeans that smelled faintly of manure, sat on another seat across the room from Kari. She alternated between casting fearful glances toward the door her mother had disappeared through and tapping away at her phone despite the large sign on the wall above her that said, "Please turn off all cell phones."

Finally, a tall, harried-looking man with a patrician nose, medium-length dark hair, and tired eyes walked through the door from the medical section and glanced around the waiting room. He tugged his white coat into place before walking over to stand in front of Kari.

"Mrs. Smith?" he asked. "I'm Doctor Patel. I'm the doctor on duty tonight. You're here about your husband, Charles?"

Kari decided this wasn't the time to insist on the "ex." "Ms. Stuart, actually. Kari. I kept my own name." She shook her head. "Sorry, you don't care about that. Can you tell me how Charlie is doing?"

A muscle twitched in Dr. Patel's jaw, but otherwise his expression remained unreadable. "I'm very sorry, Mrs., I mean, Ms. Stuart. We did everything we could, but I'm afraid Mr. Smith didn't make it. You have my sincerest condolences."

"I, what?" Kari felt her mouth drop open and had to force herself to shut it. "He's dead? But that's not possible. He was just at my house for brunch this morning. He seemed a little under the weather and left early, but I thought he just had a stomach bug or something. Are you sure you are talking about the right man?" She glanced over at the other woman, wondering if it was possible they'd somehow gotten Charlie confused with the man who had come in by ambulance.

The doctor gave her a sympathetic look, his brown eyes warm behind round wire-rimmed glasses. "I'm afraid there is no mistake," he said. "You said he was at your house this morning? Can you tell me what symptoms he was manifesting at the time?"

Kari blinked hard, still trying to digest the news. "Uh, he had an upset stomach, I guess. He was at Oktoberfest last night and thought he'd eaten something that might have disagreed with him. I know he had to run into the bathroom before he left, so I'm guessing bowel issues as well, but I didn't ask for specifics."

"Anything else?" the doctor asked. He was typing the information into some kind of handheld device, but she wasn't sure if it was something that linked to the hospital computers, or just a way of making notes for himself. Everything medical seemed so much more computerized these days. "Slurred speech? Dizziness?"

"No, neither of those," Kari said, thinking back. "He seemed to be walking and driving fine, although right before he left he appeared to be a bit confused. I guess I figured he was just distracted by not feeling well, but I did notice his eyes looked kind of foggy. Was he running a temperature? Should I worry about catching something?"

Dr. Patel frowned slightly. "No, not at all. In fact, your husband died of acute organ failure—liver and kidney failure, to be precise. We did everything we could, but he was already past the point of saving by the time he got here."

Kari's hand flew up to cover her mouth. "Organ failure? I don't understand. Charlie was seriously ill? I mean,

I hadn't seen him in years, but he seemed just fine when he got to town a few days ago."

"You misunderstand me," Dr. Patel said. "Mr. Smith wasn't suffering from a long-term ailment. In fact, all indications are that he was poisoned."

🐈 Eight

"Poisoned?" Kari said. She had to lock her knees to keep from dropping back into her chair. "Not a heart attack? You're sure?"

Dr. Patel nodded gravely. "His symptoms were consistent with certain types of poisoning, but we won't know exactly what caused it until we get the toxicology reports back. There are a number of different things that can bring on sudden catastrophic organ failure, even in surprisingly small amounts."

He gave her a piercing look, as though scanning her for signs of any similar ailment. "Presumably if you had ingested whatever caused your husband's death, you would already be seriously ill too, but please come in immediately if you develop any unusual symptoms."

He glanced back over his shoulder at the door he'd come through. "I'm afraid I've got to get back to my other patient, but the police would like to talk to you before you leave. They're on their way and it shouldn't be long, but we have a room you can wait in. The receptionist can get you some water if you need it."

"Police?" Kari repeated. She felt as though she was missing something. "Are you saying you don't think whatever poisoned Charlie was accidental? You don't think he took some kind of overdose, do you? Because that's really not like him."

"We are required to notify the police in cases where the cause of death is undetermined," Dr. Patel explained, somewhat vaguely. "Do you know if he was on any kind of medication?"

"Not the last time I knew," Kari said. "But we hadn't seen each other in a long time, so I can't be sure."

He nodded, apparently not the least bit curious about why a husband and wife might not have seen each other for years, or possibly just too tired to care. He directed Kari to a door at the side of the waiting room, which she had assumed was a closet, or an entrance to the rest of the hospital. Once inside, the doctor left her alone and she sank into one of four wood chairs set around a square wooden table with a scratched-up surface.

There was an uncomfortable-looking brown vinyl couch at the far end, under smudged windows that overlooked a parking lot, and the room was painted a depressing institutional green. The only soft touch to the space was a floral box of tissues set in the middle of the table, no doubt for the benefit of grieving relatives.

Sadly, she couldn't even muster a tear for Charlie. She hadn't loved him in a very long time, and in the end, hadn't even liked him, but she still felt oddly shaken by the suddenness of it all.

Kari pulled out her phone and called Suz, figuring that if the woman in the waiting room could ignore the "no cell phones" sign, so could she. Although she'd try and keep it short.

"Hey," Suz said when she picked up. "Where are you? I stopped by the house a little while ago, but you weren't there. Out on another hot date with our favorite veterinarian? If so, why the heck are you calling me?"

"Very funny," Kari said, pleased that her voice sounded calm, even though her stomach was still doing flip-flops. "Actually, I'm at the hospital. And before you panic, I'm fine. It's Charlie."

"There's something wrong with Charlie?" Suz said. "Let me guess—brunch didn't go well and you finally lost your temper and hit him over the head with a cast iron frying pan." She laughed.

"I wouldn't kid about that, if I were you," Kari said, tapping the ugly scarred table with her fingers. "Charlie's dead, Suz. And they think he was poisoned."

There was silence for a minute on the other end of the phone. "You're not serious," Suz said finally. "Charlie is really dead? But you just saw him this morning, didn't you?"

"I did," Kari said. "But he wasn't feeling well and left not too long after he arrived. I guess he was already sick. I feel kind of guilty for not realizing there was something really wrong with him. The landlady at his bed-and-breakfast phoned me a few hours ago to tell me she'd had to call an ambulance for him."

"That's awful," Suz said. "I never liked the man, but still . . ." She paused for a minute. "Wait, you said he was poisoned. Do they think he ate or drank something he shouldn't have, or took something? Or do they think it wasn't an accident?"

"I'm really not sure," Kari said, biting her lip. "The

doctor who worked on him said he died of liver and kidney failure, and they weren't sure what caused it. Dr. Patel said something about a toxicology report. Meanwhile, he told me the police wanted me to wait here so they could talk to me. I'm not sure how worried I should be about that."

"Crap," Suz said with feeling. They'd both had unfortunate run-ins with the law in the last year, Kari back in June when she'd discovered the body of the local dog warden right in the sanctuary's backyard, and Suz when she'd been suspected of murdering a woman who bred Bichon Frise at a dog show in August. "Not again."

"Hopefully they just want to ask me a few routine questions," Kari said. "I'm sure it's nothing."

"Do you want me to come down there?" Suz asked.

While Kari wouldn't have minded the company, she couldn't think of anything useful Suz could do to help. At the sound of voices outside the door, she said, "No, that's okay. I'll be fine. I'll call you when I get home."

"Okay," Suz said. "But just remember I'm good for bail money if you need it."

Kari ended the call, standing up and tossing the phone into her bag just as the door opened and two uniformed officers walked in. One of them was quite familiar.

"Ms. Stuart," Sheriff Richardson said, not looking at all surprised to see her. Presumably the people at the hospital had given him her name. "We have got to stop meeting like this." He gave her a stern look. "Seriously, I mean it."

Dan Richardson was in his mid-fifties, with the stocky, muscular build of an ex-jock gone slightly soft with age and a desk job. His brown hair was always neatly trimmed, with only the beginnings of silver starting to show, and his gray eyes missed nothing. The younger man who trailed after him into the room had a buzz cut and broad shoulders, but was otherwise unremarkable.

"This is Deputy Carmichael," the sheriff said. "He's going to be taking some notes on our conversation, if you don't mind." He paused and cleared his throat. "Also, I'm sorry for your loss. Shall we take a seat?" He gestured toward the table.

Kari sat down, wishing she had taken the doctor up on his offer of a glass of water. Her mouth was suddenly very dry.

"It wasn't really a loss," she explained, hoping she didn't sound too callous. "I hadn't seen Charlie in four years before he showed up in town last Wednesday, and to be honest, I would have been happy to go the rest of my life without seeing him again. The divorce was reasonably amicable, but we hadn't stayed friends afterward."

"Yes, the divorce," Richardson said. "Let's start with that. There seems to be some confusion. Mr. Smith had apparently been referring to you as his wife, and yet you say the two of you were divorced. Which is it?"

Kari sighed. "Both? The reason Charlie came here was to tell me that he had discovered that our divorce papers had never been officially completed, which he said meant we were still married. As far as I was concerned, we were divorced, but there is some possibility that in the eyes of the legal system, he was right."

Richardson raised one bushy eyebrow. "It seems odd

that he would show up out of nowhere after all this time. Did he give a reason for doing so?"

Kari barely restrained herself from rolling her eyes. She had a strong suspicion that the sheriff already knew the answer to that question. Not only was it a small town—and he ate at the diner, which was gossip central—but he was familiar enough with her situation to be able to guess at the motive. Was he trying to trap her into telling him a lie? If so, she wasn't going to fall for it.

"Money," she said in a flat tone. "Charlie found out about my lottery win somehow, checked into the divorce paperwork, found I hadn't filed mine correctly, and came here to demand half of my winnings. Although when I told him I'd already spent a lot of it on the shelter, he told me he would take that instead. Apparently he'd made plans for the land before he even got here."

"The Serenity Sanctuary? That's pretty important to you, isn't it?" the sheriff asked. "I can't image you were too happy he was trying to take it away from you."

Subtle. "No, I wasn't. But we were still discussing things, and I had every reason to believe we could come to some kind of agreement," Kari said. "Besides which, I am still not convinced he was right about us not being divorced. I'm waiting for a call from the office where the paperwork was supposed to be filed, in case it has turned up."

"I'd like the number of that office," the sheriff said. He flipped through some notes in his ever-present note-pad. "I understand from the doctor that you told him you saw Mr. Smith earlier today? Is that correct?"

Kari clenched her fists under the table. "Yes. He was supposed to have brunch with me so we could talk about all of this. But he wasn't feeling well when he got to my house, and he only stayed a few minutes."

"You're sure he was already ill before he got there?" Richardson's gray eyes seemed to drill into hers. "Not after he ate whatever it was you served him?"

"He barely had a bite," Kari said. "And yes I'm sure. Besides, I was going to eat all the same foods. I would hardly poison my own quiche. There was bacon in it, for goodness sake."

The sheriff made a noncommittal sound, and scratched down another note, despite his deputy frantically typing into his phone, probably making his own notes. "I made a few calls on my way over here, and it seems as though you spent some time with your husband last night as well."

"EX-husband," Kari said.

"Well he certainly is now," Carmichael muttered under his breath. He gave her a suspicious look he'd probably been practicing in the mirror since he went to the police academy.

Richardson ignored him. "About that," he said. "I find it a little odd that you never mentioned Mr. Smith before he showed up in town."

Kari cocked her head. "And do you go around talking about all your exes, Sheriff?"

He grunted. "I don't have all that many, but no, I do not."

"There you go," Kari said. "As far as I was concerned, he was ancient history. When I came back to Lakeview, I was determined to put the past behind me and move forward. So, no, it isn't odd I never mentioned him."

"Mmm," the sheriff said. "And yet you were together at the Oktoberfest celebration last night."

"We most definitely were *not* together," Kari said, shaking her head. "I was there with Angus McCoy, Suz and Bryn, and Sara Hanover and her husband, Dave. Charlie just muscled his way in to our group, the way he always did." She gave Richardson a crooked smile. "If you don't believe me, I'm sure Sara would be happy to confirm it." She took out her phone. "I can call her if you like."

Richardson waved a hand at her. "No, no, that won't be necessary. We don't need to bother Mrs. Hanover on a Sunday." He'd had a son in Sara's class and, Kari suspected, found her just as intimidating as every other parent and student who had dealt with her. "I take it that Mr. Smith seemed to be in perfect health when you saw him last night?"

Kari nodded.

"Did he eat anything suspicious that you noticed?" Richardson asked.

"The only thing I saw him eat was a jalapeño popper," Kari said. "Which he swiped off my plate and then nearly choked on because it was so spicy. But I can't imagine that was what made him sick. Angus ate at least three of them from the same plate and as far as I know, he's just fine." She had talked to the vet first thing in the morning when he came by the shelter to check on a sick kitten, so she wasn't too worried. About him, anyway. Her own position was starting to look a bit precarious.

She crossed her arms and stared at Richardson. "Sheriff, I did not poison my ex-husband. I won't pretend I was fond of him, or that I was happy when he showed up unexpectedly making wild claims about us still being married. I certainly wasn't going to let him take the Serenity Sanctuary away from me after everything I—and everyone else—did to bring it back from the brink of closing." The very thought made it feel as though there was a giant rock in her stomach.

"But if I hadn't been able to prove we really were divorced or persuade him to settle for a much smaller amount of money and just go away, I would have resorted to lawyers, not poison." She shook her head. "I'm guessing you will find that whatever killed him was completely accidental. But if it wasn't, you're going to have to look somewhere else for your killer."

Richardson raised an eyebrow. "Mr. Smith had only just gotten to town. As far as I can tell, you are the only person here he knows."

"Ha," Kari said triumphantly. "Actually, I'm not. He introduced me to a man named James Torrance at Oktoberfest. Said they were working on a business deal together." She scowled. "Turning my land into a glamping retreat, if you can believe it."

"Really?" the deputy said. "Glamping is so cool. And it is really big bucks these days."

Both Kari and Richardson glared at him and Carmichael subsided over his note taking.

"Is that so?" Richardson said to Kari. "Any idea where I could find this supposed business partner?"

She shook her head. "Sorry, none. But he was in the diner asking questions on Friday, so maybe Cookie would know something more about him. She has a way of getting information out of people that makes me surprised the CIA hasn't tried to recruit her."

Kari thought for a moment. "There was also a woman he said was staying at his bed-and-breakfast who showed up at our table. I saw him talking to her earlier, and I wondered if maybe she was chasing after him. Women did, you know. He was handsome and success- ful and charming when he wanted to be."

"So your alternate suspects are a business acquain- tance who stood to make a lot of money working with him, and some random woman who might or might not have found him attractive." Richardson didn't sound im- pressed. "I'm afraid that none of them sound as though they have nearly the motive—or the opportunity—you did, Ms. Stuart."

"Oh come on," Kari said, her exasperation finally getting the better of her. "I did not kill Charlie Smith, sheriff. I'm telling you, if I were going to, I would have done it years ago when we were still married."

Richardson tapped his pen thoughtfully against his notebook. "According to Mr. Smith, you still were. Which reminds me; I should look into whether or not you are still mentioned in a will, or a beneficiary of his life insurance."

Kari didn't bang her head on the table, but it was a near thing. "I'm sure he changed that all as soon as we walked out of the divorce court. He didn't give me one extra penny then, and I can't imagine he ever planned to do so at any time in the future."

She was exhausted from the various ups and downs of the day, and all she wanted to do was sit in her own living room and hug a cat, a dog, or both. "Are we done here, Sheriff? Because I don't think there is anything else useful I can tell you, and I'd really like to go home."

"Fine," Richardson said, standing up from the table. "We'll just follow you over there and collect anything that might have gone into this brunch you served. I'd like to have the forensics people take a look at it, just in case."

Kari was too tired to argue. "Whatever," she said. "I think I've permanently lost my appetite anyway."

Nine

"They took your pots and pans?" Sara said in the appalled voice of someone who had a matched set of high-end chef quality cooking implements. "That's terrible."

Kari shrugged as she emptied a shallow litter box into the large black garbage pail in the middle of the shelter's front room and wiped it out with a paper towel. She followed this with a spritz from a bottle of the special animal-safe cleaning fluid they used and wiped it more thoroughly. They went through a *lot* of paper towels at the shelter. Not to mention a lot of litter.

"They were just some random pans I'd collected over the years" she said. "And the sheriff told me I'd get them back after they'd tested them for anything that could have made Charlie sick."

She, Sara, Bryn, and Suz were all together at the Serenity Sanctuary, and Kari was giving her friends an update on the day's events. She'd gone over as soon as Richardson and his deputy left. Suz occasionally popped in to help with the evening cleanup on Sundays, since she didn't groom dogs on that day, and Kari thought it would be easier to talk to her friends at the same time, instead of trying to update them all separately. A couple of volunteers were out back cleaning the dog kennels, and the other women had already finished the main feline room before Kari had gotten there.

Sara and Bryn wore matching red *Serenity Sanctuary* tee shirts, since they'd both been working that afternoon, helping to connect visitors with the animals they were interested in, and returning phone calls. Some days their answering machine had so many messages on it, it could take hours to respond to them all. Suz, on the other hand, was in a purple and pink plaid flannel shirt and worn blue jeans, with a purple bandana tied around her cropped lavender hair.

"Did they take all the food in your refrigerator?" Bryn asked as she moved a couple of kittens and their semi-feral mother carefully from a holding crate back into their newly scrubbed cage. Fortunately the mama cat was quickly distracted by a fresh bowl of smelly tuna-flavored wet cat food, and only took a couple of half-hearted swipes at the young woman. "I mean, how did they know what you put in the brunch you cooked?"

Kari scowled. In the end, the cops had nearly emptied her kitchen. "Most of it. All the completed dishes I had left over, plus spices, sugar, salt, even the ketchup. As if anyone puts ketchup on quiche." She shook her head, and the braid she'd pulled her dark hair into almost fell into the bowl of water she was filling at the sink at the far end of the room. "That stuff I probably won't get back, so I guess I need to go grocery shopping when we're done here." At least the shelter had closed at five, so as soon as they were finished, she could lock up for the day.

"Do you want to go out to dinner, since there isn't much left to eat in your house?" Suz asked, giving Kari a sympathetic look. The groomer didn't cook much, so she had takeout menus for every place in town. Suz liked to say that the height of her culinary skills was adding more cheese to boxed macaroni and cheese.

"No thanks," Kari said. "I'm sure the word has spread by now that Charlie is dead, and I'm not feeling up to dealing with the sideways glances and whispering comments. I think I have some pizza in the freezer that the sheriff didn't consider a possible murder weapon."

"Surely Sheriff Richardson doesn't really believe that you killed Charlie," Sara said. She had popped into the small kitchen off the main room to wash the dirty water and food dishes they'd taken out of the cages, but she'd been listening to the conversation over the clink of metal bowls and the low hum of the running water.

"There doesn't seem to be anyone else in town who has a motive," Kari explained. "And the spouse is always the main suspect, as far as I can tell. Richardson seems to think that I would kill to save the shelter from falling into Charlie's hands."

She stopped what she was doing for a moment to think about it. She'd put her heart and soul into this place, and it had given her life a purpose she'd needed badly.

"I'd go to some pretty extreme lengths to save the Sanctuary, and all the animals in it," she admitted to the others, remembering back to how she'd risked her life to find the person who had killed the former dog warden. "But I'd like to think that murder would be a step too far, even when Charlie was involved."

Kari fastened the latch on the final cage and grabbed the bucket and mop that were leaning against the wall by the desk. There was a certain satisfaction in slapping the mop head against the floor, even if it did get her sneakers wetter than they'd normally be. The whole situation was so frustrating. The pungent odor of the pet-safe floor cleaner they used instead of bleach filled the air, even though it was extremely diluted. Luckily the upgraded ventilation system would make short work of it.

"Mind you, back when we were married there were plenty of people who had reasons to be angry with him," she said. "Charlie could sweet-talk anyone into almost anything, and when a deal went sour, the folks who lost money tended to take it personally. Maybe we just need to find out who might have a reason to be upset with him now. Besides me, that is." She whacked the mop against the floor again and Suz walked over and gently removed it from her hands, taking over the task with a little less vigor.

"At least the sanctuary is no longer in danger," Bryn said, sounding relieved. She'd been dedicated to the place long before Kari had even gotten there, and still spent most of her time there when she wasn't in classes. "So that's one piece of good news."

"Not necessarily," Sara said in a thoughtful tone, a dish towel hanging forgotten from one hand. "If Charlie really did have a claim on some of Kari's winnings, it is possible his next of kin could, too."

"Ugh," Kari said, making a face. "The last I knew, that was his mother. She never liked me. Thought I wasn't nearly good enough for her precious son. She doesn't need money, but she'd probably go after mine just out of spite."

"You should reach out to her before she finds out you're a suspect in his murder, then," Suz suggested. "Maybe a nice sympathy call during which you can subtly ask if she is still his closest family. For all you know, he's had two more ex-wives in the time you've been split up."

"I'm not sure she'd even talk to me," Kari said. "But I suppose I could try. I want to make sure to give the sheriff time to officially notify her of Charlie's death first, though. I definitely don't want to be the one to break it to her."

"Kari?" Bryn said. She was peering out the window in the direction of the parking lot. "Did you know there is some guy out there walking around with a clipboard and some kind of electronic distance measuring device? You don't suppose he's with the cops, do you?"

Kari glanced over Bryn's shoulder and growled under her breath. "No, he's not. That's James Torrance, the man who was working with Charlie on the glamping plan. He was at the brewery last night, remember?"

Bryn ducked her head shyly. "I, uh, wasn't really paying attention," she admitted. Suz grinned. The two of them had mostly been focused on each other.

"I'm going to go out and see what he's doing here," Kari said, rolling her eyes at her friend. "He's certainly not interested in adopting a cat."

She stalked outside and made her way over to where Torrance stood, gazing at the mountains in the distance. Kari had a feeling he was seeing dollar signs, not the beauty of the local scenery. Torrance's pale blond hair looked almost white in the fading early evening light, and his suit jacket seemed to be struggling to accommodate his broad shoulders.

"Can I help you with something, Mr. Torrance?" Kari asked, folding her arms over her chest. "Because if you're not here to make a donation or adopt an animal, this is private property and I'm afraid I'm going to have to ask you to leave."

The blond man looked startled, stepping back from her and blinking rapidly behind his black-rimmed glasses. "Oh, hi," he said. "I didn't realize you were here. And please call me James. After all, we're going to be working together on this great project."

Kari sighed. "No, James, we're not going to be working together. The truth is, we were never going to be working together."

"What are you talking about?" James asked. The cheerful look that seemed to be a permanent expression slid off his face. "Charlie assured me that the two of you had come to an agreement about the land. He told me you were going to sign over the shelter and the property, and we already have preliminary paperwork in place to move forward on the glamping compound."

"You haven't heard, have you?" Kari said, almost feeling sorry for him, despite the fluorescent shoelaces and too-hearty manner that got on her nerves. He was just another victim of the Charlie Smith charm offensive.

"Heard what?" James asked. He waved an arm around to point at the hills. "I've been driving through the area all day to get the lay of the land, so to speak. Did you know that cell service is incredibly spotty out here?"

Kari snorted. "I did, actually. I suspect your camping people wouldn't be all that thrilled to find out that they couldn't check their phones constantly. We have a land-line up here at the sanctuary, and I have one at my house because cell phones rarely work. But that means the po-lice haven't gotten in touch with you. You should prob-ably call them as soon as you get back into range."

James gaped at her, open-mouthed. "The police? Why would the cops want to talk to me? I haven't done anything wrong. I was just driving around."

She took a deep breath and let it out slowly. "Char-lie's dead, Mr. Torrance. He died at the hospital a little while ago after falling ill this morning." One more breath and she added, "They think he was poisoned. They want to talk to you because you're one of the few people in town who he knew."

"Dead? Dead? How can he be dead?" James said, his ruddy face turning pale with shock. "I just saw him last night and he seemed fine." The blond man took another backward step and pointed an accusing finger at Kari. "Wait a minute. He was supposed to have breakfast with you this morning."

"Yes, he was," Kari said through gritted teeth. This was that last time she invited an ex-anything over for brunch. "But he was already feeling sick when he showed up, and he left soon after he got to my house. I assure you, I had nothing to do with whatever happened, and I'm still not convinced he didn't just accidentally ingest something toxic. But the police will want to talk to you nonetheless."

James shook his head, as if he was having a hard time taking in what she was saying. "Dead. I can't believe it. What a disaster for the project."

"Well, it's not great for Charlie either," Kari said mildly. "But I'm sure you'll find another site. One that's a lot more suitable for your needs. And, you know, doesn't already have an animal sanctuary on it."

"You don't understand," James said. He ran his fingers through his hair. "Charlie told me you two were still married. That he had the rights to the land, and there weren't going to be any problems moving ahead. We signed a contract, and I've already given him a lot of money to get the ball rolling. A *lot* of money."

"I'm sorry about that," Kari said. "Charlie had an unfortunate habit of bending the truth to fit his version of reality. He didn't see it as lying, exactly. I think he thought he could bulldoze the universe into doing things his way. It worked more often than not, but when it didn't, the results could be pretty explosive. It was one of the reasons I left him." She shrugged, suddenly tired. "I'm afraid in this case, neither the universe nor I was going to do what he wanted."

James took a step forward, his broad shoulders and bulldog manner taking on a more threatening feel. "I don't believe you," he said in a low voice. "He said you'd agreed. I think you were in on the deal, and now that Charlie is conveniently dead, you're backing out and keeping my money. Well, we'll see about that, Ms. Stuart."

"What? No!" Kari threw up her hands. "I didn't know anything about any agreement between you and Charlie. I told him more than once that I wasn't going to give up the shelter. I don't have your money. The only reason I was even talking to Charlie about all this was to try and persuade him to take a smaller amount of my winnings and go."

"You're lying," James said, thick eyebrows meeting in a scowl. "And even if you're not, I have a signed contract, and as Charlie's wife, you're going to have to honor it. I have a legitimate claim on this land, and I'm going to get it, if I have to bring in every lawyer in the state."

He stomped off toward the parking lot, where a large Jeep the same flashy orange as his sneaker laces was parked across three spots, pulling his cell phone out of his pocket and muttering to himself when he realized he still had no signal.

Kari watched him pull out with a speed and fury that sent gravel flying through the air, leaving two matching grooves in the otherwise neat lot. He'd seemed legitimately surprised when she'd told him about Charlie's death, but she had to wonder if his protests were a little over the top. Perhaps he'd already learned that he'd been double-crossed and killed Charlie because of it. There was certainly quite a temper lurking under that avuncular demeanor.

She'd been wondering who else could have been angry with her ex, and she'd certainly found one person who was. What had James Torrance known, and when had he known it?

Ten

Kari was looking into her sadly depleted refrigerator for something she could fashion into dinner, the kitten poking her head inside as if she might spot an option Kari had missed, when there was a knock on the front door. Kari hoped it wasn't the cops, coming to haul her off to jail. Although if they did, at least they'd probably have to feed her.

Queenie trotted at her heels as Kari walked over to open the door. To her surprise, she was greeted by the diminutive figure of her closest neighbor, Mrs. Lee. Mrs. Lee was one of those Asian women who could have been anywhere in her fifties or sixties or maybe even seventies, with straight black hair twisted into a bun and only a few tiny wrinkles around her eyes. The Lees lived behind the sanctuary, not far from the edge of the property line, and Mr. Lee had been a thorn in Kari's side since the day she bought the place. Although to be fair, he probably saw it the other way around.

"Mrs. Lee, good evening," Kari said. "What can I do

for you?" Queenie stood up on her hind legs and sniffed, meowing loudly. Kari hurriedly scooped her up before she could get cat fur on Mrs. Lee's pristine black pants or colorful quilted jacket.

"I brought you dumplings," Mrs. Lee said in her lightly accented voice. She held out a casserole dish from which amazing smells emanated. No wonder Queenie had gotten excited. Mrs. Lee's dumplings were famous at every local pot luck dinner. "I heard there was a death in the family. You have my sympathies."

Kari swallowed hard at the unexpected kindness. She'd known that the small-town grapevine would spread the news, but she hadn't anticipated this sort of reaction.

"That's very kind of you, Mrs. Lee," she said. But she didn't want to accept the dumplings under false pretenses, as much as her mouth was watering at the aromas of pork and five spice powder. "But Charlie was my ex-husband and not really family."

The older woman made a clicking sound with her tongue that was clearly meant to imply disagreement. She held the casserole dish out even farther. "No, no, you take it," she said in a stern voice. "It does not matter. When someone dies, you bring food. That is how to be a proper neighbor."

"Oh, well, thank you," Kari said, giving in and putting the kitten down so she could accept the container. "I very much appreciate it."

Mrs. Lee waved a tiny hand dismissively through the air. "It also does not matter that people are saying that you killed him." She leaned down to pet Queenie, who was twining around her ankles affectionately. "I do not believe that anyone who cares so much for animals could be a murderer."

Kari could feel a lump forming in her throat at this unasked for vote of confidence. "Thank you for saying so, Mrs. Lee. I hope that the new noise baffling system we were finally able to get installed in the kennels last week has made Mr. Lee happy." He'd been calling regularly about the barking since the days when Daisy still owned the place.

"Quiet is good," Mrs. Lee agreed. "My husband teaches history and sociology at the college in Perryville and he says he needs his sleep to be able to deal with annoying young people. He is definitely pleased with the reduced noise."

"Great," Kari said. The project had been on her list since she'd bought the sanctuary, but there had been so many more urgent needs, it had taken them a while to work their way down to the ones that had more to do with aesthetics than safety. "So, does Mr. Lee also believe I'm innocent?"

Mrs. Lee gave a tinkling laugh that reminded Kari of bells. "Oh, no. He is quite sure you killed your husband, and cannot wait for you to go to jail." She smiled gently at Kari to take the sting out of her words, although there was little doubt they were true. "Do not bother to bring back the casserole dish. Seeing you will only make him cranky. I will pick it up again in a few days."

She turned to leave and then swiveled around again as if she'd forgotten something. "Oh, I meant to ask— you are friends with that nice veterinarian with the red hair, are you not?"

"Angus McCoy?" Kari had to suppress a grin at just

hearing his name. "Yes, I am. He is very helpful with animals at the sanctuary, as well as taking care of my own cats and dog when Dr. Burnett, my regular vet, isn't available." Queenie meowed, as if to say she thought so, too. "Why do you ask?" She knew the Lees didn't have any pets of their own. Mr. Lee had made that clear on a number of occasions.

"Oh, it is just that I saw him eating lunch with a pretty blond lady," Mrs. Lee said. "Won't it be nice if he finds a good woman to settle down with?"

"Lovely," Kari said in a faint voice.

Mrs. Lee walked off down the road in the direction of her own home and Kari took the casserole dish and Queenie inside, shutting the door a tad too forcefully behind her.

The dumplings, which had smelled so wonderful a minute ago, suddenly turned her stomach. Of course, it might not have been the food.

"What the heck is going on, Queenie?" she asked the kitten.

Her only answer was a pink-tongued yawn. Apparently no one was going to tell her anything tonight.

Kari picked at a couple of dumplings. They were delicious, as expected, with tender doughy outsides and slightly spicy salty-sweet interiors that steamed when you opened them up. But Mrs. Lee's parting comment had ruined Kari's appetite, and eventually she put the rest away until she could eat them with the appreciation such a culinary masterpiece deserved. She thought maybe it would clear her thoughts and soothe her spirit if she went for a walk by the lake instead.

Blue Heron Lake, for which Lakeview was named, was typical of the lakes in New York State, many of which had been formed by glacial movement centuries ago. It was about seven miles long, with the town situated at about the center of its length. A river led into it at one end and out the far side on its way to neighboring Perryville and beyond, and it was popular with both tourists and locals alike who wanted to take a canoe or a small boat out for a day of fishing, or simply paddling around and taking in the sights.

There were various brown sandy beaches scattered along the shoreline, many of them with boat ramps, picnic areas, and swimming sections. But Kari's favorite spot was a couple of miles from the sanctuary, where the shoreline was too narrow and rocky for much of anything other than walking along. She often went there when the stresses of running the shelter got to be too much for her and she needed a break.

Five Mile Beach, as it was known, because it was five miles from the center of town, was often deserted, especially in October when the tourists were concentrating on leaf peeping and the locals mostly thought it was too cold. It was wonderful to have the long stretch of sand to herself, with only the occasional person out walking his or her dog to break the meditative peace of the wind and the gentle sound of the subtle waves washing against the shore.

The air smelled fresh and crisp, with just a hint of smoke from a campfire somewhere further down the lake. She'd pulled on a lightweight denim jacket over her long-sleeved tee shirt and jeans, and replaced her sneakers with sturdier hiking boots. The last thing she needed right now was to twist an ankle.

Kari had brought Fred with her, since he loved a good stroll along the shore as much as she did. Although he was a little more likely to bark at the herons who frequented the lake than she was. Fortunately, most of them had taken off for warmer winter climes. As usual, Queenie had insisted on coming along, although she was getting a little too big for her favorite perch atop Kari's shoulder. Instead, Kari had trained her to walk on a harness—or possibly Queenie had just trained Kari to take her on walks.

The truth was, Queenie never ran off, whether or not she was wearing her harness, much preferring to stick close to Kari, or run along with her buddy Fred. The regulars on the beach had gotten used to seeing Kari with the rangy mutt on one side and the small black cat on the other, and hardly even batted an eye as they passed.

Tonight the space was even more quiet than usual, which Kari appreciated. But as she stood at the edge of the water watching the sun begin to set, she was hailed by a familiar voice.

"Hi there," Angus said, walking up to her with Herriot, his white pit bull, following along, the dog's progress slowed by the apparent need to sniff at every rock and footprint in the sand. When they got to Kari, Herry and Fred touched noses and exchanged a sociable *woof*. Queenie, who got along with pretty much all other animals and had met Herry before, meowed at him briefly before sitting down to lick at a hind leg with studied feline indifference.

"I wasn't expecting to see you here," Angus said, brushing a lock of red hair out of his eyes. The breeze immediately blew it back. He turned to the dog. "Sit,

Herry." The pit bull sat without hesitation, his broad bottom making a quiet thunking noise as it hit the sand.

Kari didn't even bother to try that with Fred, who mostly considered commands to be suggestions of the vaguest sort. He'd sit if he got tired, but otherwise she was content to let him wander up and down the shore, as long as he stayed nearby.

"Hi," she said back. "This is a pleasant surprise. I was going to call you later, but it has been a long day, and I needed to gather my thoughts first."

Angus gave her an inscrutable look, although the concern in his blue eyes was clear enough. "I'm not surprised. I heard that your husband died. Are you okay?"

"Ex-husband," Kari said automatically. She shrugged, pulling her jacket a little tighter against the rising breeze. "And I'm fine. Well, not fine, exactly, but it isn't as though we were close. I didn't even like the man. It was just kind of a shock."

"I can imagine," Angus said, but he didn't reach out to give her the hug she would have expected.

To be fair, she didn't reach out for him either. Things just felt strange between them, somehow. Of course, her ex had shown up out of nowhere, horned in on their last two dates, picked a fight with Angus in the diner in front of half the town, and then died under suspicious circumstances. She supposed that could put a strain on a relationship that was far more established than theirs was. Maybe Angus had decided being with her was more trouble than it was worth. She wouldn't blame him. Much.

"Mind you, it doesn't help that Sheriff Richardson seems to have nominated me for the role of primary suspect," Kari added. "He and a deputy came to my house and took away half the contents of my kitchen, just because Charlie came over for brunch this morning. A meal he didn't even eat, I might add." She hunched her shoulders inside her jacket, less because of the increasing wind and more because of an internal chill she couldn't quite seem to shake.

Angus gave her a tight smile. "Well, they say the spouse is always the most likely perpetrator. Or is that just on television?" He leaned down to pet Herry and added in a casual tone, "So you had Charlie over for brunch?"

"It's true in real life too," Kari said. "But I didn't kill my ex-husband. I didn't even put salt in his coffee instead of sugar. And yes, I invited him to brunch to try and talk to him about this idiotic plan to turn the Serenity Sanctuary into some kind of fancy campground. He wanted to go to dinner, but I thought breakfast would be more neutral and less intimate." She sighed. "It turned out not to matter, because he wasn't feeling well when he got to the house, and only stayed for a few minutes."

"I assume you told that to the cops," Angus said.

"I did," Kari said. "I'm not sure they believed me. The sheriff told me they're going to do an autopsy and a toxicology report, and presumably they'll be able to tell from his stomach contents that at least I was telling the truth about him not eating my food. I have no idea what the tox screen will say."

She slumped, suddenly feeling as if gravity was twice as heavy as usual. She'd been a suspect in a murder before, when she'd discovered the body of the crooked town dog warden out by the fence behind the sanctuary, but this time it felt a lot more personal. She really did have a motive, although she couldn't believe that anyone who knew her would actually think she'd kill somebody.

She said as much to Angus, and he tilted his head thoughtfully. "He was a jerk," Angus said. "And he was trying to take away the sanctuary, or half your lottery money, or whatever. Nobody would have blamed you if you'd felt threatened by that."

Kari stared at him. "There's a big difference between feeling threatened and actually murdering someone because of it."

Angus held up one hand in defense. "Of course there is. I didn't mean to imply that you'd actually done it." He pushed that errant strand out of his face again impatiently. "I should probably get going. I've got to be at the office early in the morning for a difficult surgery." He patted her awkwardly on the shoulder. "I'm sorry about your—about Charlie."

Kari didn't think he really was sorry, although she didn't blame him for that either. "Look, I was wondering, um, that is, a couple of people mentioned that they saw you out to lunch with Tanya, that woman who came to the table with Charlie last night. Do you know her from somewhere?"

She couldn't be sure in the waning light, but she thought that Angus might have blushed. As it was, he didn't quite meet her eyes when he said, "Oh, no, not really. She took the nature walk I gave on Saturday morning, and she seemed kind of lonely, not knowing anyone in town. So I invited her to lunch. Not a big deal. Just trying to be friendly."

Sure. Then why hadn't he told her about it before this? Of course, she hadn't told him about inviting Charlie over either. It didn't mean she was guilty of anything—they just weren't at the stage where they told each other about every little thing on their schedules. And one of the things she liked so much about Angus was his big heart. It probably really wasn't a big deal. She was just being paranoid, and a little oversensitive because she'd had such a rough day.

"That was nice of you," she said. "And you're right, I should get home, too. It has been a really long day and I'm pretty wiped out." She reached up and gave him a quick kiss on the cheek. "I'm glad we ran into you though."

"Me too," Angus said, and this time his smile looked more genuine. "I'll talk to you tomorrow, okay?"

"You bet," she said. Hopefully by then the police would have information that would clear her, and life could get back to normal. She had to admit, that would be a huge relief.

🐈 Eleven

Late on Monday morning, Kari got a call inviting her to stop by the sheriff's department. At her earliest possible convenience. If not sooner. Apparently the sheriff was eager to speak to her. The caller's tone of voice made it clear her attendance wasn't optional.

She had been intending to man the front desk as soon as they finished the daily cleaning and opened to the public at noon, but fortunately Bryn didn't have a class that day and was available to come in and cover until Kari got back. Assuming, of course, that the sheriff didn't lock her up and throw away the key. Kari didn't *think* that was going to happen. But she dropped Queenie off at the house just in case the visit took longer than expected.

"Love you, Monkey," she whispered as she kissed the kitten on the head. Queenie licked her nose as if to say, "Love you too, Mama," before running off to pounce on an unsuspecting Robert as he slept curled up on the couch. The large yellow cat pounced back, and then chased the kitten up the stairs. Kari decided that if they weren't worried, she'd try not to worry either. Queenie had an uncanny nose for trouble, and if she thought things were okay, they probably were.

Probably.

When Kari arrived, she was escorted back to the sheriff's office by a short stocky woman in uniform. Like its occupant, it was plain and no-nonsense, with a scuffed linoleum floor, walls lined with shelves and filing cabinets, and an oversized wooden deck stacked high with folders, all of them precisely aligned. A computer sat off to the right side of the desk, with its screen turned away from her so Kari couldn't see what was on it. It could have been anything from notes on the case to a game of solitaire. The only personal items on the desk were a framed picture of Duke, the sheriff's golden retriever, catching a Frisbee on a beach, and a mug that said in big black letters, *"To quote Hamlet, Act III, Scene III, Line 87, 'NO.'"*

Kari bit back a laugh as she read it. The sheriff clearly had both hidden depths and an unexpected sense of humor. Sadly, neither of those was likely to help her in her current situation.

The man himself was sitting in a large black leather chair on wheels behind the desk, scowling at something on the computer monitor. As usual, his uniform was neatly pressed and his short slightly graying brown hair looked as if he had had it trimmed that morning. As Kari was ushered into the room, he swiveled around to face her and gestured toward one of the two hard wooden chairs provided for visitors.

"Have a seat, Ms. Stuart. Thank you for coming in at such short notice. I know you probably have a busy day planned, but there were some questions I had that couldn't wait," he said.

Richardson had approved the adoption of a police dog for his force from the Serenity Sanctuary, plus he'd spent some time out there during a previous investigation, so he had a fairly good idea of how much work was involved in running the shelter.

"Can Sergeant Foreman get you a cup of coffee or anything?" he asked. "This might take a while."

Oh, great. Kari debated between the merits of something comforting to drink versus becoming even more wired than she already was, but as always, the thought of coffee won. "I wouldn't mind a cup, if it isn't too much trouble," she said. "One sugar, a splash of milk." She pointed at his desk. "Any chance I can get it in a cup like that one?"

Richardson actually laughed. "No, I'm afraid that's the only one in the building. My son got that for me when we were at the butting heads daily stage and he clearly felt as though my answer to everything he asked was 'no.' I'm afraid you're going to have to settle for standard issue disposable."

They waited in silence until the sergeant had returned with Kari's coffee and put it down on one of the few empty spaces on the desk, then left, closing the door behind her with a loud click that made Kari jump.

"So, uh, I guess this visit means you have new information?" Kari ventured, picking up the cup and cradling it between both hands. She glanced across the desk, but as usual, Richardson's granite face was giving nothing away.

He picked up a folder from the top of a stack by his left elbow and flipped it open on the desk in front of him. "A surprising amount of new information, in fact," Richardson said. "The lab and the coroner's office can get backed up and sometimes takes days or weeks to get back to me. Fortunately, we seem to have hit them during a lull between bodies." Kari couldn't tell if he was joking or not.

"So I assume you didn't find anything poisonous in the things you took out of my kitchen," she said in a confident tone. There wasn't much she was sure about in this case, but she did know she hadn't poisoned Charlie.

The sheriff tapped the paper on top of the file. "We did not. Nothing in the food. No traces on the pans or plates. Even the cleaning fluid we tested wouldn't have harmed anyone, unless they drank the entire bottle. Maybe not even then." He looked almost disappointed. It would undoubtedly have made his life much easier if the answers were that simple.

"I have animals," Kari said as if that explained everything. Which for her, it did. "I don't keep anything toxic in the house. If I have an ant infestation, I use borax. I rarely have issues with mice because of the cats, but on the rare occasions rodents get into the walls or some other place the cats can't reach them, I have humane traps I bait with peanut butter." She shook her head. "I did tell you I didn't poison Charlie."

Richardson stroked his chin thoughtfully. "Well, you didn't poison him at brunch, anyway. That doesn't eliminate the possibility you did it at some other time and place." He turned over another piece of paper and scanned its contents. "So, you said when I first talked to you that Mr. Smith claimed not to be feeling well when he arrived at your home for brunch?"

Kari took a sip of coffee and almost spat it out. Talk

about trying to poison people. She replaced the cup gingerly on the desk and answered the sheriff's question. "Yes, that's right. As I said, he complained that his stomach was upset, and then ran for the bathroom. He was also a little pale, and I thought his eyes looked off. But I'm not a doctor. I just thought he was hungover from drinking too much beer at Oktoberfest, or possibly coming down with a bug."

She clasped her hands together tightly in her lap. "I had no idea he was really sick, sheriff. If I'd known, I would have taken him to the emergency room myself. He just seemed a little off."

"Mmmm," Richardson said, jotting a note down on one of the papers. She couldn't tell if he believed her or not, which was completely disconcerting. No doubt the intended effect.

"Well," he said finally. "As it happens, it would probably have been difficult to tell at that stage. The owner of the bed-and-breakfast where Mr. Smith was staying said that his symptoms got increasingly severe after he returned from seeing you, until they finally got bad enough that she called for the ambulance."

"Do you know what caused his illness?" Kari asked. "I mean, now that you've eliminated my cooking." She gave him a sardonic look, which he ignored without apparent difficulty.

"Are you familiar with the destroying angel mushroom?" Richardson asked, gazing at her intently. "Technically known as *Amanita bisporigera*, if you are scientifically inclined."

Kari blinked. "Destroying angel? That sounds awful. I've never heard of it." She rubbed her fingers on her jeans. "Is that anything like the death cap? I know that

one grows in New York State and you have to be careful
when you pick wild mushrooms, because it can mimic
edible varieties."

She reached for the coffee again but stopped, remembering how dreadful it was. "Angus McCoy, the veterinarian, leads nature walks sometimes. He told me about
the death caps, but I probably only remembered because
they sounded so creepy."

"Did he now?" the sheriff said, raising an eyebrow.
"How interesting. And yes, the death cap and the destroying angel are actually in the same family. They are
among the most toxic of all known mushrooms, and
they do in fact grow in this area, on the edge of wood-
lands, near trees and shrubs, even in lawns. They can be
mistaken for edible mushrooms like button or puffball,
and are responsible for most of the mushroom-related
deaths every year."

He sounded like he was quoting from a botany text.
He'd probably been doing research since he'd gotten the
test results back. Richardson was nothing if not thorough.

"That's horrible," Kari said, suppressing a shudder.
"Is that what killed Charlie? A poisonous mushroom?"
Somehow it seemed like a very banal ending for such a
charismatic man, to be taken out by something so small
and seemingly normal.

"According to the coroner, yes," Richardson said,
sounding grim. "The toxin is quite distinctive, and there
were also still traces of it in Mr. Smith's digestive system, although they might have missed them if they
hadn't been looking for the cause of his symptoms."

"There weren't any mushrooms in the brunch I
made," Kari said.

Richardson waved off her comment. "I know that,

Ms. Stuart. I told you everything from your kitchen came back clean." He looked down at his notes again. "Apparently the symptoms of amatoxin poisoning don't appear for anywhere from five to twenty-four hours after the mushroom is ingested, so if your husband already felt ill when he arrived, your breakfast couldn't have been responsible."

He took a sip of his own coffee, without any noticeable reaction to its taste. Clearly he was a much tougher person than she was. No surprise there.

"Interestingly," he went on, "by the time symptoms—which can include cramps, vomiting, diarrhea, delirium, and convulsions—appear, the damage to the victim's liver and kidneys is almost always irreversible."

"So you mean . . ." Kari couldn't quite get the words out past the sudden lump in her throat.

"Indeed," Richardson said dryly. "When Mr. Smith arrived at your house for brunch, he was already dying." He sat back in his chair and stared in her direction. "Which raises the question, are you the kind of woman who could sit across the breakfast table from a man she'd poisoned and watch him suffer without saying anything?" He raised an eyebrow. "Are you, Ms. Stuart?"

Kari pressed her lips together so she wouldn't say anything impulsive that would get her into even more trouble than she was already in, and took a deep breath through her nose before she spoke. "No," she said in a flat tone, staring back into his gray eyes. "I most definitely am not."

"Hmph," the sheriff said. "Not even if that person was trying to take away the new life you've built for yourself and everything you valued the most?"

Kari sighed. "Not even then, Sheriff. I assume you've been looking into my background and you are well aware that there were plenty of times when I had next to nothing. I survived it then and I'd survive it now."

She shook her head. "At most Charlie could only have taken away half of my lottery earnings. If he'd somehow managed to steal the sanctuary from me, and that was by no means a certainty, I would have rebuilt. And I'd still have my friends and my animals, who I value more than any money or property. Was I happy he was here? No. Was I concerned about the havoc he intended to wreak on my world? Absolutely. But none of that was reason enough to kill him."

"Maybe," Richardson said, rolling his pen back and forth between his fingers. "Or maybe not. You would be amazed at the things people will kill over." He glanced down at his notes again and flipped over another piece of paper.

Kari was beginning to hate those pages.

"Of course, now that we know the cause of death, perhaps it is possible that Mr. Smith simply picked the mushroom himself and ate it by mistake. Maybe this whole thing was just a tragic accident, and not murder at all." The sheriff shrugged.

She thought back to the years she'd been married, and the multitude of Charlie's various likes and dislikes, all of which he had made abundantly clear every time she cooked. "I don't think so," she said reluctantly. "Charlie always hated mushrooms. Once he threw an entire pot of spaghetti sauce against the wall because I'd forgotten and added mushrooms to it. I was cleaning up red stains for a week."

Kari shook her head. "I suppose that could have changed in the years since we split up. People's tastes do shift. I used to hate kale and now I love it. But once Charlie made up his mind that he didn't like something, he was rarely willing to try it again, so it doesn't seem likely. Although there were mushrooms on the Oktoberfest buffet."

The sheriff gave her a small crooked smile, barely a twitch of the lips. "That matches what Mr. Smith's mother said when we talked to her," he said. "She swore he would never have voluntarily eaten a mushroom if he knew that was what he was being served. Plus no one else who ate the mushrooms at the brewery has gotten ill. So I'm afraid that brings us back to someone giving it to him intentionally, disguised as something else. This is still very much a murder investigation."

Wonderful. He'd been testing her. Kari wasn't impressed. After all, knowing her ex disliked mushrooms was such a small thing, she could have forgotten all about it. Only the memory of scrubbing stains off the kitchen tiles on her hands and knees had made it stick in her mind so vividly.

"Assuming I didn't do it," Kari said, scowling at him. "And since I know I didn't, I'm definitely going with that assumption; do you have any other possible suspects? I don't for a minute believe that I'm the only person who was angry at Charlie. He could be incredibly charming, but he also never hesitated to run over anything or anyone who stood in the way of what he wanted."

"Some people are saying that one of the things he wanted was you, Ms. Stuart," the sheriff said. "Rumor has it that he was planning to convince you to return home with him. I assume that might have upset your veterinarian friend, Dr. McCoy. Diner gossip says you've been dating him for the last few months. Is that right?"

Kari rolled her eyes. "Yes, Angus and I have been seeing each other, but the relationship is still in the early stages. Plus I told him repeatedly that I had no intention of returning either to Long Island or to my marriage, no matter what fairy tales Charlie told himself and everyone else. I have made a lot of mistakes in my life, Sheriff, but I try never to make the same one twice."

"I see," Richardson said, looking down at his notes again. "But as you yourself mentioned, Dr. McCoy leads a nature walk aimed at foragers. He would certainly have been able to identify the destroying angel mushroom if he saw one. Plus, he was seen having a very public fight with the victim. A fight over you, from what everyone who was there says."

He looked back up at her. "You say you and the good doctor haven't been dating for that long. Are you certain you know him well enough to be sure he wouldn't kill a rival out of jealousy?" He leaned back in his chair until it creaked dangerously, then pulled forward again to put his face closer to hers. "Completely certain?"

Was she? Angus had been acting strange the last couple of days, and she didn't know why. But she couldn't imagine the man she'd seen gently removing porcupine quills from a whimpering puppy's nose while whispering quiet reassurances doing anything violent or deadly.

"I've been with men who were jealous and possessive," Kari said firmly. In fact, that described Charlie to a tee. "Angus just isn't like that. The only time I've ever seen him really angry is when someone deliberately hurt an animal. Other than that, he's one of the kindest people I know."

"That doesn't explain the fight in the diner," Richardson said.

Kari sighed. "Charlie could have tried the patience of a saint," she said. "He purposely got in Angus's face and provoked him. There was some minor shoving, but nothing worse than you'd see on a schoolyard playground between two boys. Hardly a reason to accuse someone of murder."

Richardson tapped his pen lightly on the desk. "That may be so, but Doctor McCoy was somewhat evasive when we asked him where he had been and who he'd been with in the twenty-four hours leading up to your husband's death. He's not off the hook yet. Of course, neither are you. So far, you two are the only ones we can see who have a clear motive."

"What about James Torrance?" Kari asked. "He's the one Charlie was working with on trying to turn the sanctuary land into some kind of glamping retreat. I found him at the shelter yesterday night, checking out the property. He *said* he'd been out all day driving around the area, and he had no idea that Charlie was dead. But he also told me that Charlie had assured him the deal was all set and that I had agreed to it."

"Is that right?" the sheriff said, looking intrigued. "I assume you had done no such thing."

"Absolutely not," Kari sputtered. "There was no way I was going to kick needy animals out of the only refuge they had, just so rich people could camp out without having to put up a tent." She caught herself before she continued ranting, since she was just reinforcing her supposed motive.

"Anyway, Torrance told me that he'd already given Charlie a lot of money toward the project. I don't know if that was true or not, but the man was really incensed when he left, muttering about lawyers and how the project wasn't going to be stopped just because Charlie was dead." Kari gnawed on her lip. "I have to admit, I wondered at the time if maybe he already knew Charlie had lied to him, and was just pretending to be surprised by the news. There was nothing fake about his anger, though."

Richardson peered across his desk at her. "You sound as though he scared you. Did he threaten you in any way?"

"Only with legal action," Kari said. "But he flipped from friendly to furious like someone flicked a switch, and he was pretty aggressive about his intention to go ahead with his plans no matter what."

She took another sip of coffee to give herself time to calm down before she chewed through her own lip, not even caring about the taste this time. "Um, sheriff, you don't think he could actually have some sort of claim on the shelter, do you? He said he and Charlie had signed paperwork."

"I doubt it," the sheriff said, looking thoughtful. He made another note, hopefully one that wasn't about her for a change. "Did you sign anything with Mr. Smith?"

"Except the disappearing divorce papers a few years ago?" Kari said. "No. Not since he came to town. I was just stalling him long enough to try and figure out what to do. I guess I'd better talk to a lawyer, though." She still hadn't gotten around to calling Carmen Rodriquez, although in Kari's defense, she had been a little busy.

"It couldn't hurt," Richardson said, not unsympathetically.

"But you'll look into James Torrance?" Kari said. "And that blond woman I mentioned?"

"I look into everything, Ms. Stuart," Richardson said. "That's my job. I even talked to Paige Adams, because a receipt from her bookstore was in Mr. Smith's wallet, dated that Saturday within the time frame we were looking at."

"Paige?" Kari said. "Oh yes, Charlie did ask me where he could get a book to read and I suggested Paging All Readers. But surely there isn't anything suspicious about selling someone a book."

"There isn't," Richardson said. "Unless you deny that you've done so, when the police have proof otherwise. For a few moments there, Ms. Adams managed to get herself onto our suspect list."

Kari thought about Paige. She was certainly Charlie's type—pretty in a wholesome, sporty way, with straight light brown hair she wore in a swingy ponytail, brown eyes, and a tall slightly curvy figure. Paige was cheerful and enthusiastic, especially when it came to books, and often attended the book club. She took turns hosting it in her shop, although that was a smart decision, since the members usually picked up a few extra books while they were there.

Paige had even adopted a large white cat she named Shakespeare from the shelter last month to be her official shop cat. She lived in an apartment over the store, so he went upstairs with her every night. Kari liked the other woman, who had moved to town and opened the bookstore about a year ago, but she didn't know much about her past before that. Could Paige have known Charlie before she moved to town?

"Was there some kind of connection between them?" she asked. Charlie certainly hadn't said anything when she'd mentioned Paige, other than to complain about the cuteness of her shop's name.

"Not exactly," the sheriff said. "As it turned out, there was a fairly innocent explanation for Ms. Adams's lie. Apparently Mr. Smith made a serious pass at her, which she initially responded to by accepting an invitation to have drinks sometime. After he died, and she found out that he was your husband—or ex-husband, whatever—she felt bad about it and didn't want word to get back to you. So she panicked when we asked her if she had seen him that morning, and said no. But once we explained that we were tracing his movements throughout the day and knew he had bought a book there, she admitted the truth."

Kari shook her head. "That sounds like Charlie, all right. So you took Paige off your suspect list in the end?"

"We did, for the most part," Richardson said. "We have yet to establish any other connection between the two of them, and it seems unlikely that she would have murdered him for asking her out for drinks."

He sighed, probably at the folly of people who lied to the police for what he would consider to be a ridiculous reason. "We also checked into Mr. Smith's first wife, since she apparently had a restraining order put out on him at the time of their divorce. But she has since remarried and lives in San Francisco, so it seemed extremely unlikely that she would be involved."

"That's it?" Kari asked. "Except for the people we've talked about already? Like James Torrance and his supposed deal with Charlie?"

"As far as Mr. Torrance is concerned, I will see what I can find out. But I doubt you have anything to worry about. Unless you decided to solve your problems by poisoning your husband. In which case you might want to find a lawyer who belongs to a firm that handles both business law and criminal law. Because if that's the case, Mr. Torrance's glamping scheme is going to be the least of your worries."

☙ Twelve

By the time Kari left the sheriff's department, it was almost one o'clock. She figured she might as well stop at the diner and pick up some lunch for herself, and something for Bryn to thank her for covering. Plus a few extra things, in case there were other folks working who hadn't eaten yet. It was easy to get caught up in all the demands of the shelter and forget to stop and refuel. She did it herself all the time.

But she regretted the decision almost as soon as she walked through the door. Before the bell had stopped its cheerful jingle, almost everyone in the place had turned around to see who had come in. Those who didn't got a nudge from whoever was sitting near them. Conversations stopped and there was a momentary hush before voices picked up again, slightly louder than before, as if everyone was trying hard to pretend the pause had never happened.

Kari nodded at some of the folks she knew as she made her way across the black-and-white checkerboard floor to the section of the long counter where takeout orders were placed. A few people nodded back, but others didn't meet her eyes, or looked away as soon as they had. Normally enthusiastic greetings were muted and subdued, although a few people ventured a hesitant, "Sorry for your loss."

Mrs. Vandercook, a Sunday school teacher whose classes occasionally took field trips to the sanctuary, pursed her thin lips as Kari passed by, and said something in a low voice to the thin, gray-haired woman sitting with her, who looked enough like Mrs. Vandercook to be her sister. Clancy Duckworth, a local handyman who had done a few small jobs out at the shelter, dropped money for the bill on his table and left without even saying hello, even though he practically had to walk past her on his way out the door. Even Paige Adams, who owned the bookstore, couldn't meet Kari's eyes as they crossed paths while Paige was on her way out, although she did mumble something sympathetic. Of course, Kari was pretty sure she knew the reason for that, based on what the sheriff had just told her.

Funny, but it hadn't even occurred to Kari that the local folks might actually believe she was guilty of killing her ex-husband. But it must be that, or they were uncomfortable with the possibility she had. Or perhaps the diner rumor mill had gotten things wrong (as sometimes happened) and they believed that she was actually selling out to some outside investor. Either way, it was pretty clear that for the moment, her presence was about as welcome as the plague.

As she stepped up to the counter, Cookie, her blond bouffant hairdo topped with a bright yellow bow, bustled up to wait on Kari, her round face split by a broad smile. Kari was happy to see that at least someone didn't think she'd suddenly turned into a crazed killer.

"Hi, Cookie," she said, studiously ignoring all the whispers behind her. "I'd like to get a few sandwiches to take to the sanctuary. Make it two turkey on whole wheat, two ham and Swiss on rye, and one hummus wrap, please." That ought to cover everyone, including Bryn who was a vegetarian. She thought for a second. "And two big orders of fries." It had been a fries kind of morning, and the ones the diner served were stellar, hand-cut with the skins still on, crispy on the outside and soft on the inside, with just the lightest dusting of their own seasoned salt.

"You bet, Sugar," Cookie said in a cheerful tone. "So they didn't lock you up, eh? That's good."

Kari blinked at her. "Uh, yeah, I think so. Especially since I didn't do anything wrong."

Cookie wiped her rag over a puddle of coffee marring the gleaming chrome top of the counter. "Of course you didn't," she said stoutly. "I'll get that order right in for you."

"Men," she added, shaking her head. Not a strand of hair moved out of place. "Nothin' but trouble, ain't that the truth?" She turned around and hollered the order at the cook through the open window that led to the kitchen area. Then turned back around and glared at a young woman in a blue version of the diner's uniform, who was whispering to a customer as she filled his coffee. "Bernadette, if you don't have anything better to do than stand around and chat, there's a sink full of dishes back there that aren't going to clean themselves."

"Don't you worry," Cookie said to Kari in an only slightly lower voice. "This whole thing will blow over, just you wait and see. Nobody here really thinks you killed your husband, even if we didn't know you actually had one. And if you did, I'm sure he deserved it." She patted Kari's hand where it rested on the counter on top of her wallet.

"Ex-husband," Kari said with a sigh. "Thanks, I think." She only hoped that Cookie was right, and the entire nightmare would be over soon. But in the meanwhile, Kari was pretty sure the kitchen staff was taking bets on how soon she'd be arrested. For now, the diner was going to have to be off limits.

When she got back to the shelter, Sara was at the front desk filing papers, with Bryn sitting on a stool at the other side of the L-shaped counter, returning the phone calls that had stacked up on the answering machine during the time they were closed or too busy cleaning to be able to pick up the phone.

Most days there were as many as twenty or thirty messages, and the regular staff and volunteers took turns responding to them. Some of them were simple—what were the shelter hours, how could someone adopt an animal, or maybe an inquiry from someone looking for a specific type of cat or dog. Others were more complicated, though. People called with animals they wanted to turn in to the shelter, either because they'd found a stray, or a mama cat with kittens who had given birth in their shed, or their child had developed an allergy, or they were moving and couldn't take their pets with them. Or they were looking for an inexpensive spay/neuter clinic, or had fallen on hard times and needed help caring for their animals until they got back on their feet.

The needs of the community seemed endless. Kari had developed a new respect for the other shelters in the area, many of which had been doing this work for decades, and a fresh understanding of why the woman she had met at the shelter where she'd first tried to take Queenie had seemed so frazzled and overwhelmed.

The Serenity Sanctuary tried to help all the animals who fell through the cracks, but it was an ongoing struggle. Thankfully, Angus shared their goal of reducing the amount of unwanted kittens, and donated his time and skills doing spays and neuters twice a month. They offered a sliding scale based on what people could afford, as well as neutering all the animals the sanctuary adopted out to prevent future issues.

The work was rewarding, but often frustrating, so Kari always tried to make sure that both her paid workers and her volunteers knew they were appreciated. Hence the lunch delivery, among other things.

"Hey," she said to Sara and Bryn, as the young woman hung up the phone and filled in the information sheet they used to track calls. "I stopped off at the diner and bought myself lunch. I brought enough for everyone, in case you hadn't gotten a chance to eat yet."

She placed the large brown paper bag on the desk, and opened the top so the delicious aromas could circulate through the air, easily surmounting the usual faint odors of cleaning fluids and cat litter. As if summoned by magic, Jim appeared from the door leading to the kennels out back.

"Please tell me you brought—" he grinned at the sight of the bag on the counter. "Lunch. Excellent. I was getting ready to fight Louie the basset hound for that new bone we gave him this morning. Are there fries?"

Sara stuck her nose inside the bag and inhaled. "Definitely fries." She gave Kari a mock scowl. "You know I was going to start a diet this week." She pulled out a hand full of fries anyway, munching on them as she headed into the kitchenette to get some paper plates and napkins.

Jim snorted, going over to the sink at the side of the room to wash his hands before he ate. Sara was always going to start a diet, and never did. It was something of a running joke. Kari sympathized, since they both tended to be just a little bit curvier than they'd like. But it wasn't going to stop her from eating the fries either.

"Let me call Rachael in," Jim said. "She's outside walking Sparky." Rachael was a local woman who volunteered at the shelter a couple times a week, coming to take some of the dogs currently in residence out for much needed exercise and fresh air.

Sparky was a Dalmatian mix whose owner had had to go into a nursing home. When they'd first taken him in, he'd been a little subdued, but he was compensating for that now with renewed exuberance that made long walks a necessity. They were hoping to place him in a home with kids and very, very patient parents. Luckily, they'd already had one family in to meet him, and they were scheduled to return for another visit next Saturday, so Kari was keeping her fingers crossed.

In the meanwhile, having someone to walk Sparky and the other dogs freed up the regular staff to do the million and a half other tasks that went along with running a shelter, so Kari was extremely grateful for volunteers like Rachael.

"I got hummus for you," Kari said, handing the wrap to Bryn, who nodded her thanks and continued to document the call she'd just finished. "There's turkey or ham and cheese for everyone else," Kari said to Sara as she returned with the plates and spread paper towels over the front desk to spread it all out on. "I don't really care which one I have, as long as I get some of those fries."

Sara reached for half of a turkey sandwich. "How did things go down at the sheriff's department?" she asked.

Before Kari could answer, Jim came back in. He was alone.

"Where's Rachael?" Kari asked. She knew the woman came in at eleven, and often stayed until her kids got out of school, so unless she'd brought a lunch with her, the volunteer had to be hungry. "Isn't she joining us?"

Jim's face slowly turned pink and he wouldn't meet Kari's eyes. He was a veteran whose PTSD made it tough for him to work at regular jobs, and he tended not to be great around most people. His arms and neck were covered with tattoos and he clearly wasn't very well educated. But he loved the animals, didn't mind doing the dirtiest jobs, and had eventually gotten used to Kari after she replaced the previous owner Daisy, who he'd idolized. Right now, though, he looked as though he'd like to bolt back into the kennels and hide.

"She said she's not hungry," he mumbled, looking at the floor. "Said she'd eat when she got home."

"Ah," Kari said. She didn't buy that story for a minute. But could the woman actually believe that Kari might start randomly poisoning sandwiches? Apparently so.

"If you'd rather not eat the food I brought either, Jim, I'll understand," she said in a soft voice. The French fry she'd been nibbling on seemed to turn into sand in her mouth.

His head shot up and he stalked over to the desk and grabbed a sandwich at random, not even looking to see what it was. "Not a chance," Jim mumbled around the large bite he took. "I'm starving." He swallowed, then added, "And I'm not an idiot like some people. I know there's no way you killed anyone." He plopped the other half and a handful of fries onto a plate with a defiant look and then walked outside to eat it at the picnic table outside.

"He's a good man," Sara said in a quiet voice after the door closed behind him. "And I'm sure nobody really believes you killed Charlie."

"Yes he is," Kari agreed. "But I'm afraid you might be wrong about the second half of that sentence. You should have seen the people in the diner. It was like half of them expected me to lunge at them with a knife and the other half were making book on how long it would be before Sheriff Richardson arrested me." She sighed. "This is getting old fast. I can't believe that Charlie is ruining my life, even after he's dead. That's so typical."

"What did the sheriff say?" Bryn asked. She nibbled at her wrap delicately, somehow managing not to drip lettuce down the front of her shirt the way Kari just had. "Was your husband really murdered?"

"Ex-husband," Kari and Sara said in unison.

"Ex-everything," Bryn said.

There was no arguing with that. "They found evidence that he was poisoned by some kind of wild mushroom," Kari said. The sheriff hadn't told her it was a secret, after all. "Something called a destroying angel."

Bryn's normally dark complexion paled noticeably. "Oh, no," she whispered. "That's terrible." She put her wrap down with a thud and wiped at her eyes with the hand that hadn't been holding it. "That's a horrible way to die."

Sara and Kari exchanged glances.

"That sounds like you know something about it," Sara said in a gentle tone.

Bryn blew her nose on a napkin. "I had a cousin when I was younger. He and I would stay with my aunt for a few weeks every summer, to give our parents a break." She gave a watery smile. "Of course, I was a very sophisticated nine and Bobby was only seven, so I thought he was kind of a pest when he tried to follow me around, but mostly we had a good time."

She shook her head, lost in memories for a moment. "That last summer, we had watched an old movie called *My Side of the Mountain*. It was based on a book my aunt was reading to us every night." Bryn smiled. "One of the perks of staying with a librarian. It was like having our very own story hour."

"I remember that book," Sara said. "I loved it both because it was about a boy surviving on his own in the wilderness, and because it was set right here in the Catskills." Sara had grown up in Lakeview and other than the years she spent at college, had spent most of her adult life here, too.

"That's the one," Bryn said. "We were completely fascinated about the idea of being able to live off the land, with no help from grownups. Bobby and I spent days out in the backyard, pretending we were hiding out in the mountains. My aunt's house butts right up against a tract of woods, so it was perfect. Until Bobby found some mushrooms growing in the grass and decided we should eat them, just like the boy in the movie ate things he found growing wild."

"Oh, no," Sara said.

"Yes. It was a destroying angel." Bryn wiped her eyes

again. "He didn't get sick right away, and by the time my aunt figured out what was going on, it was too late. I'm not sure either one of us has ever forgiven ourselves. I didn't eat mine because I didn't like mushrooms, or I would probably have died, too."

"It was an accident," Kari said. "And you were a little kid. There was nothing you could have done." She felt terrible about bringing back such a bad memory, although it gave her an interesting glimpse into Bryn's past. "I'm so sorry that happened to you."

"I remember hearing about that at the time, but I didn't realize it had anything to do with you. I'm so sorry, Bryn." Sara looked at Kari thoughtfully. "But the police are sure that your ex-husband's poisoning wasn't an accident?"

"Charlie hated mushrooms," Kari said. "He never would have eaten one on purpose. So they're pretty sure that means someone slipped it to him somehow." She glanced at Bryn. "It wasn't me, I swear, Bryn."

"Of course it wasn't," Bryn said, blowing her nose one last time and then picking her wrap up again, as if to signal that her part of the conversation was done. She tended to be a bit reserved, unlike her outgoing and bubbly aunt. "Like Jim said, only an idiot would think that. But somebody did it."

She gave Kari and Sara a fierce look. "And we're going to find out who, right? Not just because we don't want Kari to go to prison for something she didn't do, but because anyone who would do that to someone on purpose deserves to be punished."

Kari couldn't have agreed more.

🐈 Thirteen

As they were finishing up the evening cleaning, and running one last load of laundry through the industrial machines Kari had purchased along with her many other upgrades, her cell phone rang. A glance at the screen told her it was Angus, so she hurriedly dropped the towel she was folding and accepted the call.

"Hey," she said. "What's up?"

She moved out of the laundry area, which was tucked into one corner of the kitchenette, so she could get away from the rumble of the dryer. From her new position right inside the main room, she could see Bryn and a volunteer named Fern cleaning litter boxes and filling food bowls. Sara had already gone home for the day, since, as she often explained, her husband was apparently incapable of cooking anything that didn't involve a barbeque grill.

The slightly fishy smell of wet cat food clashed with the more acrid scent of the sanitizer in the spray bottle Bryn was wielding, but the odor just reminded Kari of how happy she was to be here, doing these mundane tasks every day. Serenity Sanctuary had turned out to be her sanctuary, too. She hoped nothing was going to happen to take that away from her.

The sound of Angus's voice brought her back from her slightly depressed musings about an uncertain future. Now she could concentrate on her uncertain present instead.

"I was just wondering if we could meet up when I got out of work," he was saying. "I wanted to talk to you about some things, and I have new eye drops I want to try out on that kitten whose infection isn't responding to the Terramycin." In the background, she could hear the muted sounds of dogs barking and people talking. The veterinary office sounded a lot like the shelter.

Kari wondered what Angus wanted to talk to her about. Hopefully he wasn't going to tell her he didn't want to date her anymore while simultaneously trying to get drops into a squirming kitten's eyes. That would be a new breakup low, even for her.

"Um, sure," she said. "I'm going to be here for a little while longer. I was going to try and catch up on some supply orders after everyone else left. I just have to pop home for a couple of minutes to feed my gang before rioting breaks out, but then I'll be back."

"Great," he said. "I should be there in a half an hour or so. Maybe an hour, if the techs are still having problems keeping that one overnight IV drip from crimping up and setting off its alarm. They've been fighting with it for the last few days, and I told them I'd take a look."

"Not a problem," Kari said. "I was out for a while this morning, talking to the sheriff, so I have a lot to catch up on." She hesitated and then added, "Speaking of which, you're not afraid to be alone with me, are you? I know there are a lot of rumors going around town."

Angus coughed and sputtered, and she could almost see him choking on the coffee he insisted he could drink all day without it keeping him awake at night like any normal person.

"Kari! No, of course not," he said. "Good grief. It sounds like you've been having a rough day. I'm sorry I didn't call earlier, but it has been a zoo around here."

Kari laughed, partially at his bad animal-themed joke, and partially out of relief. "Okay, great," she said. "See you in a bit."

About forty-five minutes later, Kari was trying to type a massive food order into her computer, although she was constantly being interrupted by Queenie, who had insisted on coming back to the shelter with Kari after the cats and Fred had been fed.

Queenie had been knocking Kari's pens off the desk, which was one of the kitten's favorite games, and had added in a new target: the cute beer-shaped bottle opener from the Lakeview Lagerhaus Kari had brought back from Oktoberfest.

Just as Kari hit "send," the bottle opener hit the floor with a clunk, missing Kari's sneaker-clad foot by less than an inch. Thankfully, it was metal topped with thick plastic, so it didn't seem to be affected by the abuse.

"Cut that out, you little miscreant," she said, picking up the opener for the sixth time and putting it back on the desk. She made a mental note to take it home with her and put it on the fridge (it had a magnet on the back), out of the kitten's reach. Kari scooped up the tiny troublemaker and kissed her nose before settling Queenie onto her lap. "This game is not nearly as much fun as you think it is."

Round green eyes blinked up at her innocently, as if what Kari had just said couldn't possibly have been true. "*Mo-aw*," the kitten said, reaching a black paw out toward the decorative opener again.

There was a rap on the door and Angus poked his head in. His red hair, always on the shaggy side, was even more disheveled than usual, and Kari thought he looked tired. Maybe she wasn't the only one who had had a rough day.

"Hi there," she said, getting up from her chair and plopping Queenie gently onto the floor so they could both go over and greet him. As usual, Queenie somehow danced around his large feet without getting stepped on.

"Hi there," he said, giving Kari a quick hug. "I'm sorry," he added as her nose wrinkled. "I got peed on by a Rottweiler who is apparently a big baby when it comes to getting his shots. I would have stopped at home and changed my clothes before coming over, but as usual, I was late getting out, and I didn't want to hold you up."

With most of the lights turned off or down for the night and everyone else gone, the main room of the shelter seemed much more private and intimate than it usually did. Kari decided she really didn't care about the smell—after all, she probably wasn't exactly the freshest flower in the bunch at this point either—and hugged him back.

"It's fine," she said. "I'm glad you're here. Do you want me to bring the sick kitten out, or should we go into the back?"

The sanctuary had a separate room where infectious

or ill cats could be segregated away from the others. Right now there were only three residents: an elderly cat being treated for a urinary tract infection who needed the privacy of her own litter area and some peace and quiet, a stray who had been brought in after he lost a fight to some kind of animal who was recovering from surgery, and the seven-week-old kitten with the persistent eye infection.

Angus had been treating her for over ten days already, and while her siblings had recovered quickly and gone back in with their mother, the tiny gray-and-brown tiger cat they'd named Diana Prince was still snuffly and goopy-eyed. Luckily she was old enough that she'd been weaned, but she was being fed a slurry of wet food mixed with water through a large syringe since her stuffed nose meant she wasn't very hungry and wouldn't eat on her own.

"How's my little princess today?" Angus asked the kitten, picking her up in one long-fingered hand. They'd decided to go back and treat her in the sick room, mostly to make sure that Queenie didn't get exposed to anything. The little patient had been on antibiotics for days and probably wasn't still infectious, but there was no point in taking any chances.

The kitten squeaked up at him, peering out through eyes that were still glued half shut. A muted purr rumbled out of her tiny chest. Angus had that effect on animals. It was one of the things Kari liked about him.

Angus checked the kitten over, tutting over its snotty nose. "Well, she's not running a temperature anymore," he said. "But she should have responded to the antibiotic better and the eye drops we've got her on clearly aren't doing the job."

He pulled a couple of small bottles out of his jacket pocket. "I've brought a couple of new things to try. She's old enough now that she should be able to tolerate a stronger antibiotic, and I've had good results using these drops on the more resistant infections."

He applied the drops and somehow managed to get the liquid antibiotic down the kitten's throat without her spitting most of it back onto his shirt, which was more than Kari could usually do. Then he wrote down the dosing instructions on both bottles and put them in the box with the kitten's name on it on the shelf nearby, removing the old medicines at the same time.

Angus washed his hands at the sink to the side of the room, then took a minute to check on both of his other patients before washing his hands one last time and turning to Kari with a small smile. "Now that the fun part is over, shall we go back into the main room to talk?"

They sat down next to each other on the visitor's couch by the door, with Queenie immediately hopping up to sit on Kari's lap. The black kitten had knocked the bottle opener off the desk again while they were gone, and Kari had picked it up as they crossed the room, and now was fiddling with it as they talked.

"That was a fun night," Angus said, nodding at the opener. "Despite the unwanted company." He took a deep breath and Kari braced herself, not sure she wanted to hear whatever he was going to say next.

"I owe you an apology," he said, pushing his hair back out of his face and looking uncharacteristically diffident. "I'm sorry if I made you feel as though I doubted you. I know you would never hurt anyone on purpose. I haven't been avoiding you, I've just well . . . there is something I haven't told you about."

"Oh?" Kari said, hoping she sounded more encouraging than apprehensive. "Is this a good thing or a bad thing?"

Angus smiled at her, and the knot in her stomach loosened a little. "It's not really either," he said. "I was following a hunch about someone involved in this whole mess and I didn't want to get your hopes up until I figured out if there was anything to it or not."

Huh. That wasn't what she'd been expecting. "Really? Who?"

"That blond woman you pointed out when we were having lunch at the diner the other day. The one who showed up at Oktoberfest, too. We talked about her, right?" He pointed at the opener she was teasing Queenie with.

"Sure," Kari said, deciding not to mention that she'd been fretting about that same woman for other reasons. "What about her?"

"I thought there was something odd about your story about her coming into the sanctuary and looking at pets, even though she didn't live in town yet. So when she left the diner, I followed her." He looked slightly embarrassed, one corner of his mouth twitching upward. "I know, it sounds silly. I read too many mystery books as a kid, probably. I just had a feeling. And after Charlie was so awful to you, and I overreacted and made things worse, I wanted to see if there was anything I could do to help."

Kari felt her eyes widen. "And you thought this woman had something to do with Charlie's plans for the shelter? Why?"

Angus shrugged. "I was facing her when Charlie and I got into it at the diner," he said. "And I could swear that she was staring at us with absolute fury on her face. It was just for a minute, and it could have just been that she was angry that our childish tussle was interrupting her lunch, but there was something about her expression that looked more personal."

"So you followed her?" Kari said. "Then what?"

He flushed. "Nothing, then. She went in and out of a couple of stores and generally acted like any other tourist. So I thought maybe I was mistaken. But then the next day she turned up for my nature walk."

"Somehow she didn't strike me as the foraging type," Kari said with a smile. "But I guess you never know."

Angus nodded, pushing his hair out of his face again. If he didn't get it cut soon, Kari was going to take him to see Suz. Kari had her friend trim her own long curly hair a couple times a year, although it was pretty simple because it was all one length. Kari always told people who found this shocking that the one person you could trust to do what you told them when you said, "Just trim one inch off the ends," was a dog groomer, since many of the fancier purebred cuts were so precise. And the owners so picky.

"You really don't," Angus said. "That guy James Torrance came, too. You know, the one who said he was doing business with your ex-husband. At least he had a good reason to be interested in the nature walk, since he said he was checking it out for future glamping guests, to see if it was something to add to the brochure."

"Great," Kari said, trying not to grind her teeth. "They were already planning the brochure. Swell." She ran her fingers through Queenie's soft fur to soothe herself and got a purr for her efforts. "Did I tell you that

Torrance actually showed up here on Sunday in the early evening to scope the place out?"

"Seriously?"

"Yup," she nodded. "He said he didn't know that Charlie was dead. His surprise seemed genuine enough, but I'm not sure I bought it anyway. What I did believe was his anger when I informed him that I had never agreed to let Charlie have the property, and there was no actual deal, no matter what Charlie had told him."

Kari gave a small shudder, remembering how threatened she had felt as the wide-shouldered man had loomed over her in that moment. "He *really* wasn't happy about that. Now he's insisting that since Charlie signed a business agreement with him—which Torrance apparently gave him quite a bit of money for—and I was supposedly still married to Charlie, that means I have to honor the agreement. He mentioned lawyers. Loudly."

Angus gave her a quick hug, making sure not to squash Queenie in the process. "That sounds terrifying," he said. "I'm sorry I wasn't there. But I doubt his claims would stand up in court." He grimaced. "That Charlie of yours sure was a piece of work."

"Not mine," Kari reminded him. "That was the whole point of the divorce. But yes, he certainly was." She steered the conversation back to where it had started, eager to get an explanation for the reports she'd gotten. "But you were telling me about this woman. What was her name again? Toni? Tammy?"

"Tanya," Angus said. "Tanya Baldwin. I don't know much about her. But she seemed kind of sad and a little lonely when we were chatting after the nature walk, so I invited her to have lunch with me. I thought maybe I could find out if she had any connection with Charlie or maybe his business partner. She and this guy Torrance didn't act like they knew each other, but she was clearly lying about something."

"Where did you go?" Kari asked, as though that were at all important. "Someplace nice?"

Angus snorted down his nose. "I took her to the Good Karma Deli. I was hoping that she'd have a couple of beers to wash down the spicy chicken tikka masala and vindaloo and end up letting something slip."

Kari raised an eyebrow. "Sneaky. Did it work?"

"It did, although she just had water to drink. She was still pretty chatty," Angus said with a chuckle. "In fact, she told me something very interesting. So interesting that when the sheriff asked me where I'd been on Saturday, I kind of dodged the question, because I wanted to tell you first."

Ah. That explained what Richardson had said about Angus being evasive. She hoped that whatever he had learned got one or both of them off the suspect list. And not more firmly on it.

"Well, are you going to tell me this interesting fact you learned, or am I going to have to sic this kitten on you?" Kari demanded.

Angus's blue eyes twinkled with merriment. "Okay," he said. "But you're never going to believe it."

"What?" Kari said, picking up Queenie and holding her in midair. The kitten just kept purring.

"Tanya told me she followed Charlie to town to find out what he was up to." He held up one hand to stave off the inevitable follow-up question. "Because she was his girlfriend."

Fourteen

Kari's jaw clicked closed and she put the kitten down carefully on her knee. "His what?"

"According to Tanya," Angus repeated, "she was his girlfriend. Of course, I only have her word for that, since we can't exactly ask Charlie."

"Holy moly," Kari said. "I can't believe Charlie was trying to get back together with me when he already had another girlfriend." She thought about it for a moment. "Oh, wait. Yes I can." They said a tiger never changed its stripes. Apparently that went for skunks as well.

"Well, to be fair," Angus said, "Tanya said they had only been going out for a few months. But she insisted the relationship was serious."

"It probably was for her," Kari said. "Whether that means it was for Charlie is a whole other issue. You said she followed him here? Why on earth would she do that?"

Angus had found what looked like a shoelace in his

pocket and was using it to play with Queenie. Kari didn't even bother to ask why he was carrying one shoelace. The vet had a tendency to pick up stray bits and pieces and pull them out later with no idea where he'd picked them up. She actually found it kind of adorable. Or was that adorkable?

"According to Tanya, Charlie told her he was going out of town for a couple of days on business, but then she'd found an article about your lottery win on his desk. She said your name and the section about the shelter were circled in bright red, which is why she noticed it when she stopped by to water his plants," Angus said. "When she looked you up and found out that the two of you used to be married, she got worried and followed him to Lakeview."

"If that's true, he can't have been happy when she showed up," Kari said. "Since he clearly had plans that didn't include her, at least at this stage of the game." She chewed on her lip. "Are you sure they really were in a relationship? The whole thing seems kind of odd."

"I don't know," Angus said. "Can you think of someone from your old life you could call and ask if Charlie was dating anyone?"

Kari thought about it for a minute, and got a sinking feeling in her stomach. But she'd been intending to make the phone call anyway. She'd just been putting it off because she had a bad case of "don't wanna."

"What?" Angus asked. "You have a funny look on your face." He stifled a laugh. "Like a cross between indigestion and someone remembering a horror movie they saw."

"That sounds about right," Kari said. "I think I'll have to call my former mother in-law."

"Ouch," Angus said. "Didn't you tell me that she didn't like you much?"

"I don't like zucchini much," Kari said with a grimace. "Shirley *despised* me. She never thought I was good enough for her son. Mind you, I'm not sure she ever thought anyone was good enough for her golden boy." She sighed, suddenly feeling sympathy for the woman who had helped to make her married years a living hell. "She must be devastated, though. Charlie was everything to her."

"So she wasn't married?" Angus said.

"Oh yes," Kari answered, rolling her eyes. "But it was sort of an odd marriage. Charlie's father did something in finance and was always away overseas, and when he was around she criticized every move he made. She actually referred to him as 'Mr. Smith.'"

"Sweet," Angus said.

"Yeah, not so much," Kari said. "He was kind of a cold fish, so I'm not sure her sniping bothered him at all. I think maybe Charlie learned how to charm her at an early age to keep on his mother's good side, and it just kind of morphed into who he was as an adult."

She sighed, remembering the way he'd swept her off her feet when they met right after her mother had died of cancer. She'd been visiting family on Long Island and had been introduced to Charlie at some pretentious social function they'd dragged her to in a fruitless effort to cheer her up. Her mother had just died, leaving her with a drunk father and a wild seventeen-year-old brother. Nothing in the universe could have cheered her up.

But Charlie had made a good stab at it. Eleven years older than her, handsome, successful, sophisticated, and oh so charming—once he'd made up his mind that she was what he wanted, she didn't have a chance. A few months later she graduated from college and they got married right away. But she wasn't the broken, malleable woman he thought she was, and their marriage soon descended into bitterness and acrimony.

None of which had been helped by Charlie's mother, who took his side with increasing shrillness and who had probably thrown a party the day Kari moved out. And now she had to call the woman and express condolences before quizzing her about her dead son's love life. Swell. Kari would rather be cleaning dog pens. With a toothbrush and a spoon.

Kari didn't even have the excuse of not knowing the phone number, since the digits had apparently been permanently carved into her memory over the course of her marriage. Oh well, no point in putting it off any longer. The sheriff had already called Charlie's mother to inform her of his death, although Kari had no way of knowing exactly what Richardson had told Shirley.

"Hang on a minute," she said to Angus. "I doubt this will take long." She pulled out her phone and keyed in the number, clutching Queenie a little closer for support.

An involuntary chill ran down her spine as the familiar voice said, "Smith residence. Shirley speaking."

"Uh, Mrs. Smith, this is Kari. Kari Stuart. I just called to say how sorry I am about Charlie. I know how close you two were, and what a terrible loss this must be." Kari stopped for breath, feeling like she was babbling.

"Kari?" Shirley sounded more baffled than angry. "I appreciate the sentiment, but how did you even know that Charles was dead? I only got the call yesterday." There was a honking noise in the background, as Shirley blew her nose vigorously enough to echo out of the phone.

Good grief. Apparently Charlie hadn't told his mother what he was up to. "He, uh, he was in Lakeview. Where I live now," Kari explained. "He showed up unexpectedly to visit me last Wednesday. You didn't know?"

There was a momentary pause. "No, I did not. It had been my understanding that he was off on vacation with his new girlfriend." She gave a sniff, this one sounding more indignant than bereaved. "A totally inappropriate woman, I must say, even for Charles. Her taste in clothing was appalling, she was nowhere near his intellectual equal, and her hair dye came from a *box*." Shirley added, as if this were the final straw, "She worked in an office. And not even something classy, like a law office, although I can't remember exactly what kind it was."

Kari bit back a sigh. "Well, I worked in an office part time when Charlie and I were married," she said.

"Yes, dear," Shirley said. "But you were working for your husband. That is a completely different kettle of fish."

This whole conversation was as unpleasant as a week-old kettle of fish, but at least Shirley had answered Kari's question about the girlfriend, without Kari even having to ask it, or explain why she wanted to know. She supposed that was something.

"What was Charles doing in, what did you call it, Land's End?" Shirley asked. "When that sheriff called, I was in such shock, I didn't think to ask him. Why on earth would he go to visit you after all this time?"

"Lakeview," Kari said. "The town I grew up in?" Not that she really expected Shirley to remember. "And it's actually kind of a strange story. Charlie came to tell me he'd discovered that our divorce paperwork had apparently never been filed correctly, so we were still married." She decided there was no point in mentioning the lottery win or that Charlie was trying to get money from her. The woman was mourning her son, after all. Besides, it might give her ideas Kari would rather she didn't have.

Shirley made a choking noise. "You what? That's impossible."

"That's what I said," Kari agreed. "I'm sure it will all turn out to just be some kind of paperwork mix-up. Somebody filed it in the wrong drawer or something. But in the meanwhile, Charlie had a business deal he was working on here, so he was still in town when he, uh, died."

She glanced up to see Angus give her a crooked smile. He could obviously tell, just from her end of the conversation, that it wasn't an easy one. He shifted a little closer so his knee was touching hers. Just a small thing, but it helped.

There was another brief pause and then Shirley said in an unusually subdued tone, "That sheriff said my Charles was murdered. It doesn't seem possible. Everyone loved him. Do you think there was some sort of mistake? I don't really trust some small-town police officer to know what he is doing."

"Actually," Kari said, twisting a curl of hair around one finger, something she sometimes did when she was nervous, "Sheriff Richardson is very competent. I've, uh, seen him work before." The fact that she had been a suspect in one case, and Suz in another one, not to mention that she was Richardson's main focus in *this* particular case, seemed like information that Shirley wouldn't find reassuring.

"Hmph," Shirley said. "If you say so." She gave a tiny cough, and then added in a reluctant tone, "I have never approved of any of the women my son chose, but I have to admit, you were far from the worst of them. At least you have a backbone, and a certain amount of brains. Not like that Sylvia. I swear, that woman had the IQ of a goldfish. Although her father did have a lot of money."

Kari blinked at her phone, then put it back up to her ear, wondering if she had actually just gotten a compliment from Charlie's mother. Not a great one, but still.

"Uh, thank you, I think," Kari said.

"My son was a good man," Shirley went on as if Kari hadn't spoken. "He deserved better than to die in some backwater town. Murdered, no less. I need to know what happened to my son, Kari." Her voice cracked. "I need you to find out what really happened to my boy. Please tell me you will. I don't trust this sheriff. I've never met him. But you were married to Charles. You must have loved him once. Promise me you'll find out the truth."

Kari opened her mouth, then closed it again. What could she possibly say? Queenie gazed up at her with wide green eyes and gave Kari's hand a lick.

"Okay," Kari said. "I'll do my best. And again, I'm sorry about your loss."

There was a sigh on the other end of the phone, and Shirley hung up without another word.

What on earth had just happened? Had Kari really agreed to hunt down the person who murdered her ex-husband to please the former mother in-law who hated her? She shook her head, eyes closed.

Oh well, it wasn't as though she wasn't already trying

to figure out what happened, both to clear her own name and to satisfy Bryn's need for punishment for the person who had used the mushroom that had taken her cousin's life to murder someone. Now there was just one more reason to get to the bottom of Charlie's murder. No pressure. No pressure at all.

You okay?" Angus asked, giving her a sympathetic look. "Do you want me to make you a cup of tea or something?" The kitten gave a tiny "*meep*" as if to add her concern to his.

"I'm fine," Kari told them both. "It wasn't exactly a fun conversation, but it went better than I'd expected. She did confirm that Charlie had been seeing someone, although she didn't mention Tanya by name. The description sounded about right, though."

"Huh," Angus said. "So Charlie's mother had no idea he was here in Lakeview, or what he was up to?"

"Nope," Kari said. "Nor had he mentioned the whole 'we're still married' thing. So other than confirming your information about Tanya being Charlie's girlfriend, I'm not sure we got anything helpful. We're pretty much right where we started."

Angus leaned back against the couch and crossed one long leg over the other knee. "So let's see what we actually know. Maybe something will pop out at us if we go over it piece by piece."

Kari couldn't come up with any better suggestions. "Okay," she said, scooting around so she was sitting sideways and facing him. Queenie settled in on her lap, small black paws kneading Kari's thigh.

"So this all started when Charlie showed up out of

nowhere, claiming we were still married, and that this meant he was entitled to half of my lottery earnings," Kari said. "The jerk."

"Something which we still don't know was true," Angus added with a scowl. "Either the part about the divorce or if he would actually have been able to persuade a judge to hand over the money you won years after you left him." He thought for a second. "Although we're definitely sure about the jerk part."

Kari carefully removed one sharp claw from where it had become stuck in her jeans. "Well, I did call the county clerk's office where the divorce papers should have been filed, and the woman there said she couldn't find them. Considering how discombobulated I was after I left, it is certainly possible that part of his story was true. As for the money, I guess we'll never know. But he could have made things very difficult for me, which was why I was playing along and trying to figure out if there was a way to get him to go away without getting everything he wanted."

"Except that what he wanted turned out to be the sanctuary and the land it is sitting on," Angus said. "Because he already had a plan to create this glamping retreat with James Torrance."

"Who we know was here in town when Charlie died, because we saw him at Oktoberfest, and then he came here to the sanctuary later the next day," Kari added. "He was really angry when I told him there was no way the project was going forward. If he knew that Charlie's plan wasn't working out the way they had intended it to, and he had already given Charlie a lot of money, he could have had a motive to kill him."

"That's true," Angus said. "But wouldn't he have had

a better chance of getting his money back if Charlie was still alive?"

Kari shrugged. "Maybe? Or maybe that money was specifically tied to this particular project. If so, Torrance would have lost the money either way." She thought for a minute, then went on.

"He was furious about Charlie lying to him. I could see it in his eyes. Torrance comes across as such a pleasant, fun-loving guy with his funky sneaker laces and hearty 'Hey, how ya doing' personality, but if you had seen the look on his face when I told him I wasn't giving up the sanctuary and had never agreed to do so, you wouldn't have recognized him as the same man."

"Okay," Angus said. "So Torrance is on the suspect list. Who else would have a motive?"

"This mysterious girlfriend, maybe?" Kari said.

Angus looked dubious. "Maybe? But why? Jealous of the beautiful ex-wife?"

Aw, he just said she was beautiful. Kari got distracted for a second, but then pulled her attention back to the matter at hand. "Doesn't seem like much of a motive, does it?" she said. "I mean, maybe if he had dumped her, but it doesn't sound like he did. He was just here trying to get my money."

"And you," Angus reminded her. "You said he was trying to persuade you to come back home with him."

"Hah," Kari said. "That was never going to happen. And honestly, I think it was just a ploy to get his hands on the rest of my lottery money. He could easily have told this Tanya woman he was going to string me along and then go back to her. Did she say anything that gave you any idea of what she was thinking?"

"Not really," Angus said. "I'm not sure she realized

that you and I were dating. After all, she only saw us together briefly at Oktoberfest when she stopped by the table, and we were with a bunch of other people. I think she was just venting about not trusting Charlie. It seemed pretty innocuous."

He thought for a minute. "In fact, if jealousy was the motive, I'm a bigger suspect than she is."

"Well, the sheriff certainly seems to think so," Kari agreed. "But since we both know you didn't do it, I suspect we should keep focusing on the other facts of the case."

She chewed on her lip for a moment, thinking. "Okay, so what about the murder itself? The toxicology report said he was killed with a poisonous mushroom. But the problem is, that doesn't narrow down the time he was actually poisoned much, since apparently it can take anywhere from five to twenty-four hours to do enough damage to be noticed."

"We know he was already sick when he came to your house for brunch," Angus said, still not looking happy at the reminder. "And he died that afternoon. Which theoretically means he could have been poisoned anytime between Saturday morning and early Sunday morning. That doesn't help us much, does it?"

He tapped one long finger against his chin. "Do they know what kind of mushroom it was?"

"Oh," Kari said. "I guess I haven't talked to you since my meeting with the sheriff. Apparently it was something called a destroying angel. I'd never heard of it, but Sheriff Richardson said it grows in this area, and can be mistaken for edible varieties of mushroom by people who don't know any better."

"Destroying angel," Angus repeated, his eyes wide.

"That's a nasty one. I occasionally see them when I'm leading my nature walks, and make sure I point them out to everyone." He swallowed hard. "I've never known anyone who had that kind of poisoning, but from everything I've read, it sounds like a terrible way to die."

Kari sighed. "I know. I wouldn't wish that on anyone, not even Charlie. Bryn lost a cousin to that mushroom when she was just a kid and it sounds devastating." She thought about it for a minute. "Do you think someone picked that particular method because they wanted him to suffer? Or was it just a matter of convenience? You know, they happened to spot one and thought, 'Gee, that's handy. I wanted to kill this guy and didn't know how I was going to do it. Look, a poison mushroom!'"

"No idea," Angus said. "I suppose it could be either. Or even both." He reached out and patted Queenie, who was playing with the bottle opener again. "Is it possible your ex-husband simply picked it himself and it was all just a horrible accident?"

Kari shook her head. "No, I don't think so. Charlie hated mushrooms. He never would have eaten one on purpose. For that matter, he wasn't the type to eat something he found growing wild in nature. He wouldn't even let me have a garden, because he said that there would be bugs all over everything."

"Well, he's not wrong," Angus said with a laugh. "I have a small patch out behind my house and it's not unusual to find an uninvited guest in my salad. I just love how fresh everything is, and don't worry about it much."

"Charlie believed that food should come from the grocery store wrapped in plastic, like God intended," Kari said ruefully. "So no, it isn't likely he would have eaten it by accident. Sheriff Richardson seems quite convinced that its murder."

"And that you're the most obvious suspect," Angus said with a grimace.

"Unfortunately, yes," Kari said. "On the surface, it certainly looks like I had the most to gain by his death. The sheriff even said he was going to check into whether I was still a beneficiary on any of Charlie's insurance policies."

"Were you?" Angus asked, looking startled.

Kari shrugged. "I have no idea. I doubt it, but I suppose he could have forgotten to take me off after the divorce. But he told me that when he divorced his first wife, a few years before he met me, he made sure she didn't even get the points on their shared grocery store card. He was petty about stuff like that."

"Huh," Angus said. "But if it turns out that you were still married, wouldn't you inherit everything?"

"Good grief," Kari said. "I hope not. I mean, it's not as though I need the money, and if it turns out that's true, the sheriff will just think it gives me an even greater motive." She swallowed around the sudden lump in her throat. That possibility hadn't even occurred to her. "I'm sure he has a will. Probably leaving everything to his mother. Or his favorite golf course, on the condition that they name a charity event after him, or something."

She really wasn't sure, though. They'd talked about getting their wills written up by a lawyer when they were first married, but Charlie didn't even want to discuss it. She'd never been sure if it was because he didn't want to leave anything to her, or if he was just uncomfortable facing his own eventual mortality. She had no idea if that had changed after she left.

"I guess the sheriff will find out one way or the other," Kari said. "In the meanwhile, let's focus on the rest of what we know already. You said that you've seen this destroying angel mushroom around here. Is it common?"

Angus scratched Queenie's chin. "I wouldn't say common, exactly. I've only spotted them a few times. But not rare, either. Our local conditions are perfect for fungi, because the ground can be quite moist."

"Oh, I know," Kari said. "When we had those five days of rain last month, I literally had mushrooms popping up in the middle of my lawn. I pulled them out because I was afraid the chickens or the dog would get at them, and I didn't know if eating them could make them sick."

"Probably not," Angus said. "We've never had an instance of a pet being poisoned by a mushroom at the veterinary hospital. I think they don't find them appealing. No idea about chickens, but either way, the mushrooms that came up in your lawn were probably perfectly harmless."

"So how can you tell the difference?" Kari asked.

"There are a few distinguishing features," Angus said. "For instance, the destroying angel has what's called a volva, a kind of veil that covers the entire mushroom when it is young. It fractures as the mushroom grows, but you can often find patches of the material on the stalk or cap. It's one of the things I point out to people when I spot one on the nature walks. But I also warn everyone that when foraging, it is important to be extra careful with wild mushrooms."

Privately, Kari thought she might never eat the things again, wild or otherwise.

"I'm not sure I'd be able to spot the signs," she said.

"Oh, it can be tricky to tell the difference between edible and inedible with a lot of plants," Angus said. "For instance, the roots of Queen Anne's lace are actually wild carrots, and you can eat them. But the plant resembles poison hemlock, which is, as the name would suggest, deadly. I always suggest that people steer clear of wild carrots, just in case."

"Why on earth would people go foraging, if it is so dangerous?" Kari asked, making a face.

Angus rolled his eyes. "Those are just two examples," he said. "There are plenty of plants that are safe and easy to find. People do it for a lot of reasons. The plants found in nature are usually organic, more nutritious, and of course, free. Plus it is a way to connect with nature, and our ancestors—who survived as hunter-gatherers for thousands of years—and a reason to get outside and stroll around." He smiled at her.

"I guess," Kari said.

"There's a booklet, too," he added. "Paige Adams, who owns the Paging All Readers bookstore, orders them for me at a discount, and most of the people who go on the nature walks buy one to take with them. It's an easy reference guide to identifying safe and unsafe plants."

Kari sat up straighter. "So both James Torrance and this Tanya woman would have had these booklets?" she asked.

"Along with the other twenty or so people who took the walk with them this weekend," he said. "Not to mention the folks who have taken it previously, some of whom live in town or are repeat visitors. I have a couple of regulars who own a second home in the area and bring their guests with them every time they're here."

"Oh," Kari said, subsiding back against the couch. "That kind of widens the pool of suspects, doesn't it?"

Angus gave her a wry grin. "The nature walk has turned out to be surprisingly popular. Of course, it is mentioned in the 'What to Do in Lakeview' pamphlets that are in all the bed-and-breakfasts in town, plus the information racks at the diner, town hall, and anyplace else tourists might end up. Thankfully, there are a few of us who take turns leading the walks, so I don't have to do it every weekend. But odds are that Tanya and James were just bored and looking for something to do, and it was just a coincidence that they were both on the nature walk."

"Well, it looks like we're right back where we started," Kari said with a sigh. "I guess I'm going to try and find out where Tanya is staying and see if she'll talk to me about Charlie. At Oktoberfest he said they were both staying at the same B and B, but since we know he was lying about knowing her before, he was probably lying about that, too."

"Uh, as it happens," Angus said, suddenly finding his sneakers very interesting, "she's staying at the Lakeshore Haven. It's a couple blocks past the end of the Main Street business district, where it starts transitioning into residential buildings. It's not fancy, but it is right on the lake, so the views are nice."

"You don't say." Kari stared at him, wondering how he knew and why he hadn't wanted to tell her.

"I walked Tanya back there after lunch," Angus said. "You know, just trying to be a gentleman."

"Okay," Kari said. "I actually know the woman who owns it, Dora Hudson. She's part of the book club I belong to, and we've met at her place a couple of times. You're right, the place is more homey than ritzy, but it is a great spot for a B and B."

She glanced at her watch and stood up, scooping Queenie onto her favorite shoulder perch. It was already past seven at night, and Kari still hadn't eaten dinner. "It's probably too late for me to go over there tonight, so I'll try in the morning after I finish up with things here."

Angus stood up, too. "I should get going. Herriot will be waiting for his evening stroll and sniff expedition. And I need to get out of these disgusting clothes."

Kari, who had just opened her mouth to ask him if he wanted to grab dinner with her, closed it again. "Yeah, sure," she said, feeling strangely disappointed. "I hear you. Thanks for the new meds for the kitten, and for going over all this with me."

Angus gave her a brief hug before heading for the door. "Anytime," he said.

He paused, one hand on the knob, and turned around to give her an intent look. "Go easy on Tanya when you talk to her tomorrow," he said. "I know that the whole situation is kind of weird, with her dating your ex, but remember that she just lost someone she was close to, and presumably loved, if she was concerned enough to follow him here. You don't want to make the conversation any more difficult than it has to be."

As he closed the door behind him, Kari had to wonder, was he more concerned about it being difficult for her, or for Tanya? And how worried should Kari be if it was the latter?

Fifteen

By around ten thirty Tuesday morning, Kari had finished the bulk of her part of the cleaning duties and answered a few phone calls and emails that only she could handle, so she headed out to the Lakeshore Haven Bed and Breakfast. After the usual argument with Queenie (which the kitten lost for a change), Kari shrugged into her denim jacket, since it was still a little cool out, and got into her new Toyota for the brief drive into town.

As she headed down the steep Goose Hollow Road, slowing often as it twisted and turned, Kari admired the glorious colors of the fall leaves, all yellow and orange and red, as though Mother Nature had decided to paint all the trees with her favorite hues. Meadows normally filled with crops lay fallow and waiting for spring planting, some of them dotted with the large round humps of rolled hay bales that always made Kari think of resting buffalo.

Tall spires of goldenrod lined the road in riotous profusion, with the occasional patch of more demure wild asters and black-eyed Susans sprinkled among them. One of the infrequent houses she passed had a huge line of late sunflowers, their heads turned to follow the sun.

A man out walking his dog raised a hand in greeting and Kari waved back out her partially opened window. She loved all the changing seasons of the Catskills, but autumn was probably her favorite. The crisp, clean air, occasionally touched by a hint of wood smoke as she passed a house whose occupants were burning leaves, the murmured lowing of cows in a field as they munched on the last of the summer grass, and the stately oaks and maples with their burnished foliage, all of these things said home to her. Not only had she grown up here, but since her return, she had done her best to build herself a new life in this place. She was determined not to let anything ruin that for her.

The Lakeshore Haven Bed and Breakfast was on the aptly named Lakeshore Drive, which ran around the edges of Blue Heron Lake for about three miles before turning into Country Route 7 on its way to neighboring Perryville. The houses on the lake side of the road tended to be smaller homes and three-season camps, but there were a few larger houses that had once belonged to the wealthy families who had founded the town.

Dora Hudson's house had three stories and sprawled across two lots, although there wasn't much land separating it from its nearest neighbors. Lakefront property had always been at a premium, so little space had been wasted on yards. An eight-foot white fence lent the bed-and-breakfast residents some privacy on one side, and on the other a gravel drive led to a small parking area shaded by trees. What little lawn there was had mostly been given over to bright flower beds and hanging baskets filled right now with colorful mums that echoed the changing leaves, with neatly trimmed grassy paths in between.

The house itself was painted a cheerful yellow, with vivid blue shutters and a matching front door. A sign hanging from a wrought iron holder said *Lakeshore Haven Bed & Breakfast. Dora Hudson, Proprietor.* A smaller sign hung underneath currently read *No Vacancy* and probably would until the end of the season.

Kari rang the bell and waited for a minute until she could hear footsteps approaching from the other side. When the door swung open, it revealed a plump older woman with dramatic auburn hair in a riot of short curls (both clearly owing their state to regular visits to the Bashful Beauty Boutique, although there was nothing bashful about either the hair or its owner). She was wearing royal blue Capri pants, a blouse covered with grinning orange jack-o'-lanterns, and scuffed leopard-print slippers. A flowered apron tied around her ample waist was dusted with flour, and she was wiping her hands off on a dish towel as she opened the door.

"Hello, Dora," Kari said. "I'm sorry, it looks like I've interrupted your cooking."

"Kari! What an unexpected pleasure," Dora said. "Come in, come in," she said, waving Kari in the direction of the kitchen, from which the tantalizing aromas of baking emanated.

"I was just making some muffins for the guests. Running a bed-and-breakfast means there always needs to be a plentiful supply of baked goods on hand." Dora patted her substantial belly and grinned, "Some of which never make it to the guests, alas." She didn't seem genuinely disturbed by this state of affairs.

"So, what can I do for you?" Dora asked as they entered the kitchen. It was as homey as the rest of the place, but despite its quaint feel it featured a state-of-the-art oven and stainless steel refrigerator. Kari felt a pang of envy, thinking about her battered stove and ancient plain white fridge. She *really* was going to have to deal with upgrading her own house, now that the shelter had mostly been brought up to the standards it deserved.

A set of red enamel bowls sat on the counter next to an open carton of free-range eggs that Kari recognized as coming from a vendor at the local farmer's market and a canister of flour, among other things. Already greased muffin tins were lined up next to them, while the last batch—blueberry, from the smell of them, cooled on metal racks on the farmhouse table that dominated the center of the room. A hanging copper rack showed off a wide array of pots and pans, and colorful ceramic pots full of herbs lined the windowsill.

"I think you must have the best kitchen in the county," Kari said with a sigh. Dora flushed with pleasure.

"Can I get you a cup of tea?" the older woman asked. Kari thought she was probably in her mid-sixties, although the dyed hair made it hard to tell, and her round face barely showed any wrinkles, except a few laugh lines around her bright green eyes.

"No thank you," Kari said. "I've actually stopped by to see one of your guests, if that's okay. A woman named Tanya? I think she's staying here."

Dora's face brightened. "Oh, yes. Tanya Baldwin. Lovely girl. She got here on Friday night. She was lucky because I had a last-minute cancellation or I wouldn't have had a room for her. A little nervy, but very sweet.

"Do you know, she actually asked to borrow a mason jar to put leaves and stones into? She told me that everywhere she goes, she makes up a little collection of things she picks up as she walks around, so she has a piece of every place she visits. Isn't that nice? I'm thinking of adding that to my guest offerings." Dora gazed at Kari. "I didn't realize she knew anyone in town."

"I don't know her, exactly," Kari said. "We just had a mutual friend. My ex-husband, actually. I was hoping to talk to her about him."

"Oh, honey, I heard about that," Dora's smile slid away and she patted Kari's hand. "I'm so sorry for your loss." She shook her head. "Terrible thing to happen. We can't have people coming here and getting poisoned. It will simply ruin the tourist trade."

Kari blinked. "Well, it's not as though it is a regular occurrence. But I see your point. Is Tanya here, by any chance?"

"You just caught her," the landlady said, her eyes darting toward the oven. "She's checking out in an hour."

Yikes. "I guess it is a good thing I came when I did," Kari said. "Look, you clearly need to get back to your cooking. Why don't you tell me how to find her room, and I'll get out of your way."

"If you don't mind showing yourself up, I do need to get this next batch in," Dora said. "I've got some guests I promised to pack picnic lunches for—that's an extra fee, you know—and I should really get these muffins finished and start in on that. Tanya is in the Tulip Room, top of the stairs and on your right."

"Thanks so much, Dora," Kari said.

"No problem at all," Dora said, already turning back to her mixing bowls. "I'll see you at the next book club meeting."

Kari went out of the kitchen and back where she'd come in. Opposite the front door there was a set of stairs that led to the second floor, and presumably, on to the third floor as well. The wooden treads had faded paisley carpeting, which she followed to the second-floor landing. When she turned to the right, the first door she came to had a stencil of a large pink tulip on it. The door across the way had a red rose. The Rose Room, no doubt.

She knocked twice, briskly. The door swung open and Tanya, wearing skinny jeans and a low-cut red sweater that didn't really suit her shape or coloring, said, "I'll be right down to pay my bill." When Tanya saw Kari there instead of Dora, she took an involuntary step backward, which was enough space to allow Kari to slip inside.

"Hello," Kari said in a pleasant tone. "I hope you don't mind, but Dora told me where to find you, and said it would be okay to come on up."

As Tanya fumbled for a response, Kari took the opportunity to glance around the room. She had only ever been in the living room downstairs when she came for the book group meetings, and it was interesting to see how the other half slept, as it were.

As might have been expected from the name, the Tulip Room had a flower theme. The queen-sized bed had a comforter covered in bright pink tulips on a cream background, and the curtains were a dusky rose satin with lighter pink ties. The wood-planked floor had a few cream-colored throw rugs, and a flowered chair sat in a corner next to a small desk. Photographs of tulips by a local artist adorned the walls, and a vase full of the cut flowers sat atop an antique dresser, next to a pile of leaves that were just beginning to curl at the edges, and a few rocks that looked as though they might have been gathered on the shore of the lake.

A quick peek into the en suite bathroom showed the same pink theme, mini soaps in the shape of tulips, and an assortment of cute little bottles of shampoo, conditioner, lotion and such with the bed-and-breakfast's name on them. Nice. The entire place was cozy and welcoming, and Kari was tempted to book a stay here the next time she needed a break, even though it was only a few miles from home.

"Uh, hi," Tanya said. "You're Kari, right? We met at the Oktoberfest celebration last Saturday. Is there something I can help you with?" She glanced toward the suitcase that lay open on the bed, and the closet, which still had a few dresses hanging on padded pink hangers. "I'm kind of in the middle of packing."

"So I see," Kari said. "I wanted to talk to you about Charlie, if you can spare a couple of minutes."

Tanya turned pale under her heavily applied blush and clenched her hands into fists at her side. "Charlie?" she said in a high voice.

"Yes, Charlie," Kari said. "You know—my ex-husband, your current boyfriend?"

"Oh," Tanya said, and sat down on the edge of the bed. "How did you find out?"

"It's a small town," Kari said, not wanting to bring Angus into it. "Everyone eventually knows everything."

"I'm sorry," Tanya said. She looked miserable, and wouldn't meet Kari's eyes. "I know I shouldn't have come here. It was just . . ."

"So you *were* dating?" Kari said, just to clarify.

"Yes, we were," Tanya said. "It had only been a couple of months, but things had been going so well." She patted her hair. "I'd changed my whole look to fit in better with his friends, and I was trying to lose weight. He even took me to meet his mother."

"That must have been fun," Kari said, feeling an unexpected sympathy for someone she'd frankly expected to dislike. "Not. I take it Charlie didn't know you were planning to come to Lakeview?"

Tanya shook her head. "He told me he was on a business trip, but his birthday was coming up and I thought I could surprise him. I even bought him a gift." She pulled a long flat box out of her suitcase and showed it to Kari.

Inside was a tie with a golf theme in green and gold. Kari didn't have the heart to tell the woman that Charlie would have hated it. He only wore expensive designer ties and hated novelty anything. "Cute," was one of the worst insults he could apply to a gift. The tie definitely fell into the cute category. But tears were already gathering at the edges of Tanya's eyes and Kari didn't want to do anything to make her feel worse.

"Nice," Kari lied. "But isn't it true that you actually followed Charlie here to check up on him because you found out he was coming to visit me?"

Tanya dug a tissue out of a pocket in her jeans and ran it under her eyes, leaving a black streak from her mascara. "It is," she said in a whisper. She didn't seem to question how Kari could know that. "Like I said, it was a horrible mistake. I should have just stayed at home. But I was so worried. I saw your picture in that newspaper clipping and you were so pretty. *And* you'd won all that money in the lottery. How could I not worry?"

Kari scooted the flowery chair over to where the other woman was sitting. "I promise you, anything between me and Charlie was over a long time ago. I hadn't even talked to him since the divorce, and I had less than zero interest in getting back together with him."

"But he was such a catch," Tanya said.

"Not once you got to know him," Kari said flatly. "The only reason he came here was to try and get his hands on half of my money. It had absolutely nothing to do with me personally. This wasn't about love. It was about greed."

Tanya wiped her eyes again. "It wasn't greed," she said. "He needed that money to get his business back on its feet again. He had big plans. He told me we'd get married after he got everything on track. But he didn't tell me he was going to come see you, or how pretty you are." She glared at Kari, shifting so rapidly from grief to anger, it almost made Kari fall off her chair.

"In a way, this was all your fault," Tanya said. "He was so mad when he found out I was here. He said I was going to ruin everything. That you two were going to get back together. That if you found out who I was, you wouldn't agree to go into business with him. I'd never seen him so furious." She burst into tears, sobbing into her now soggy tissue.

Kari sighed and got up to get a new one from a fabric-covered box on the dresser next to the leaves and stones. After a moment's thought, she grabbed the entire box and handed it to Tanya before sitting back down.

It occurred to Kari that if she had been the one to end up dead, she definitely would have pegged Tanya as the person with the strongest motive. But the woman seemed genuinely grief-stricken over Charlie, which frankly was more than he deserved from the sound of it.

"Look," Kari said in a gentle tone. "I promise you, there was never any chance of me going into business with Charlie, and even less chance of me getting back together with him, no matter what he might have said. I'm sure he loved you very much."

She cleared her throat. "But I'm afraid you're going to need to talk to the sheriff before you leave town. I happen to know he wanted to ask you some questions, and that was before I found out you were Charlie's girlfriend."

Tanya gazed up at her, eyes wide like a deer caught in the headlights. "But why would he want to talk to me? I didn't do anything."

Except stalking your boyfriend and buying the world's ugliest tie. But Kari was pretty sure that last one wasn't a criminal offence.

"It's all routine, nothing to worry about," Kari said. "Believe me, Sheriff Richardson is just concerned with getting all the facts." Hopefully, facts that would prove Kari hadn't killed her ex-husband, although after talking to Tanya, she doubted anything Tanya had to say to the sheriff was going to help.

"Would you go with me?" Tanya asked tearfully. "I know you don't owe me anything, but I'd feel better if I had someone there who was on my side."

It was all Kari could do not to let her mouth fall open. What on earth made this woman think Kari would be on her side? Still, she did feel sorry for her, if for nothing else than the fact that she'd been yet another victim of Charlie's persuasive charm. Kari supposed that while that didn't put them on the same side, exactly, it did mean they were both members of a not-very-exclusive club.

"Fine," she said, trying not to sound too reluctant. "Come on then. Let's get this over with."

Somehow she didn't think this was what Angus had had in mind when he suggested she not make things difficult.

Sheriff Richardson gave Kari an odd look when Tanya explained who she was and that she wanted Kari to stay in the room while he asked his questions.

But all he said was, "Interesting choice. Most people would rather have a lawyer." Then he ushered them into his office and indicated they should both sit in front of his desk.

"Thank you for coming in," he said to Tanya. "If I could please get your full name, home address, and your relationship to the deceased?"

Aw, nuts.

Sure enough, Tanya burst into tears again.

Ten minutes later, after Richardson had sent a sergeant to fetch tea and yet more tissues, Tanya had told him more or less the same story she'd told Kari. Kari thought the tears were real, but when Tanya described Charlie as sweet and loving, never impatient or critical, Kari had to wonder if the woman had been dating some other Charlie Smith.

She supposed it was possible that he'd never showed his true self during their time together, or maybe, like a much younger Kari, Tanya had simply been too naïve to recognize the signs of an abusive personality. Or maybe he'd been on his best behavior for some reason, until he finally snapped at Oktoberfest, when she'd seen them arguing.

Richardson added another note to his ever-present pad and gazed dispassionately at Tanya. "Can you tell me where you were in the twenty-four hours before Mr. Smith was taken ill?" He looked down at his pad. "I'll need you to account for your whereabouts starting on Saturday morning, please."

Tanya blinked wet eyelashes, her mascara smeared under her eyes like two dark half-moons. "Well, let me think. Saturday morning I got up and had breakfast at Lakeshore Haven. You know, that Dora makes the most incredible omelets. And her muffins, oh dear me. I swear, I think I gained ten pounds since I got here." She stared down at her cup of tea, which Kari suspected wasn't much better than the station coffee. "I also had a delicious pot of Lapsang souchong. It was so good, I lingered longer than I should have."

"And Mrs. Hudson can vouch for that?" Richardson asked, jotting it down.

"Oh, yes," Tanya said. "She actually came and sat down for a cup of tea after I'd finished breakfast. I asked about things to do around town, since it was such a beautiful day, and she recommended the nature walk."

Tanya blushed and glanced down at her tea. "It was led by a lovely man named Angus. Maybe you know him? He's a veterinarian, and he was so knowledgeable about all the local flora and fauna. After the walk was over, he invited me to lunch, so we were together until about three, I think."

The sheriff raised an eyebrow in Kari's direction before saying, "Is that so? Yes, I'm familiar with Dr. McCoy. He's a very respected member of the community. I take my own dog to him, in fact."

Kari answered his questioning look with a tiny shrug, which she hoped he would be able to interpret as, "Yes, I knew about this already. No, I'm not bothered by it." Part of which was actually true.

"And after you left Dr. McCoy?" he asked Tanya, pen poised over paper.

"I had a little bit of a headache, so I went back to the bed-and-breakfast to lie down," Tanya said. "I stayed in my room until around five-thirty, when I decided to go check out the Oktoberfest celebration at the brewery. That was in the brochure Dora gave me too, plus she showed me a flyer with a description of the music and such. To be honest, it really wasn't my kind of thing, but she was so persuasive, I thought I'd at least go check it out."

"I see," Richardson said. "I gather from Ms. Stuart and some of the others who were there with her that you actually arrived at their table in the company of Mr. Smith, and that you were seen arguing together before that. Can you explain what you and Mr. Smith were discussing, and why when you reached the table, he told everyone that he knew you because you were staying at the same B and B, something we have established is in fact untrue?"

Tanya flushed, glancing at Kari and then away again. "Uh, it wasn't really an argument, exactly," she said. "Charlie wasn't happy to see me at the celebration, because he didn't want Kari to know that we were dating. I said I didn't understand why it was such a big deal, since he swore he wasn't interested in her romantically, but he wanted me to leave. I told him it wasn't a problem, that he could just say we met in town, so that's what he did. I didn't like lying, but it seemed harmless."

"How long did you stay at the party?" Richardson asked. "I've asked around, and no one seems to have seen you after you stopped by Ms. Stuart's table for those few minutes, and then said you were going back to the snack table."

"I ended up leaving right away," Tanya said. "My headache from earlier turned into a migraine after Charlie and I had our little disagreement, and it really wasn't my kind of event anyway. So I just went back to the bed-and-breakfast. Dora was in the kitchen baking when I got there, so she made me a cup of chamomile tea and I went upstairs. I ended up taking a pill and going to bed early."

The sheriff looked down at his notes again. "You said Oktoberfest wasn't your kind of event? Why not? And if it wasn't, why did you go?"

"Like I told you, I thought it might hurt Dora's feelings if I didn't, because she seemed to think it was the best thing ever. And I was hoping to run into Charlie, since I'd barely seen him since I got to town." She sighed. "I told you how well that worked out. Anyway, it isn't my kind of thing because I don't drink."

"You don't drink beer?" Richardson said. "I could see why Oktoberfest wouldn't be much of a draw, although there is always the music and the food, too."

"I don't drink at all," Tanya said. She rooted in her purse and pulled out what looked like a fancy coin with words engraved on it around a central triangle. "Look, I got my ten-year chip from AA in July. I quit when I was pregnant with my son, and haven't had one drink since." She tucked it back in her wallet and looked earnestly at the sheriff. "Charlie was still there when I left, and I didn't speak to him afterward. I didn't even know he was dead until Dora told me on Monday."

"Dora told you?" Richardson said. "Why would she do that?"

Tanya blew her nose again. "She'd seen us talking together in her garden a couple of times. Charlie came to the Lakeshore Haven because he didn't want us to be out in public where Kari might spot us and ask awkward questions. He originally told me he was trying to convince Kari to give him the shelter property, but he had no intention of hanging around after it was a done deal."

She sniffed. "Obviously, Dora didn't know anything about that. I told her Charlie was just a nice man I'd met while I was on vacation. But when she heard the news down at the diner, she thought I'd want to know."

"That must have been very difficult for you," Richardson said. "Being told that the man you loved had died and not being able to say anything."

"It was terrible," Tanya said, her tone so sad it broke Kari's heart. "I just nodded at her then went up to my room and cried and cried. This morning, I finally decided there was no point in staying here any longer, and pulled myself together enough to start packing. That was when Kari came and told me I needed to talk to you before I went home."

She sat up straight. "I've done that, so can I please go finish packing? I've already stayed here longer than I'd originally planned."

The sheriff tapped his pen against his pad and thought for a moment. "I'm afraid I'm going to have to ask you to stick around for a couple of days longer, Ms. Baldwin. This is a murder investigation, and your relationship with the victim—not to mention the fact that you lied about it—means that I might have more questions for you as things develop."

Tanya shoved her chair back and stood up, causing both the sheriff and Kari to jump, although admittedly the sheriff's reaction was a lot subtler.

"No!" she said. "I have to get home. You don't understand."

Richardson made a "sit down" gesture with his hand. "Then why don't you explain it to me?" he suggested in a calm voice.

"I need to get back to my son," Tanya said, wringing her hands as she took her seat again. "He has cerebral palsy, and he's not used to me being away for longer than a couple of days. My parents are taking care of him, but you have no idea what's involved in caring for a child with special needs. Thankfully, my job is very understanding, and though the pay isn't great, the health insurance is. But that doesn't mean I can stay here indefinitely. I need to get back to work, and back to my son."

"I see," the sheriff said. "I have sympathy for your situation, and I promise, we'll do our best to get you home as soon as possible. Hopefully it won't be more than another day or two. In the meanwhile, you're free to go for now. Thank you for coming in."

Tanya got up again, her purse clutched tightly against her chest. "I guess I'd better get back to the bed-and-breakfast and make sure Dora can let me keep the room." She nodded tersely at Kari. "Thank you for coming in with me."

Kari didn't really feel like she had been much help, and finding out about Tanya's son made her feel even worse. "Let me know if there is a problem with your accommodations," she said. "If you need to find another place to stay, I can ask around."

After Tanya left, the sheriff and Kari stared at each other for a minute. Richardson finally said, "That was interesting. Thank you for tracking her down and saving me the trouble. I suppose it would be a waste of my time to tell you to stay out of police business and let me handle this case."

Kari decided that now probably wasn't the time to remind him that the last two cases of his she'd gotten dragged into, she'd ended up finding the killer. Especially since in one of them, she'd almost gotten killed herself.

"I have no intention of interfering," she said instead, getting up from her chair with what she hoped was a modicum of dignity. "I was just trying to help. And you have to admit, finding out that Charlie had a secret girlfriend who was in town when he was killed had to be at least a little bit useful. After all, you're the one who said that the killer is often someone close to the victim."

Richardson cocked an eyebrow. "Yes, I did. And I will certainly check into Ms. Baldwin's story. But it sounds as though she has a number of people to vouch for her whereabouts during the pertinent times, including your friend Dr. McCoy."

Kari tried not to scowl, since that wouldn't help anything. "Yes, but—"

"There are no 'buts' here, Ms. Stuart. You are correct

in that we usually look at those who are nearest and dearest to the victim, as well as those who have the most to gain from their death. And at the moment, that is looking a lot more like you than anyone else, despite your attempts to steer us in another direction."

He looked pointedly at his desk, which was piled high with folders as usual. "Now, if you don't mind showing yourself out, I have work to do."

Kari didn't mind at all, since she was afraid if she stayed for one more minute she was going to end up saying something she'd regret. Possibly a number of somethings, some of which would have gotten her mouth washed out with soap by her mother when she was a child.

He might have work to do, but so did she. Because clearly, if she didn't find out who really killed Charlie, there was a very good chance she was going to go to jail for a crime she didn't commit.

❦ Sixteen

She almost made it. But just as she was leaving the sheriff's department, James Torrance came in the door, escorted by a young uniformed deputy with Asian features and short black hair. James wore a smart suit, clearly tailored specially to fit his unusually wide shoulders, and today's sneakers had rainbow laces tied in a jaunty double knot. But his whitish-blond hair was disheveled and there was a scowl on his normally cheerful visage. A leather bag about the size of a briefcase was clutched in one hand, its shoulder strap dangling perilously close to his feet, and the strong aroma of musky aftershave wafted in her direction.

"You!" Torrance said when he saw her. "This is all your fault!" He turned to the officer and pointed at Kari. "I don't know why you're bringing me in for questioning. This woman was clearly responsible for Charlie's death. Why aren't you interrogating her?"

"Hi, Deputy Clark," Kari said, giving the officer a lopsided smile. She'd dealt with him earlier in the year, when Suz had been accused of murdering a dog breeder at the local kennel club show, and had found him to be a reasonably decent sort. For someone who accused her best friend of murder.

"Ms. Stuart," Clark nodded at her. "I take it you two have met?"

"Met!" James exploded. "She's trying to rip me off for millions. She was clearly in on it with that husband of hers. Just arrest her and let me get out of this one-horse town."

Sheriff Richardson stuck his head out of his office. "Is there a problem here, Deputy Clark? Because I think the folks at the ice cream shop down the street are going to start complaining about the noise."

"I protest being dragged in here when I am the injured party," James said, shoving his black glasses up on his nose so hard Kari was afraid either the glasses or the nose would give. "You should be questioning this woman. She did it, I'm sure of it."

The sheriff sighed, no doubt thinking about the paperwork waiting for him in mountainous stacks on his desk. "Let's all step into my office for a moment, shall we?" He herded James and Kari in that direction, trailed by Deputy Clark, who had the look of a man who knew he was going to get a talking to later about his inability to do his job without dragging his boss away from his own work.

Once inside, Richardson shut the door behind him and pointed James and Kari toward the chairs in front of his desk. The young deputy came to stand by the side of the desk, holding his hat in his hands.

"James Torrance, I presume," the sheriff said, sliding

into his own seat. "Would you care to explain to me what all that fuss was about?"

"This officer dragged me down here while I was in the middle of an important Zoom meeting," James said. "And then when I got here, I saw *her*." One stubby finger stabbed the air in Kari's direction. "I don't understand why you're wasting my time when you already have the murderer right here."

Kari fought the impulse to drop her head into her hands and just leave it that way until this entire conversation was over. Maybe the whole day. She wished she'd brought Queenie with her, since at least the kitten could have gotten away with hissing at the man.

"I assure you, we are talking to everyone involved in this case, Ms. Stuart included," the sheriff said smoothly. "I'm sorry we disturbed your meeting, but we'll make this as quick as possible."

James grumbled but subsided back into his chair. "I should hope so," he said. "I really don't see what you expect to find out from me. I barely knew Charlie Smith. We'd crossed paths a few times in the past at business functions, but I hadn't had much to do with him until he called me about a month ago to talk to me about possibly going in together on a project."

"That would be this glamping resort?" Richardson asked, looking down at his notes. Kari was beginning to suspect that he actually knew every single thing in them by heart, and just used them for effect. "The one that was supposedly going to be built on the land currently owned by Ms. Stuart and being used for the Serenity Sanctuary animal rescue organization?"

"What a waste of a great piece of property," James

said, rolling his eyes. "You can put animals anywhere. That site is just perfect for glamping. Convenient driving distance from multiple states and big cities. A quaint town with an unusually vibrant Main Street and interesting activities for those who want a vacation from the urban life, but don't want to just hang around doing nothing. Stellar views and a lake right down the road!"

He gestured in the approximate direction of Blue Heron Lake, as if to prove his point. "Plus there's a great microbrewery. I'm telling you, this project will be like printing money."

"Except that as I understand it, Mr. Smith lied to you about the deal," Richardson said. "He got you to sign on based on his promise that Ms. Stuart had agreed to give up the rescue and allow the two of you to repurpose the property, when in fact she hadn't agreed to any such thing. I was told that you invested quite a lot of money based on this assurance. You must have been very angry to discover you had been lied to."

"Ha!" James said. "But I wasn't lied to."

Kari leaned forward. "I'm sorry, what?"

James grabbed his leather bag and yanked it open, reaching inside to get something. Deputy Clark put one hand on his gun, clearly alarmed by the sudden movement, but the sheriff waved at him to stand down.

The developer pulled out a manila envelope and slid a sheaf of papers onto Richardson's desk "I have the paperwork right here," James said. "It's got both their signatures on it. Charlie's and hers." He pointed at Kari. "I'll tell you what I think happened. I think she changed her mind about selling that shelter, and she killed Charlie to get out of it. But she didn't realize he'd already given me a copy of the agreement."

"I did no such thing," Kari said, sticking her chin out. "I didn't sign any paperwork, and I certainly didn't kill anyone. Not even Charlie."

"If you don't mind," Richardson said, reaching out one hand to pick up the papers. "I'd like a look at those."

He perused them thoroughly for the next couple of minutes, flipping from one page to the next, not saying anything, while Kari tried not to squirm in her chair and James sat back looking triumphant. Finally, Richardson folded the stapled pages over until the last one was on top and handed them over to Kari.

"So you're saying that's not your signature, Ms. Stuart?" he asked in a neutral tone.

Kari gazed at the scrawled name in mixed shock and fury. "It certainly looks like it, Sheriff. But I assure you, I never saw this agreement before in my life. I definitely never signed it, or any other papers having to do with this deal." She handed it back to him, her stomach clenched into a knot to rival the ones on Torrance's sneakers.

"Then how do you explain this?" the sheriff asked. "It looks genuine enough to me."

"Charlie must have forged them," Kari said, pressing her lips together. "He probably had plenty of things with my signature on them from when we were married that he could have copied it from. But I'm telling you, I never signed those papers."

Richardson handed the paperwork back to James, looking dubious. "I suspect you're going to need to have that signature examined by an expert," he said.

"That won't be necessary," James said, looking smug. "I already have a top lawyer on his way from New York City. I have every intention of holding Ms. Stuart to this agreement."

"Even though your business partner is dead?" Richardson said mildly. "I would have thought that might put a crimp in your plans."

James shrugged his wide shoulders. "It's inconvenient, but not an insurmountable obstacle," he said.

"I see," the sheriff said. "So you could, in fact, have forged Ms. Stuart's signature yourself somehow, killed Charlie Stuart, and still managed to continue on with the project you have so much invested in?"

"I, uh, no. I mean yes, theoretically, but I didn't," James stuttered.

Kari felt minutely better, although the lump in her stomach remained.

Richardson moved his notebook closer and poised his pen over it. "Just in case, I'd appreciate it if you could tell me where you were on the Saturday before Mr. Smith died."

"You're wasting your time," James said, glaring pointedly at Kari. "But if you insist." He pulled out his phone and tapped on it to bring up what was probably some kind of calendar function. "I'm staying at that little motel on Route Eight," he said. "I had to get up early for a call to Tokyo. It was seven a.m. our time and eight p.m. there, so it wasn't optimal for anyone, but that's business for you. Then I went to breakfast at that funky diner in town. Surprisingly good food for such a weird retro dive."

Cookie would be thrilled, Kari thought. Or she'd stab the man with a fork the next time he came in. That would be good, too.

"And after breakfast?" Richardson asked, hardly twitching at all at the insult to his favorite eatery. "Where did you go then?"

"I saw a pamphlet at the diner about things to do in town, and there was a nature walk that sounded interesting. I am very serious about my work, and always check out the local offerings so I know what to suggest to my glamping clients," James said smugly.

"After the walk was finished, I rented a bicycle—very clever idea, bicycle rentals, by the way—and I biked around the lake." He patted his thighs, which were almost as massive as his shoulders, and seemed to be giving his well-cut trousers a run for their money. "I like to stay in shape. Fit body, fit mind, I always say."

Richardson glanced down at the slight thickening of his waist that came from so many hours stuck behind a desk and sighed. "Indeed. What about the rest of the day?"

"Nothing special," James said with a shrug. "I spent most of the afternoon in my hotel room working until I went to the Oktoberfest around five."

"Oh?" the sheriff said. "So beer is part of your fitness regime?"

James grinned. "I'm a big fan of microbreweries," he said. "Man cannot live on green drinks alone. Besides, it was a good place to meet up with Charlie. He'd told me he was going to be busy all day, so we made plans to see each other there. One beer, two stones, as it were." He gave a honking laugh.

"What time did you see Mr. Smith, assuming you met up as planned?" Richardson asked.

"I think it was about five-thirty or six," James said. "I saw him at a table with a bunch of other people, including his wife," he said, his mouth turned down.

"Ex-wife," Kari muttered under her breath. "Freaking ex-wife."

James ignored her and went on. "We left the table a few minutes later and went off to talk on the patio, where we could be closer to the food and the beer. He seemed just fine to me. A little annoyed by something, maybe, when we first started talking, but he got over whatever it was and we spent the next couple of hours chatting and making plans. He definitely didn't seem sick." He glared at Kari. "Then. Who knows what she did to him before or after I saw him."

"I see," Richardson said, putting down his pen. "Thank you for your time, Mr. Torrance. I appreciate you coming in. Can you tell me if you were planning to leave town anytime soon?"

James's head shot up and he looked startled. "I'm not a suspect am I? I told you, she did it." He pointed at Kari. "She's the only one who stood to gain from his death. She probably thought she'd be able to hold on to all her lottery winnings, plus the money I'd already given Charlie as an investment in the glamping project."

"It's still early days in the investigation," the sheriff said, getting up from his chair. "We have various people's stories to check out, including yours, as well as other lines of inquiry to follow up on. It would be helpful if you stayed in the area for a bit."

"Well, really," James said, making a hmph-ing noise. "Luckily, I can do most of my work from anywhere, as long as I have my laptop and an Internet connection. Besides, as I said, I have a lawyer coming into town to consult with me on this paperwork." He waved it in the air before stuffing it back into its envelope.

"Ah, yes," Richardson said. "I hope you won't mind if I get a copy of that for my records." Before Torrance could protest, the sheriff had plucked it out of his fingers and handed it to Clark. "If you want to follow the deputy out into the main office, he'll make a copy and give you back the original. It won't take more than a minute. Thank you for your cooperation."

James trailed Clark out of the sheriff's room, leaving Kari alone again, facing him across the folder-strewn expanse of his desk. *Déjà vu.*

"I did not sign that agreement, Sheriff," Kari said in a quiet voice. "I swear to you."

He looked at her without blinking for a moment, his usual poker face firmly in place. She had no idea if he believed her or not.

"Maybe you did. Maybe you didn't," he said. "Either way, it doesn't look good, does it?"

No, Kari agreed. It certainly did not.

Kari went back to her house briefly to check on the animals and let Fred out to pee, then went up the path to the shelter trailed by the kitten, who insisted on going along, although she got temporarily distracted by a bright orange butterfly along the way.

Once there, Kari poured herself a cup of coffee and sat down at her desk, but couldn't concentrate enough to get anything useful done.

"How did things go this morning?" Sara asked, fetching her own cup and then coming over to perch on the edge of Kari's desk. "Did you find that Tanya woman?"

Kari scooped Queenie up and settled her on her lap, snuggling the kitten for comfort. "I did," Kari said. "It turns out that Angus was right and she was Charlie's girlfriend. Apparently she followed him here to surprise him for his birthday with a really ugly golf tie."

"Seriously?" Bryn said, coming over to join them. "I mean, I didn't know the guy, but that doesn't seem like his style."

"Oh, believe me, it wasn't," Kari said. "I'm not sure how anyone could have dated him for more than a week and not figured that out. But either way, her real motivation was jealousy of me, of all things, and her fear that he was coming here to get back together with me."

"Ugh," Sara and Bryn said in unison. "I hope you straightened her out," Sara added.

"I did," Kari said. "There was a lot of weeping. On her part, not mine," she clarified. "Then I told her the sheriff wanted to talk to her and there was more weeping. For some reason she said she'd feel less insecure if I went with her, so I did."

Bryn rolled her eyes. "That's just weird."

"You're telling me," Kari said. "But what was I supposed to say? The woman had just lost her boyfriend, who she clearly still had pleasant delusions about. Plus it turns out that she has a son with health issues."

"Huh," Sara said. "So did the sheriff seem to think she might have had something to do with Charlie's death?"

"I don't think so," Kari said. "Although he did ask her to stay around town for another couple of days. I think he wanted to check up on a few things."

"Too bad," Sara said. "So we still don't have any good suspects?" Worry lines furrowed her forehead.

"Not really," Kari said. "Plus Angus gave her an alibi for much of the day."

"Angus? Your Angus?" Bryn's mouth dropped open. "That's, uh . . ."

"Yeah." Kari sighed. "Don't worry. I already knew about it. Apparently Tanya's landlady at the bed-and-breakfast suggested Tanya take his nature walk in the morning. Then he invited her to have lunch at the Good Karma Deli because he thought there was something suspicious about the way she'd acted around me and he wanted to see if he could find anything out. So they were together from about ten until three, what with one thing and the other."

"That sounds innocent enough," Sara said, some of the wrinkles smoothing out again. "Thank goodness, because I've had about ten people come up and tell me they saw him out with her. So that's how he found out she was Charlie's girlfriend?"

Kari had shared Angus's news about Tanya that morning, but not how he'd gotten it. Mostly because there had been too many other volunteers around and Kari hadn't felt like getting into it.

"Yes," Kari said. "For all the good it did us. Sheriff Richardson came right out and told me I'm still his primary suspect." Her shoulders slumped. "And then things got worse."

"Worse than being suspected of killing your husband?" Bryn said. She held up one hand. "Sorry, ex-husband."

"Well, a different kind of bad, but maybe, yeah," Kari said. "James Torrance came in just as I was leaving. You know, the developer who was supposed to do the big glamping project with Charlie."

"Why is he still here?" Sara asked. "I would have thought he'd have left as soon as Charlie died and the project went from unlikely to definitely not happening.

Unless the sheriff asked him not to leave town for some reason?"

"The sheriff did ask him to stay around, but only after he'd not only accused me of being the one to murder Charlie, but produced signed paperwork saying I'd agreed to the deal. Paperwork signed by me," Kari said.

There was a moment of thunderous silence after she dropped that bombshell. Sara and Bryn looked at each other and then both stared at her.

"What?" Sara said finally. "Why would you do that?"

Kari rolled her eyes. "I wouldn't, of course. And I didn't. But somehow Torrance had a written agreement between him, Charlie, and me with my signature on the bottom."

Queenie stretched, arching her back, and let out a little growl. It was a much more adorable version of how Kari felt.

"How is that possible?" Bryn asked.

"All I can think is that Charlie forged my signature," Kari said. "Or Torrance could have, I suppose, but presumably Charlie would still have papers I'd signed while we were married. But Torrance is insisting that my signature means the project is still on, and he said he has called in some big-gun lawyer from New York City. He's not going to let this go. He seems to have sunk a lot of money into the plan already."

Bryn glanced around the room, her gaze encompassing the cages full of playful kittens, the beautiful L-shaped oak front desk that greeted every visitor, as well as the pictures on the wall of all the animals available for adoption, and her big brown eyes filled with tears. "Are we going to lose the sanctuary?" she asked.

"After everything we went through to save it?" Sara said. "Not a chance. Not after all the money and the work and the volunteers who gave up hours of their time. Absolutely not."

"What can we do?" Kari asked. "At least with Charlie, there was a possibility I could get him to just take less money and go away. But James Torrance wants this land and only this land. I mean, he'd have to pay me for it, but we'd have to start all over somewhere else."

She felt a little bit like crying, too. She'd put her heart and soul into this place, and it had given her a purpose and a sense of belonging for the first time in her life. They could rebuild, if they could find another space that was suitable, but what would happen to all the animals who lived there right now?

Long-term residents like Tripod, the three-legged yellow cat who was missing most of his teeth and spent his days napping on top of the dryer or wandering though the shelter and drooling affectionately on everyone, or One-Eyed Jack, who had lost an eye to an infection as a kitten and had never found anyone who could see past his imperfections to the sweet cat behind them. They had dozens of dogs and over thirty cats in residence right now, not counting kittens. Where would they all go if Torrance succeeded in kicking them out of their home?

"I'll tell you what we're going to do," Sara said, a determined expression on her face.

Kari had seen that look before—she called it Sara's "irresistible force" look. Not much could stand up against it. Inexplicably, Kari suddenly felt better. "What?" she asked.

Sara pulled out her phone and started scrolling through her contacts list. This took some time, since she knew pretty much everyone in town from all her years of teaching. Virtually all the long-time residents had either been in her classes or had a kid in one. Or both.

Finally she found what she was looking for. "What we're going to do," she said firmly, "is get our own lawyer. Not Carmen Rodriquez, since she's a divorce lawyer. Who, incidentally, tells me you still haven't called her." She gave Kari a stern look.

"Brian Gallagher is a criminal attorney, but he also knows a lot about business law. He'll be able to give us advice about this latest development." She set her jaw, looking for just a moment remarkably like the bulldog they'd adopted out last week who had an unfortunate habit of grabbing things and refusing to let them go. In this case, Kari thought that was probably a good thing.

"Thank you," she said, feeling her shoulders sag in relief. "I feel as though things just keep getting farther out of my control, no matter how hard I try to figure this all out. I can't believe Charlie is dead and he's *still* messing up my life."

Sara got up from her perch on the corner of the desk and put one arm around Kari in a brief hug. "We're all in this together, honey. Tomorrow we'll see if we can get Suz to come over for a brainstorming session after work, and I'll contact Brian and get him on the job. Don't you worry. Everything is going to be fine."

Kari looked down at the kitten. "See, Queenie. Nothing to worry about. Don't you feel better?"

Queenie reached up and licked Kari's chin, then

jumped onto the desk and batted the Oktoberfest bottle opener onto the floor, where it landed with a clank.

"Seriously?" Kari said. "Not again. You're not helping, you little monkey." But she picked up both the opener and the kitten and gave Queenie a kiss. Maybe everything was going to be okay after all.

Seventeen

The next morning, Kari was getting ready to head over to the shelter when Queenie stared at the door and hissed. Kari stopped spreading jam on her toast and put her coffee cup down. *What the heck?* It clearly wasn't Charlie, since he was, you know, dead. But Queenie was rarely wrong. And by rarely, Kari meant never.

So she opened the door with no small amount of trepidation, only to breathe a sigh of relief when she saw it was Sheriff Richardson.

"Sheriff, good morning," she said, opening the door wider. "Did you have some more questions? I'm just getting ready for work, but I'd be happy to get you a cup of coffee. Or did you find out something about that fake signature on the papers James Torrance had?"

Richardson looked uncharacteristically grim, even for him, and there were two deputies standing behind him.

"I'm sorry, Ms. Stuart," he said. "I realize it is early, but I have a warrant to search your property."

Queenie hissed again, from somewhere near Kari's feet, and Kari hushed her absentmindedly. "A warrant?" she repeated, feeling like she was missing something. "I don't understand. There's nothing here. You already took most of the contents of my kitchen."

She waved her piece of toast at him, as though that would make her point. "What are you looking for now?"

"I'm afraid I can't say," Richardson said, showing her the search warrant. "But we got a tip that there is an item pertinent to the case hidden here, so we're going to have to take a look."

Kari blinked at him. "Uh, okay," she said, opening the door wider. "Did you want to come in?" After all, she knew she had nothing to hide.

He shook his head. "Actually, the warrant is for us to search any outbuildings on the grounds."

"Outbuildings?" Kari thought she was starting to sound like one of those birds that repeated everything it heard. "I don't have any outbuildings." She peered outside past him and the deputies. "Unless you count the carport, the tiny shed where the gardening tools are kept, and the henhouse."

Richardson's lips pressed together. "Would you mind showing us this henhouse?"

Kari slid her feet into the sneakers standing by the door, not bothering to tie the laces. "Of course not, but there's nothing in there but chickens, straw, and if I'm lucky, a couple of fresh eggs."

"Nonetheless, we'd like to take a look," the sheriff said. He waved the search warrant as if to remind Kari that it really wasn't optional.

Kari shrugged and led them down the slightly slanted dirt path that led to the chicken coop. It was a wire and wood box with enclosed areas for the hens to roost in the back and an open space for them to walk around toward the front. Kari shut them inside at night, because of predators like foxes and weasels, but during the day they wandered in and out and all around the yard at will. These particular chickens, which she had inherited along with the house when she'd bought the shelter from Daisy, tended to take free range to an entirely new level. She was pretty sure she spotted one out of the corner of her eye, happily settling in on top of the sheriff's car.

"Get out of the way, Fancy," she scolded one brown and white hen with fluffy feathers on her legs and feet who had let out a particularly loud squawk as they approached the henhouse. "Nobody is coming to get you." Kari turned to Richardson. "Fancy is a little neurotic, even for a chicken," she explained. Deputy Clark, who along with his partner Deputy Kent, had accompanied the sheriff, snickered behind one raised hand.

Kari stopped in front of the entrance to the coop, arms crossed over her chest. "Here you go," she said. "Have at it." She pointed at a basket hanging on a nail right inside the gate. "If you find any eggs, you can put them in there. Save me the trouble of looking for them later."

The three men started to go inside, but it rapidly became clear that the space was too small for all of them at once. Richardson stepped back and gestured at Clark. "Go on, you get the honors. Try not to get chicken poop all over your shoes. It will stink up the station like crazy."

The deputy sighed as he pulled on a pair of latex gloves. "What am I looking for exactly, besides eggs?"

Richardson grimaced. "Something small, so check everywhere. Look through the hay and in all the nooks and crannies."

"What if there is a chicken sitting on the hay?" Clark asked plaintively.

"Then look under the darn chicken," Richardson said.

They all stood around for a few minutes while poor Deputy Clark worked his way around the perimeter of the henhouse, feeling his way along the ledges where the chickens roosted and even picking up their water bowl to look underneath, slopping slightly mucky fluid all over his pants in the process. He uttered a few rude words and the chickens responded with what was no doubt the equivalent in bird.

Kari was almost starting to relax when the dark-haired deputy straightened up, a funny look on his slightly bony face.

"Sir, I think I found something," he said.

The sheriff pulled on his own gloves and entered the coop, walking toward the back end where the chickens roosted at night. Kari could hear him say, "Be sure to get some picture of that in situ." A few minutes later he came back out, followed by Clark who wiped his mucky hands off on his pants and then winced when he realized what he'd done and yanked off his gloves instead.

"Do you recognize this, Ms. Stuart?" the sheriff asked. He held up a clear evidence bag containing a small plastic bottle with no label. It was half filled with a cloudy liquid.

Kari shook her head. "No, I don't," she said. "I've never seen that before, and I have no idea how it got into my henhouse." She was starting to get a really bad feeling.

"I see," Richardson said. "I should tell you that we got an anonymous call telling us that the poison that killed your ex-husband was hidden in an outbuilding on your property. I thought it was unlikely at the time, but I admit, it is a clever place to put something. No one would ever look for a murder weapon under a hen's butt."

"That's *not* mine," Kari insisted. "And I have no idea how it got there, although anyone could have gotten in. The fencing is to keep out animals, not people. It doesn't even lock."

"That may be so," the sheriff said, "but I'm going to have to ask you not to leave town anyway. If this turns out to be what I think it is, you are going to jail."

Still feeling slightly shell-shocked, Kari went over to the sanctuary to help out with the morning chores. Queenie tagged along, sticking closer than usual once they got there as if she could sense that Kari needed moral support.

Kari thought she was covering up well, but after the second time she tried to put dog food into one of the cat's bowls, Sara pulled her aside and asked her what was going on.

"Have you heard back from your lawyer friend yet?" Kari asked, shoving her hands into the back pocket of her jeans so Sara couldn't see them shaking. "Because it looks like I might need him sooner than we thought."

"Why?" Sara asked, glancing around to make sure

they were out of earshot of the rest of the volunteers. Bryn was in the back, feeding the dogs with Jim, and as much as everyone else who worked there was bound to be on Kari's side, there wasn't any point in adding to the rumors already swirling around town. "Has something happened?"

Today Sara was wearing a dark blue shirt with large turquoise flowers that matched the dyed streak in her cropped gray hair, and jeans with flowers on the back pockets that she'd probably embroidered there herself. Small silver hoops hung from her ears. As usual, she looked practical and neat, and made Kari feel underdressed in her black Serenity Sanctuary tee shirt with its stylized cat and dog silhouettes logo in white, and her own much more beat-up jeans. She sincerely hoped she'd get to change her clothes before she got arrested.

"The sheriff came by with a search warrant for my outbuildings," she admitted to Sara in a low voice. Kari knew she should have told the older woman as soon as she got there, but it had somehow felt as though saying it out loud would make it more real somehow. "Deputy Clark found a small plastic bottle in the henhouse with some kind of liquid in it. They're testing it to see if it is the poison that killed Charlie."

"What?" Sara turned pale under the tan she got every summer working in her extensive garden. "Why didn't you tell us?"

Kari bit her lip. "I think I was just hoping it would go away. I mean, I know I'm innocent."

Sara gave Kari the stern look perfected over forty years of teaching. "Innocent people go to jail every day, Kari Stuart. Really, I expect better from you. I'm calling

Brian Gallagher back right now. He needs to know things are ramping up to a new level."

She paused, her finger hovering over her cell phone. "Wait. They had a warrant for the outbuildings specifically? That seems kind of odd."

"The sheriff said they'd gotten an anonymous tip," Kari said.

Sara's eyebrows shot up. "Isn't that interesting," she said thoughtfully. "I'll be sure to mention that to Brian." She turned her attention back to her cell, patting Kari absently on the arm, her mind already on the task at hand.

"You go feed the cats. Preferably actual cat food," she said. "I'll talk to Brian and see what he thinks we should do next. He's probably going to want to meet with you as soon as he can. Oh, and if you look in that bag on the counter, I bought a new wet food for Tripod to try. I think he's bored with the old stuff. This one is duck and liver. See how he likes it."

As far as Kari could tell, Tripod liked everything they put in the special dish with his name on it, but he was something of an unofficial mascot of the shelter and everyone tended to spoil him. It was as if they wanted to make up for the rough life he'd had before he'd been rescued a few years ago and the fact that they hadn't been able to find him a permanent home.

Kari managed to finish cleaning cages and giving the residents in the main room fresh food and water without any problems worse than one kitten escape, which was promptly thwarted by Queenie, who rounded up the tiny adventurer and brought him back to Kari clutched gently between fanged teeth.

Finally, around eleven thirty, Kari had had enough. She was practically climbing the walls (sort of like that kitten had tried to do) and she was making everyone else twitch too, although most of them weren't sure why.

She decided to reverse her previous stance on avoiding the diner—if she was going to end up in jail, she wanted one last good meal first, darn it. It was worth getting stared at by gossiping locals if she got to have the steak sandwich and onion rings one more time.

She called Suz and asked her if she wanted to meet up at the diner for lunch, and her friend agreed without hesitation. They'd been talking on the phone every day, and Kari had been keeping Suz up to date on developments, but they hadn't had time to get together since the Sunday night brainstorming session with Sara and Bryn. Suz had had an unusually busy schedule with her dog grooming business, and Kari had been dealing with, well, this crap.

Not only did Kari want that steak sandwich, but she also thought it would be best to break the latest news to Suz in person, and also ask her if she could take care of Fred, Westley, Robert, and Queenie if the worst happened and Kari got arrested. Did they allow pet visitations in jail?

Twenty minutes later, the two of them were seated at their favorite booth, where they could people watch as they ate. Of course, right now that meant that people could watch them right back, but most folks had been reasonably discreet, other than one obnoxious farmer in overalls and a grimy cap who had come up to the table to berate Kari for selling out to the rich city people. In small towns, rumors spread faster than the common cold in a room full of preschoolers.

Fortunately, Cookie had been nearby, and she'd given him an earful about not believing everything he heard, and then put extra bacon on Kari's sandwich without even being asked.

"Don't you worry, hon," Cookie said, her ample bosom almost resting in Kari's plate as the waitress leaned over the table. "Nobody with half a brain thinks you'd be stupid enough to get caught if you killed someone. I'm sure everything will work out fine."

"Uh, thanks, I think," Kari said. The smell of the onion rings wafting upward was almost enough to make her forget her troubles. Almost. She breathed it in like the nectar of the gods it was, trying to fix the aroma in her memory in case she didn't get to smell it again anytime soon.

Of course, Suz was as colorful and entertaining as ever, which was almost as invaluable as her unswerving support. Her short lavender hair currently sported silver tips that matched the series of silver studs running down the edges of one ear, and Suz's trademark lavender work smock was worn over bright green pants and a deep purple tee shirt that said "All the Best People Have Four Paws." Suz had opted to duplicate Kari's lunch order, down to the chocolate malted milkshake (extra thick, because you only live once), and let out a tiny moan of happiness as she bit into the steak sandwich.

"This is amazing," Suz said after she'd swallowed a massive mouthful. "What's the occasion?"

Kari took her own huge bite, making sure she got every ounce of enjoyment out of it before she answered. "The sheriff got a hot tip and searched my henhouse earlier. He found something that could turn out to be the poison that killed Charlie. So I wanted to know if you would take care of my animals if I get sent away to jail."

Suz dipped an onion ring in the diner's homemade spicy mayo and said without missing a beat, "Of course. Can I have your new car?" Suz's car was an old station wagon she mostly drove because she could haul a lot of animals in it if necessary, and it had four-wheel drive for the harsh Catskill winters.

"You bet," Kari said. "Try not to let any dogs pee on the seats."

They both laughed, and Kari took a moment to appreciate what a gift it was to have a friend who knew she needed humor more than tears right now.

"Seriously, though," Suz said. "Is there anything I can do? Find you a lawyer? Give you an ironclad alibi for the date and time of your choice? Confess to committing the crime myself?"

Kari washed down an onion ring with some creamy milkshake. "Sara is already on top of the lawyer thing," she said.

"Of course she is." Suz shook her head so that the silver tips on her hair shimmered in the light from the dangling red retro fixtures overhead. "Alibi?"

"That's kind of tough, since we can't be sure when exactly Charlie was poisoned," Kari said. "But I appreciate the offer." She thought for a moment as she chewed another bite of medium-rare steak smothered in melted cheese and caramelized onions. The flavor alone was enough to improve her day. "Just out of curiosity, what would your motive be for killing him, should you decide to confess?"

Suz tapped her chin with one long finger. Like Kari, she never bothered with polish or trying to grow her nails out, since her hands were in water much of the time. "He made a pass at my girlfriend?" She shook her head. "No, how about, he made a pass at me?"

Kari almost snorted chocolate milkshake out her nose at the thought of Charlie ever being foolish enough to attempt such a thing, even if Suz had been his type, which she wasn't. Charlie had been crazy, but not that crazy.

"I don't think so," she said. "I'm pretty sure even Sheriff Richardson wouldn't go for that one."

Suz put down her sandwich and looked Kari in the eye. "How about, he made my best friend unhappy and threatened to take away the best thing that ever happened to her. Besides me, of course."

Actually, Kari thought Richardson might buy that. He'd met Suz.

"I appreciate the offer," Kari said. "But I'm sure we'll think of something." Hopefully something that didn't involve either of them being hauled off in handcuffs.

As they were finishing their lunches, Nancy Nash came up to their table. Nancy was a pleasant woman in her fifties with tightly curling black hair, dark skin, and deep brown eyes behind pink cat's eye glasses. Today she wore a matching pink sweater over gray slacks and comfortable shoes. Nancy owned the local liquor store, Lakeview Liquor Locker, so she spent much of her days on her feet.

She was also one of the best sources of news in town, second only to Cookie herself. So Kari was pretty sure Nancy had stopped by the table as much to pick up some good gossip as she had to sympathize. Kari didn't take it personally, and figured that at least Nancy would get her facts straight, unlike some other people.

"Hi Kari, hi Suz," Nancy said. "How are you two doing?" She gave Kari a sympathetic pat on the shoulder. "I'm sorry to hear about your loss. It's just tragic that you hadn't seen your husband in so many years and then he was killed just as you were reconnecting."

"Ex-husband," Kari said, but without much energy behind it. She felt like she should just get the word printed on a button she could pin to her shirt. Plus maybe a bumper sticker for her car. "And we weren't reconnecting, exactly. Charlie just came into town to give me some information and stayed because he had a business deal he was trying to get up and running."

Nancy looked a little disappointed Kari wasn't devastated, but the liquor store owner rallied quickly. "So, that business deal—was that the one to turn the sanctuary into some kind of tourist campground? I wouldn't have thought you'd give up the shelter, especially now that you have it fixed up so nice and everything."

"I wouldn't," Kari said firmly. "It was all a bit complicated."

"Speaking of complicated," Nancy leaned in closer and lowered her voice. "Is it true that the blond woman who was at Oktoberfest with you and Angus and Suz and the rest of the gang turned out to be your ex-husband's girlfriend?"

Suz rolled her eyes. Kari had to agree with the unspoken sentiment. Was there nothing that the people in this town didn't notice? Tanya had been at their table for all of about ten minutes. Maybe less.

"Yes, she was," Kari said. "I talked to her yesterday for a while and she seems very nice. She came to Lakeview to surprise Charlie for his birthday, or so I gather." Of course, that hadn't worked out very well, but Kari didn't figure that part was anyone else's business.

"Oh," Nancy said, clearly let down not to be able to add jealousy to the rumor mill. "I thought maybe you hadn't realized who she was." She shook her head. "I met her, you know. She came into the shop a little after eleven on Saturday morning to get a small bottle of vodka. Like you said, she seemed very nice. A little quiet, maybe, like she had something on her mind."

"Saturday morning?" Kari said, surprised by Nancy's comment. "She was on the nature walk Angus gives on Saturday mornings. Maybe you are confusing her with someone else."

"Oh no," Nancy said in a decisive tone. "I have a radio talk show I listen to every Saturday at that time, and I remember I was worried I was going to miss the beginning of it because the store was busier than usual. It must have been right after the nature walk ended. I get quite a few tourists who come in afterward. I think being that close to nature must drive them to drink." She laughed at her own joke, a loud chuckle that made the people at the next table turn around to see what was so funny.

"Huh," Suz said. She turned to Kari. "Didn't you say that she was with Angus from ten until three?"

"I thought that's what she told me," Kari said. "I must have misunderstood." She looked up at Nancy. "You're sure it was her? Blond, wears clothes that don't quite suit her and a little too much makeup?"

Nancy nodded vigorously. "Absolutely. Pretty woman, but she should have stuck to her natural hair color. She used a charge card, and I remember her name was Tanya, because I realized I didn't know anyone else with that name. Do you suppose it's one of those ones that's only in fashion for a few years, and then nobody uses it for decades?"

Kari couldn't really care less about naming fads. She wiped her messy hands on a wad of paper napkins, trying to figure out what nagging thought was in the back of her brain trying to come out.

"You know, I feel bad for the poor woman," Nancy went on, oblivious as usual to the fact that she'd lost her audience's attention. "Here she is, a stranger in a town where she doesn't know anyone, and now she has lost her boyfriend. That must be tough. Do you know where she's staying? Maybe I should take her a larger, less cheap bottle of vodka, since she's in mourning." She hitched her pink fabric purse up higher on her shoulder, poking around inside for something, maybe a pen and paper to write herself a reminder note. Kari guessed it would read: *Bring bottle of vodka to woman in mourning. Find out more good gossip.*

Kari's eyes widened. "No," she said. "I wouldn't do that." She shoved away from the table, reaching into her own bag to get her wallet and throw enough cash on the table to cover both meals and a substantial tip for Cookie.

"I'm sorry," she said to Suz. "I've got to get back to the house right away. There's something I have to deal with. Can you come with me?"

"What? Right now?" Suz's mouth dropped open. "You haven't even finished your food! It's a steak sandwich!" Clearly she thought Kari had completely lost her mind.

Kari thought that was entirely possible. But then again, maybe not.

"I'm sorry, Suz," she said, getting up from her seat. "It's important, and it can't wait. If you don't have another dog scheduled right away, it would be great if you could come with me. Feel free to have Cookie put the rest of my sandwich in a doggie bag so you can bring it home to your gang for a treat." Suz had a menagerie of cats and dogs, and even a snake. Kari was pretty sure snakes didn't eat steak, although she couldn't be sure.

Suz tilted her head to one side and stared at her, as if she could see into Kari's brain. "Figured out something, didn't you?" she muttered quietly, almost to herself. "I'm free until three," she said in a normal tone. "Let me get this all packed up and I'll meet you at your house in about fifteen minutes, okay?"

"Great," Kari said. "You're the best."

"Did I say something wrong?" she could hear Nancy say to Suz as Kari hurried toward the door.

"I have no idea," Suz said, sounding baffled. "Hey, hands off that onion ring."

Then Kari was out on the street and walking toward her car as fast as she could, well aware that she had just given everyone in the diner something new to talk about. But if she was right, it would be worth it.

Eighteen

Half an hour later, Kari opened her door to find Tanya standing on the step. The other woman looked tired, with dark circles under her eyes and her hair pulled back into a careless ponytail. She wore tan slacks that looked as though they had been shoved into a suitcase and left there until she pulled them back out, and a dark olive green scoop necked sweater in a shade that made her skin appear even more sallow than usual. Or maybe she just hadn't been sleeping. If so, Kari couldn't blame her.

"Come on in," Kari said, motioning toward the living room. "The place isn't much to look at, but it's comfortable, anyway. I hope you're not allergic to cats."

Tanya stared at her a little blankly. "No, not at all. I like cats. Dogs, too." She looked down at Fred, who had come over to sit at her feet, panting gently. "As long as they're friendly."

"Oh, don't worry," Kari said. "They don't get any friendlier than Fred. He loves everyone. He's an eternal optimist and thinks that everyone who comes in the door just might have a treat stuck in their pockets. He's rarely right, but he's always willing to check."

That elicited a tiny smile, and Tanya leaned down and said, "Hello, Fred. I'm sorry about the treat. I would have brought one if I'd known." Fred licked her hand and followed her over to the old couch Kari had hidden under a garnet-colored throw. He curled up on the braided rug that lay between the couch and the two plush brown suede chairs Kari had finally broken down and gotten a couple of months ago, when she realized that guests needed someplace better to sit than her folding kitchen seats. Suz was sitting on the chair to the left, one leg tucked under the other thigh. She nodded at Tanya, who looked startled to see her, but said, "Hi," back.

The rest of the house makeover had been waiting for work on the shelter to be finished. And for Kari to find the energy to deal with it. In the meanwhile, she liked to think of it as "shabby chic" rather than just plain shabby.

Tanya looked around the place and Kari suspected she was missing the "chic" part. But Tanya's next words proved her wrong.

"This isn't what I expected," Tanya said. "I guess I thought that someone who had won the lottery would live somewhere fancier. But I love the old pine floors, and the way the bookshelves full of books and knick-knacks make the room feel so cozy. I'll bet it is even nicer when the wood stove is lit."

She sighed. "My apartment back home is pretty boring. Just white walls with a few framed prints, beige wall-to-wall shag carpet in every room except the kitchen, and a couple of spider plants. Plus my son's toys scattered everywhere, of course."

Tanya scratched Fred's ears, making him wiggle with pleasure, his plumed tail nearly knocking a stack of magazines off the table. Robert and Westley were upstairs sleeping on the bed, but Queenie stalked over from where she'd been perched on a windowsill watching the chickens strut through the yard and hopped up on the arm of the chair Kari sat down in.

"What a pretty kitten," Tanya said. "You're so lucky to be able to have pets. My landlord doesn't allow any."

"That's too bad," Kari said. "I find having animals makes life a lot better, especially during the tough times." She felt a tug of sadness in her heart. It was ironic, really. Under different circumstances, she and Tanya might even have been friends. "This is Queenie. She's kind of the boss of me."

"She's the boss of everyone," Suz put in.

Tanya smiled at the little black kitten. "My son would love her," she said. "And Fred. Especially Fred. He's always bugging me to move to someplace where we could have a dog, but housing is so expensive on Long Island, and we can barely afford the place we've got now."

"How old is your son?" Kari asked.

"He's nine," Tanya said. She pulled her phone out of her purse and showed a photo to Kari and Suz. "This is Petey. He's a great kid, if I do say so myself. He's perpetually cheerful and never complains." She beamed down at the picture, a genuine smile on her face for the first time since Kari had met her.

Kari could see why, looking at the boy in the wheelchair, his bright eyes the same color as his mother's, with floppy brown hair and a broad grin that spread from cheek to cheek. One arm was pulled in toward his chest in what was probably a habitual spasm, and a special halter held him upright in his chair, but otherwise Petey looked like any other spirited child.

"He's adorable," Kari said with complete honesty. "You're a lucky woman."

Tanya nodded, putting away the phone. "Most people don't get that. They feel sorry for me because my ex-husband left us when Petey was one and it became clear that our lives would be a lot more complicated than we'd expected. Or they think I should be pitied because I have a child with special needs. But honestly, he is the best thing in my life, and I'd do anything for him." She gazed at Kari earnestly, as if wanting to make sure the other woman truly understood. "It's what you do, if you're a mother."

Kari had never wanted children, not after the upbringing she'd had, but for a moment, she felt a pang of envy. Maybe, if things worked out for her and Angus, it was something to consider for the future. Or maybe not. She didn't want to get ahead of herself. Queenie nudged Kari's hand with her head, as if to remind Kari that she had plenty of little ones to love right now. Even if they all had fur.

Tanya shifted on the couch, sitting up straight as if to indicate that the time for small talk was over. "I really do need to get home to my son. When you called the bed-and-breakfast, you said you had figured out something about Charlie's death that could solve the case. That would be great. Now that I'm here, will you tell me what you discovered?" She looked from Kari to Suz.

"Would you like some tea or coffee while we talk?" Kari asked, feeling like a terrible hostess, and not a particularly wonderful human being.

"No thanks," Tanya said. "I'm dying to know what you found out."

"Well," Kari started to say, but there was a knock on the door. All three women jumped, and Queenie let out a loud meow. Fred just kept on snoring at Tanya's feet. A great guard dog he wasn't.

"Sorry," Kari said. "Let me see who that is. It's probably just someone from the sanctuary coming to say they need my help with something. I'll put them off until later unless it is an emergency." She got up from her chair and crossed the room.

But when she opened the door, it wasn't Sara or Bryn standing there. Instead, Sheriff Richardson stared back at her with a stony expression, Deputy Clark one step behind him and an official sheriff's department car idling in front of the house.

"Kari Stuart," Richardson said in a flat tone, "You are under arrest for the murder of Charles Smith."

Crap.

"What?" Suz said. "You can't do that." She gripped the arms of her chair. "Kari didn't do it."

"Oh, no," Tanya said, rising from the couch with a dismayed look on her face. "I'm so sorry, Kari. You know I wanted answers, but this really wasn't the one I was hoping for."

Kari knew exactly what that felt like.

"It's okay," she said. She turned back to the sheriff. "Would you please come in, Sheriff? I didn't murder Charlie. But I'm pretty sure I know who did. Once I explain it to you, I think you'll change your mind about arresting me."

Richardson scowled at her. "If you're stalling, I'm not going to be amused, Ms. Stuart."

Kari crossed her arms in front of her chest. "I'll tell you what, Sheriff," she said. "If you don't believe me when I'm done telling you what I learned, I'll let you arrest me in the middle of the diner, in full sight of everyone and their brother. You'll get free coffee and pie for a month, just for the entertainment value."

The corner of his mouth twitched upward. "That's a truly serious offer. You must think whatever you've discovered is pretty good. Very well, I'll give you fifteen minutes. If you haven't convinced me by then, we're all driving to the diner. I love their chocolate cream pie."

He swiveled around to face Clark. "Coming, Deputy?"

"Oh yes sir," Clark said, his dark eyes twinkling. "I wouldn't miss this for the world."

After Deputy Clark had gone back and turned off the car, he and the sheriff came in and sat down in Kari's living room. The house wasn't all that large to start out with, and the two uniformed men made it feel a lot smaller. Tanya had moved to the chair Suz had been in, and Richardson and Clark took the couch while Kari dragged one of the kitchen chairs over for Suz, who sat in it with her arms crossed. Queenie stayed perched on the arm of Kari's seat, staring at the policemen as if trying to decide if they were friends or prey. She and Suz had nearly matching expressions.

Fred proved once again that hope springs eternal by giving the law officers the affectionate doggy grin that showed off his lolling tongue and black-and-pink gums. Kari wasn't even surprised when Richardson pulled a dog treat out of his shirt pocket and handed it to Fred, nearly causing Fred to fall over from sheer joy. Despite the seriousness of the moment, it was hard not to smile at her silly dog. She'd meant what she'd said to Tanya. Animals made everything better.

Well, nearly everything.

"I think you'd better call that lawyer Sara found for you," Suz said.

"Is that okay?" Kari asked Richardson. She wasn't sure if she'd need the man or not, but Sara would kill her if she didn't at least let him know what was happening, under the circumstances.

"It's your right," the sheriff said. "You can have him meet us at the station, since we'll likely be there soon."

Kari swallowed hard and punched the contact in her phone, leaving a message with a secretary.

"Can I get you some coffee or tea?" she asked. "Water?"

Richardson cleared his throat. "This is not a social call, Ms. Stuart. If you have useful information to give us, I suggest you go ahead and do so. Otherwise we can just proceed to the diner and your impending public humiliation."

Kari sighed, but she didn't blame him for his impatience, or for doubting that she would be able to change his mind. And he'd been right about her stalling, but not for the reasons he'd thought. She just didn't want to say what she had to tell him out loud and change everything forever.

"I take it the reason you are arresting me is that the bottle of liquid you found in my henhouse does, in fact, contain the poison that killed Charlie?" she said.

Richardson nodded. "Among other things. For instance, we discovered that Mr. Smith died without ever making a will, so in fact, you *do* inherit everything. But

that's motive, not proof. The arrest warrant is because of
what we found the other day." He showed her the piece
of paper, although she didn't bother to read it. It wasn't
as though he was going to make something like that up.

"Lab analysis showed that the fluid we found was a
mixture of destroying angel mushroom and alcohol. The
technician who works in the lab speculated that the
mushrooms were cut up and placed in some form of alcohol to create a tincture, since the poison in the mushrooms would be soluble if left to soak for some time.
Then the mixture could be strained so that there were no
obvious pieces in it, as you saw when we found that
bottle. It looked completely innocuous, and would be
fairly easy to administer without Mr. Smith being aware
of it. But then, you knew that already, didn't you, Ms.
Stuart?"

"I did," Kari said. "But not for the reason you think.
In fact, the killer only made one, very understandable,
mistake."

Richardson raised an eyebrow. "I'll play along. What
would that mistake be, pray tell?"

Kari turned and looked at Tanya, trying to keep the
pity out of her eyes. She already knew the other woman
wouldn't want it.

"She underestimated the power of gossip in a small
town," Kari said. "Without that, Tanya probably would
have gotten away with killing Charlie and framing me,
and no one would have ever known it was her."

🐈 Nineteen

Me!" Tanya gave a shaky laugh. "Don't be ridiculous. What reason could I possibly have to kill Charlie? I loved him. You, on the other hand, hated him. He showed up in your new life, told you he was entitled to half your lottery winnings, and threatened everything you had built here. Of course you killed him. You must be desperate if you're trying to shift the blame to me. No one is going to believe you."

"I didn't actually hate Charlie," Kari said, letting the regret she felt seep out into her voice. "No, I wasn't happy when he turned up out of the blue and told me we were still married, and I was even less happy when he went after the shelter for his own selfish plans. But that was Charlie for you. I'm not the vulnerable young woman he married, and this time he wasn't going to get what he wanted."

Kari thought that was one of the saddest parts of all this. If Charlie had realized how much she'd changed, and that it wouldn't be as easy as he's assumed to steamroll her into doing what he wanted, he might have taken a different approach and saved them all a lot of grief. And maybe he'd still be alive.

"I didn't kill him for his money," Kari said. "I didn't want it when I left him, and I sure as heck don't need it now. I won the lottery, and I don't exactly have a high-flying lifestyle." She waved one hand around the unpretentious room to make her point. "And I didn't need to kill him to keep him from getting this land and closing down the shelter, although I might have had to fight him in court."

"Then why *did* you kill him?" Tanya asked. "Was it just out of spite? Revenge for how you say he treated you all those years ago?" She shook her head. "I don't think you were as confident about winning in court as you are pretending to be, and just because you haven't fixed this place up yet doesn't mean you wanted to share any of your lottery money with the ex-husband you detested."

Kari sighed. "I didn't kill him, Tanya. Nobody knows that better than you, although I admit you had me fooled up until about an hour ago."

Richardson pulled out his ever-present notebook and a pen, although he still wore a dubious expression. "What exactly happened an hour ago?" he asked.

"I was eating lunch at the diner with Suz, and Nancy Nash came over to talk to us," Kari said.

"Ah," Richardson said, suddenly looking a lot more interested.

Tanya gave them both a baffled look. "I don't understand."

Suz snorted down her long nose. "No one does, if they don't live in a place like this."

"You see, that's the thing about small towns," Kari

explained. "It is very hard to keep secrets, and there is almost always someone who knows everything that's going on. Even the things that seem trivial."

"Nancy Nash is one of the biggest gossips in town," Clark put in. He'd taken his hat off and placed it in his lap, although he had his pair of cuffs held loosely on one hand, as if ready to slap them onto the guilty party at a moment's notice. Whoever that turned out to be.

"When I got my job with the sheriff's department, she was on the phone with my mother before I even knew for sure I'd gotten the position," Clark said. "Apparently the secretary who was in charge of sending out the letters to applicants went into Nancy's shop on her way home from work and mentioned it because she knew Nancy was friends with my mom. Small towns." He rolled his eyes.

"I don't see what this has to do with me," Tanya complained.

"Nancy happens to own the liquor store," Kari said.

All the color drained from Tanya's face, leaving her makeup standing out in stark relief. "Oh," she said. She bit her lip and visibly pulled herself together. "I don't drink, as I told you, sheriff. So I wouldn't have met her."

"That's funny," Kari said. "Because Nancy remembers you quite clearly. She even recalled exactly what you bought and that you paid with a credit card. She said it stuck in her head because she'd never met a Tanya before."

She turned to the sheriff. "No doubt you'll want to double check with Nancy, but I'm sure she has the credit card slips from that Saturday and can find the one from Tanya's purchase."

He nodded, jotting down a note. "I'm not sure where

you're going with this, Ms. Stuart, but I will admit, you've intrigued me." He made a waving motion with his hand to indicate she should continue.

"When Nancy told me you'd been in to buy a small bottle of vodka, at first I thought she must have confused you with someone else," Kari said, gazing at Tanya. "But when it became clear it had really been you in her shop, I remembered you told us you didn't drink. And I thought to myself, why would someone who didn't drink want to buy vodka?"

"Maybe I just fell off the wagon," Tanya said. She glared at Kari. "Did you ever think of that, Miss Busybody?"

"I was there when you showed the sheriff your ten-year chip, remember?" Kari said gently. "I saw how proud you were of your accomplishment. No, I think you bought the vodka so you could use it to make a tincture. Like the one the sheriff found in my henhouse."

Clark's eyes widened, but when he started to say something, the sheriff held up one hand for him to wait.

"So you're saying that Ms. Baldwin here made the poison, not you, is that it?" the sheriff said. "If that's the case, where did she get the mushrooms? She's not from around here. Are you suggesting that she brought them with her from home? Because that would imply she came here intending to kill Mr. Smith."

Kari shook her head. "Not at all. In fact, I'm fairly certain that when Tanya got to town, she still thought everything between her and Charlie was fine. She was just worried about him seeing me and possibly rekindling an old flame. Something happened to change that, although I'm not sure what."

Tanya looked at the floor, but didn't say anything, so

Kari just plowed ahead with the story she'd put together from the facts she'd already known, but which hadn't added up to anything that made sense until Nancy mentioned the unlikely vodka purchase. When they'd gotten back to Kari's house, she and Suz had gone over everything, plus the new information from Nancy, and suddenly all the puzzle pieces had fallen into place.

Well, almost all of them. Kari still wasn't sure what the motive was, but she had a suspicion.

"No, I think finding the mushrooms was an accident. Tanya took Angus's nature walk on Saturday morning, and she must have seen one in the woods and recognized it for a destroying angel. Angus didn't spot it—he told me that when he did, he always pointed them out to educate people on the dangers of poisonous mushrooms that can mimic harmless ones, and when I checked with him, he hadn't seen one on this particular walk. But I'm guessing Tanya somehow knew enough to identify it, and managed to pick it without anyone noticing."

"Hmm," the sheriff said. "That's a lot of maybes. I don't know a lot about tinctures, but don't they take some time for whatever is in them to be absorbed by the alcohol? Ms. Baxter was with your friend the vet from ten a.m. until they finished lunch at three. Then she was at the Oktoberfest festivities about two hours later. I'm afraid your timeline just doesn't work."

"It does, actually," Kari said. "As soon as you realize they weren't actually together for that entire stretch of time, even though Tanya made it sound as though they were." Next to her, Queenie made a noise that sounded like disapproval. Or possibly a hairball.

"I called Angus right before Tanya got here, and he said that the nature walk ended at around eleven, and they didn't meet up for lunch until one. That gave her a two-hour window to stop by the liquor store and then put together her tincture before going back out again."

Kari pointed at a mason jar she'd left sitting out on the kitchen counter, in clear view of the living room. "On Tuesday, when I stopped by the bed-and-breakfast she's staying at, my friend Dora who owns it told me that Tanya had asked to use a jar like that one. She told Dora she liked to collect odds and ends from everyplace she visits to take home with her as a keepsake."

"There's nothing wrong with that," Tanya said in a defensive tone. "It's a perfectly harmless hobby." She turned to the sheriff. "Do I really have to sit here and listen to this fantasy story? Clearly Kari did it. You found the poison here on her property and she had plenty of motive. She's just making up a bunch of stuff to try and shift your attention to me, instead of her."

She looked at Kari, tears springing into her eyes. "I'm sorry I was dating your ex-husband, and that I went out to lunch with your boyfriend, but that's no reason to try and pin the murder you committed on me." She started to get up off the couch. "I don't have to sit here and listen to this nonsense."

Kari wasn't as impressed with the tears as she had been the last time they'd been together, since she was beginning to think Tanya was one of those people who could cry at the drop of a hat. But she wasn't so sure the sheriff wouldn't be swayed by them.

She should have known better.

"Please sit down, Ms. Baldwin," Richardson said with a hint of steel in his voice. "If it is all nonsense, I'm sure we'll be able to find the holes in Ms. Stuart's story and you'll be free to go. In the meanwhile, I'm curious to see where this is heading."

He looked back at Kari. "What does a mason jar have to do with anything? They're not exactly a murder weapon. I've got a dozen or so in my kitchen, although most of them are filled with my mother's homemade tomato sauce."

"When I got up to Tanya's room at the B and B, I saw a bunch of leaves and rocks on the top of her dresser. I didn't really pay much attention to them, other than to figure they were her collection of bits and pieces she'd picked up around town to take home with her," Kari said. She got up and fetched the pint jar from the counter and plop it down on the low table between the couch and the chairs, where Tanya would be forced to look at it.

"But here's the thing that occurred to me earlier this afternoon, when I was starting to put it all together." Kari pointed at the jar. "Tanya was packing to go home when I got there. Almost everything was already in her suitcase. Yet the stones and leaves were piled on the dresser, instead of being in the jar she borrowed specifically to put them in. If her mementos were there, where was the empty jar?"

"Maybe she changed her mind about dragging all that crap home and simply gave the jar back to her landlady," Clark suggested. "The simplest explanation is usually the right one. Isn't that what you taught me, Sheriff?"

Richardson nodded. "Occam's razor. They teach us that in the police academy, believe it or not. It's a reminder not to get caught up with complicated and convoluted answers to a problem, when usually the correct solution is the obvious one right in front of you."

"See, I told you—" Tanya started to say.

"Still, there are exceptions to every rule," the sheriff went on. "So what is it you think happened to this missing mason jar, Ms. Stuart?"

"With apologies to Occam," Kari said, "I think Tanya used it to mix the bottle of alcohol she bought at Nancy's liquor store with the destroying mushroom from the nature walk. The glass jar would have been perfect for that, and she could have set it someplace out of the way—under the bed, or in the closet, for instance—before she went out to lunch with Angus. Once she got back, she would probably have left it until the last minute to ensure it was as strong as possible, and then put the resulting tincture into a more portable container."

Kari stared at Tanya, daring the other woman to look away. "It would be easy enough to put into some kind of small bottle that would fit into a purse or even a pocket, with no one the wiser."

"You were at the table with us at Oktoberfest, although you didn't stay for long," Suz said. "We figure that was when you did it."

Tanya pressed her lips together until they turned white. "Well since you were all there," she said, "surely one of you would have spotted it if I added something to Charlie's beer."

"We thought about that," Suz said. "There was that one moment when you turned your back on the table. You had a sample glass of the pumpkin spiced stout in one hand, which you said you only accepted to be polite and then put down on the table next to Charlie's own sample when you turned back around. I think that while you had your back turned, you slipped the poison into the cup, knowing that the strong, slightly odd flavor of the bitter stout would cover up the taste."

"I also think that because you and Charlie had been going out for a few months, you knew about Charlie's fondness for strong dark beers and could be pretty sure he'd drink the second sample, given the chance." Kari said, then made a face. "You couldn't know that Charlie would be a jerk and grab one of the extra spicy jalapeño poppers I'd gotten for Angus, and drink both beers so fast, he couldn't have tasted them anyway. You just got lucky there."

"Even if he'd noticed a slightly odd taste, he would have blamed the fact that he'd practically burned his tongue off," Suz said. "As soon as you'd given him the poison, you made excuses to leave. Was it so you didn't have to stand next to him, knowing he was already dying from the toxic mixture you'd slipped him? I could see how that would be pretty upsetting."

"Yes," Kari agreed. "You're not exactly the cold-blooded killer type. I think you just felt as though you'd been backed into a corner and you had no other choice." She sighed. "Charlie had a way of doing that to people. It was practically his superpower."

"This is quite the fairy tale you've come up with," Tanya said. She suddenly seemed strangely calm. "But I don't see any proof, except the bottle that was found in *your* henhouse. There is absolutely nothing to connect that to me."

"Ah," Kari said. "That's where you're wrong."

"This ought to be good," Richardson said under his breath.

"You see," Kari went on, ignoring him, "I didn't get

a really good look at the bottle when the deputy here brought it out of the henhouse. To be honest, I was so shocked they'd found something there, I was barely paying attention."

She shook her head ruefully. "I knew I hadn't put anything in there, so I was completely taken aback when the deputy actually found something."

"Not to mention that it never occurred to her that the real murderer might try to set her up to take the fall," Suz said, narrowing her eyes at Tanya. "Kari is too nice, and always gives everyone the benefit of the doubt." Queenie hissed in agreement and Kari shushed her.

"When I thought about it later, though," Kari went on, "it occurred to me that I had seen containers about that same size and shape somewhere not that long ago. Then I remembered that when I visited you at the bed-and-breakfast, I'd admired the cute little bottles of lotion and such that Dora put out for her guests. They were such a charming touch."

"Are you saying you believe that the bottle we found in your henhouse containing the poison tincture came from Dora Hudson's bed-and-breakfast?" Richardson asked. "You're not suggesting that Dora was somehow involved, are you?"

"Heavens no," Kari said, startled by the suggestion. "I'm suggesting it was one of the ones from Tanya's own room. It would have been easy enough to clean it out well enough that there was no lingering flavor from whatever had been inside it, and if someone had happened to notice it the night of Oktoberfest, she could have just said she'd stuck it in her purse in case her hands got dry."

"Then later, she could have soaked Mrs. Hudson's

handmade label off before planting it on Kari's property and making an anonymous call to the police to send them here to look for it," Suz said. "At that point it would have looked like any other tiny bottle, with nothing to tie it to Tanya." She looked at the sheriff. "I assume you didn't find any fingerprints on it?"

Richardson flipped open his notepad, although as usual, Kari thought he was doing it more for effect than because he couldn't remember a basic fact about the case.

"No, the bottle had been wiped clean," he said. "The lab couldn't even find a partial."

Kari tilted her head. "Did it ever occur to you to wonder why I would have wiped my prints off if I was supposedly hiding it under a bunch of chickens where I thought no one would ever find it? That doesn't make much sense."

"Not much about this case ever has," Richardson said in an aggravated tone. "And I've yet to decide if this conversation is making things better or worse."

"Maybe I can help you out with that," Kari said. She picked up the handset for the house's landline phone, which she had left on the table between them, and hit redial. She put it on speaker just in time for everyone sitting there to hear Dora Hudson's cheerful voice say, "Lakeshore Haven Bed and Breakfast, Dora Hudson proprietor speaking. How may I assist you on this beautiful day?"

Suz rolled her eyes. She didn't do perky.

"Hi Dora," Kari said. "This is Kari Stuart again. I've got the sheriff here with me and I wondered if you would be willing to share with him what you told me when I talked to you earlier." She and Suz had called Dora as soon as Kari had remembered where she thought she'd seen the little containers.

Dora's tone lost a bit of its exuberance, but she agreed readily enough. Kari had warned her to expect a call or a visit from the sheriff.

"Can you hear me, sheriff?" Dora asked.

"Yes, just fine," he replied. "You're on speaker. I gather that Ms. Stuart called you earlier to ask you about the bottles from Ms. Baldwin's room? What exactly did she ask you?"

"There were two things, actually," Dora said. "First she wanted me to check the room that nice Tanya is staying in, to see if any of the little sundry bottles were missing. You see, I like to make all my guests feel pampered and well taken care of, so I have a special assortment of indulgent goodies in every bathroom."

Her voice took on a dreamy quality as she waxed rhapsodically on about the varieties of complementary shampoos and conditioners and lotions she stocked. "There's even my own special blend of essential oils for relaxation. You add a few drops to your bathwater and the cares just melt away," Dora said. "But they're not all for women, sheriff. I have a nice unscented body wash that is suitable for those with sensitive skin, or for men who don't like the flowery smell of most of the other items. Keep that in mind in case you want a little getaway sometime."

"I live here," the sheriff muttered. "It would hardly be much of a getaway." In a louder voice he said, "And what did you find when you checked?" he asked the landlady.

"Oh, well, there was one bottle missing," Dora said reluctantly. "But I didn't think much of it. I mean, people take them all the time when they check out. That's why I use such small containers. Or maybe she'd used it all up, and just hadn't gotten around to asking me for another one yet."

"That certainly sounds like a possibility," Richardson said, giving Kari a narrow-eyed and dubious look. "Hardly proof of malfeasance."

Kari held up one finger in a "wait for it" sign. "Can you tell the sheriff about the other thing you found, Dora?"

This time when she spoke, Dora's voice sounded resigned, as if she knew she was the bearer of bad news and wished she could have given the job to someone else. Kari knew exactly how she felt.

"When Kari asked me to check on the bottle, she also asked me to look and see if there was any sign of that mason jar I'd given to Tanya for her keepsake collection. The leaves and rocks were all in the wastebasket in her room, but there was no sign of the container. I finally found it, smashed into tiny pieces, inside a brown paper bag at the bottom of the garbage can outside."

She sighed. "I wouldn't even have looked there if Kari hadn't suggested it, and even if I'd seen the ruined jar, I would have just assumed that Tanya had broken it by mistake and was too embarrassed to tell me and ask for a replacement. But it was a bit odd that she'd gone to the trouble of moving the bags of garbage already inside the can and putting it underneath them. Trash day is tomorrow, and if Kari hadn't asked me to look today, it would have all been gone."

"Is that so?" Richardson said, gazing resolutely in Tanya's direction. "That *is* interesting. I'm going to have to ask you to leave the entire contents of the can alone for now, including the bag with the broken glass you found. I'll have a deputy swing by to collect it all, and take your fingerprints, strictly for elimination purposes."

"Oh, dear," Dora said. "I hope I haven't gotten that poor woman in trouble."

"It's okay, Dora," Kari said softly. "She'd already created the trouble herself. You just helped us to prove it."

Twenty

After Kari hung up the phone, there was silence for a moment. Then Tanya seemed to collapse in on herself, as if only sheer force of will had been keeping her upright until this point. One tear slid down her face, but otherwise she seemed calm enough.

"Are we going to find traces of destroying angel mushroom in that jar, along with your fingerprints, Ms. Baldwin?" Sheriff Richardson asked in an even tone.

Tanya wiped her face and nodded. She clearly knew that there was no chance of keeping her secret once Dora had found the broken pieces in the garbage.

"Yes," she said, sounding resigned and maybe even a little relieved. "Kari was right. About all of it."

She gazed at Kari and shook her head. "Pretty *and* smart. Charlie definitely didn't deserve you. And you didn't deserve to be framed for a murder you didn't commit. I'm sorry. It was nothing personal."

Suz lifted one eyebrow. "Not even a little bit personal? Maybe because it seemed like Charlie was a bit too interested in his former wife?"

There might have been a glint in Tanya's eyes that belied her otherwise meek demeanor. "Well, maybe. But really, it didn't matter once Charlie was dead, did it? Neither of us was going to have him."

"I didn't want him," Kari said, trying not to sound exasperated at having to repeat the obvious for the twentieth time. "I left him four years ago and never looked back. I would have been blissfully happy never to have seen him again, and that was without him trying to take my money and close down the shelter. I sure as heck hope you didn't kill him out of jealousy for me, because I was never, ever, *ever* going to take him back."

Tanya shook her head, her too-brassy blond hair tangling with the clunky earrings she was wearing. "I admit, that was what brought me here, but it wasn't why I killed him." She sighed. "If only he hadn't found out you'd won the lottery and decided that convincing you to give him half your winnings would solve all his problems."

"Why don't you start at the beginning?" Richardson said. "When you followed Mr. Smith to Lakeview."

Tanya looked at him as if he wasn't very bright. "Oh, that wasn't the beginning. It really started when I met Charlie. He came into the office where I worked and he was so handsome and so kind. I thought that he was my chance to have the life I wanted, with a man who would love both me and my son, and I'd finally be able to stop worrying about how to pay the bills every month. He was a little uncomfortable around Petey, but I was sure that would change over time."

"Charlie wasn't really all that big on kids," Kari said. "I'm sure it was nothing to do with Petey's condition."

Tanya shrugged. "He told me he wanted to spend time just the two of us, so we could get to know each other better. I'd never been with a man like him; he was so charming, and I believed he really loved me."

"I feel like I'm missing something," Deputy Clark complained. "If he didn't love you, why did he go to so much trouble to date you?" He didn't come right out and say that Charlie could have done better, but it was implied.

"I work in the county clerk's office," Tanya said, as if that explained everything.

And maybe it did, Kari thought, as the other shoe dropped.

"Wait," she said. "You mean the county clerk's office where our divorce paperwork was supposed to be filed?" Kari asked. "The one where the woman who normally deals with those files is on vacation?" She pointed at Tanya. "*You* are the missing clerk?"

Tanya nodded miserably. "I've always followed the rules. Never even so much as parked in a no-parking zone. But after we dated for a couple of months, Charlie said he just wanted me to do this one little thing and then we could be together forever. We'd have all the money we needed for us, and for Petey's future. All I had to do was get rid of all the proof that his divorce to Kari had been finalized."

"You have got to be kidding," Suz said, her eyes wide. "So they really weren't still married? That was just a lie?"

"It was," Tanya said, wringing her hands together in

her lap. "Apparently he'd had Kari's copy of their finalized divorce paperwork all along. She'd goofed up and
put their mailing address as the place to send it, instead
of wherever she was living at the time. He'd hung onto
it all those years in case it came in handy for something.
When he found out about the lottery win, it gave him the
idea to pretend the divorce had never been completed.

"After that it was easy," she went on. "Once he'd convinced me to help him, there was only one set of paper
files to shred, and a couple of documents erased off the
computer, and poof, all the proof of their divorce was
gone. Charlie could go after Kari's lottery winnings. For
us, he said."

"So we really were divorced," Kari said. "That's a
relief." It was nice to know she hadn't messed up after all.

Tanya shrugged. "Not that there is any evidence of it
anymore. As far as all the records show, you really were
still married at the time of Charlie's death. Once I de-
stroyed that paper trail, it was gone for good."

Kari tried to wrap her head around this new development. Clearly, the sheriff didn't seem to find it as important
as she did.

"So Mr. Smith persuaded you to clear the way for
him to come here and try to con Ms. Stuart into believing he was entitled to half her winnings?" he said.

"He said he'd convince her that he'd make her life a
living hell if she didn't give it to him," Tanya agreed.
"That should probably have been my first clue that he
wasn't the sweet man I thought he was."

Ya think?

Kari resisted the urge to wring the woman's neck.
For one thing, it wouldn't help now. For another, it prob-

ably wasn't a good idea with the sheriff and his deputy sitting right there. But man, it was tempting.

"When did you begin to suspect Mr. Smith had been using you?" the sheriff asked.

Tanya let out a laugh with a bitter undertone. "Oh, I was pretty slow on the uptake," she said. "He told me all about how his investments had suffered from the downturn in the market, but he assured me he was onto a good thing, and if he could just get the money for this one big deal, he could build the three of us a new life. Get the best doctors for Petey, move us into his beautiful big house in the suburbs. It sounded like a dream come true."

"All you had to do was help him steal money from his ex-wife," Suz said sourly. "That's some dream."

Tanya gazed at them earnestly. "You have to understand. I hadn't met Kari then. Charlie said his ex had won so much money, she wouldn't even miss the half he'd take, and that once he'd tripled or even quadrupled it, he'd give it back to her with interest."

"And you believed him?" Kari said. Charlie was a smooth talker, and he gravitated to gullible women, but even for him this sounded like a reach.

"He was very convincing," Tanya said. She hung her head. "I suppose I wanted to believe him, so I could justify my actions. You have to understand, things have been so hard since Petey was diagnosed. It felt as though I was drowning, and Charlie threw me a lifeline."

They all sat with that in silence for a moment.

"Yet you ended up following him here," the sheriff said. "Surely if you still thought he was telling you the truth, you would have just stayed home and waited for him to return with the money."

"That was the plan," Tanya said. "Then I went to his house to water his plants and I found a file on his desk. It was tucked under the blotter, but I noticed it because one edge was sticking out.

"It had a newspaper clipping with an article about Kari's lottery win. Just a small one. I guess it wasn't very big news, but some friend who vacationed in Lakeview happened to come across it," she went on. "The clipping wasn't a surprise, but there was also a piece of paper with Kari's signature written on it a bunch of times, and a stack of photos of her."

"You mean old pictures, like from when we were married?" Kari asked. She'd left all hers behind when she moved out, not wanting to drag the memories with her.

"Some of those," Tanya said. "A couple from your wedding, and a few from what might have been your honeymoon." She sighed. "You looked so happy, and it bothered me a little that Charlie had kept them.

"But then there were a few recent ones. I think maybe he hired someone, possibly a private investigator, to check up on you. I hadn't realized how pretty you were now. Suddenly I got worried. What if Charlie had plans he hadn't told me about? After all, supposedly you two were still married. I panicked, and decided to follow him to Lakeview."

She clasped her hands even more tightly together. "I hardly ever take any time off, because I don't like to leave Petey, so I had a ton of vacation time owed me. I told my boss I desperately needed a break, and told my parents the same thing. They were happy to watch Petey for me. So I came here."

"That's why you showed up at the sanctuary that first

day!" Kari said, the other shoe dropping. "You were checking me out."

Tanya looked at the floor. "I was, yes. I thought maybe I'd overreacted, and when I saw you in person I would find out you weren't that pretty, or that you were as horrible a person as Charlie said you were."

Suz snorted. "Yeah, so classy to talk down the previous woman to the current one. I remember when I first met Charlie after he and Kari started going out. I had a bad feeling about him from the get-go, but then he started talking about how nasty and selfish his first wife was, and I knew he was bad news."

"If only I'd listened to you," Kari said.

"This has been a lovely trip down memory lane," the sheriff said, tapping his pen on his notebook. "But if you don't mind, I'd like to get back to Ms. Baldwin's story. I believe she was just going to explain her motive for theoretically killing Mr. Smith?" He sounded like he still wasn't completely convinced that Tanya had done it, despite the evidence Kari had dug up and Tanya's halfhearted confession.

"I'll bet Charlie wasn't thrilled to discover you'd followed him here," Kari guessed. "Or that you were spying on me."

"Not thrilled would be putting it mildly," Tanya said in a wry tone. "He was furious. I'd never seen him like that before. He never even raised his voice, but the look on his face . . . I honestly thought he might strike me. But then he calmed down and reverted back to his regular charming self. He even apologized for losing his temper."

She shook her head. "I thought it was just the strain of dealing with Kari, and trying to get this deal off the ground. He almost convinced me I'd imagined the whole thing. I promised him I would leave the next day, and everything seemed fine."

"But you didn't leave," Deputy Clark said, stating the obvious.

"Why not?" Kari asked. She had kind of wondered why Tanya had stuck around as long as she did.

"That first confrontation was on Thursday," Tanya said. "I really was going to go home on Friday after lunch, but after I followed you to the diner, I saw Charlie show up and get into that fight over you. When I heard him tell the man you were with that the two of you were back together again, I freaked out, and asked Mrs. Hudson if I could have the room for another couple of days. Then I called Charlie and asked him to come talk to me there early Saturday morning."

"Uh-oh," Kari said. She knew from years of experience how well Charlie dealt with being thwarted. It was a little bit like waving a red flag in front of a bull. And you were just as likely to get gored.

"Yeah," Tanya agreed. "At first he tried to sweet talk me. Swore up and down that it was all an act for your benefit, to persuade you to sign everything over to him. Told me he was just trying to get Angus to go away and give him a clear playing field." She blew her breath out in a huff. "Then he explained that he'd changed his plans a smidge, once he realized that you were more attached to the shelter than he'd expected you to be."

"He never really did have a clue about what was important to me," Kari said. "Probably because our marriage always revolved around what was important to him."

"What was the change in plans?" Richardson asked. Clearly he'd figured out this was the crux of the issue.

"Oh, nothing much," Tanya said bitterly. "Just that he was going to stick with the fake marriage for a bit. Six months. Maybe a year. Long enough to get his hands on even more of Kari's money to invest in this glamping plan he'd cooked up with some business associate, and make sure the project was bringing in the windfall he was sure it would generate."

She laughed, but there was no humor in it. "He wanted me to go home and wait. Sit tight, he said. He'd be back to me in no time. A year, two at the most. Everything with Kari would be an act, because it was me he really loved. I just had to be patient."

"I take it you weren't enthusiastic about this new plan," the sheriff said in a dry tone. "My former wife didn't like waiting for me to mow the lawn. I expect you thought waiting for him to spend a year or two with another woman was a bit much to ask."

Tanya curled her lip. "A bit. I told him there was no way I was going to go along with that. I said I'd wait around another few days until he got her to sign over the property like he'd originally said, but I wasn't leaving without him. Worse came to worse, we could go home together and he could keep working on her from there by phone and email. I'd done everything he'd asked, risked everything for him. I told him I loved him, and wanted us to be together the way he'd promised. Him, and me, and Petey."

"And what did he say?" Richardson asked.

"He laughed at me," Tanya said, swiping angrily at her eyes. "He told me that there was no way he was going to saddle himself with an unattractive, boring woman and her sick kid when he could have Kari and her millions. He hadn't planned to dump me until his plan had been completed, but once he'd seen Kari again and decided he could have all the money instead of just half if he wooed her back, I was only going to be in the way."

Kari winced. She was beginning to understand why Tanya had decided to frame her, and frankly, kind of sympathized with the woman's desire to kill Charlie. Not enough to go to jail for her, but still.

Tanya took a deep breath. "I was so heartbroken. I threatened to tell Kari, and ruin all his plans."

"That must have gone over well," Kari said.

"Not exactly," Tanya said. "Charlie just smiled at me and said that Kari would never believe me over him. He'd tell her I was a crazy woman who he'd met at the county clerk's office when he went in to look for the divorce paperwork. That I'd developed a delusional obsession and started stalking him." She gazed at Kari sadly. "I knew how convincing he could be. And look at me, compared to him. The story makes more sense than him actually picking someone like me to go out with, if you don't know what his actual motive was."

"I think you're being too hard on yourself," Kari said. "I was actually jealous of *you* when I found out Angus had been out to lunch with you."

"Really?" Tanya looked amazed. Then her face fell. "It's too bad we never compared notes. It might have made this story end a lot differently."

"So you're saying you killed him because you found out he'd used you?" Richardson said, sounding skeptical. "I mean, obviously, that was a lousy thing to do, and it must have come as quite a shock to you to discover that the man you loved had fooled you all along. But that kind of thing happens to women—and men—all the time, and most people don't murder over it."

Tanya's eyes opened wide. "Oh, no, that wasn't it. That part was horrible, but if he'd stopped there, I probably would have gone home and cried into my pillow for a few weeks, cursed his name, and then moved on. But he was so very angry at me for saying I might try to wreck his plans, he told me he was going to teach me a lesson."

Kari's stomach knotted. She'd heard him use that phrase more than once. It usually preceded his most cruel retaliation for whatever he'd perceived as crossing the line.

Tanya went on, as if she couldn't stop now that she'd gotten to this part of the story. "He said he was going to tell my bosses about me destroying paperwork," she said in a quiet voice, barely above a whisper.

"He was going to make sure I lost my job. I would have had a really hard time getting another one without a recommendation and with that kind of black mark on my record. But even worse, I would have lost the health insurance that came with the county job. Petey's quality of life depends on it. We wouldn't have been able to afford his physical therapy, or occupational therapy, the special wheelchair he needs, or his medications." She suddenly looked surprisingly fierce. "It would have been bad enough for me, but it would have been a disaster for my son. I couldn't let that happen."

It was ironic, Kari thought. Tanya's fatal error had been in not understanding the power of the small-town grapevine. But Charlie's had been in underestimating the power of a mother's love for her child. He might not even have intended to follow through with his threat, since exposing her crime could have jeopardized his own plan to insist that he and Kari were still married. But there was no way Tanya could have taken that chance, and he was, as she'd said, very convincing.

"After he left, I needed to clear my mind, and I remembered one of the pamphlets Mrs. Hudson left in my room. I thought the nature walk might help me to calm down while I tried to figure out what to do. It did, too, at least a little, and Angus was so nice." She gave Kari a crooked smile. "I knew from the scene at the diner with Charlie that you two were dating. I promise I wasn't trying to steal another man from you when we went to lunch. He was just being friendly, and I was feeling so alone."

Kari didn't bother to tell the woman that Angus had also been spying on her to try and find out what she was up to. It didn't matter now anyway.

"Ah, the nature walk," Richardson said. "I wondered if that would come into this tale somewhere."

Tanya's glance strayed to the empty mason jar on the table in front of them. "Kari was right about that, too. I was desperately trying to figure out what to do. Could I go to my boss first and tell her I'd been conned, and I'd never make the same mistake again? Should I quit before they could fire me, and hope that if Charlie did rat me out, they wouldn't pursue the matter? But then I'd still have to try and find another job with such good health insurance, and I knew from experience that was nearly impossible."

"Then I spotted it. The destroying angel mushroom." Her expression lightened. "I knew in that moment what

I had to do. I would never be safe as long as Charlie was still alive. My son would never be safe.

"My dad is addicted to nature shows, and I recognized the mushroom from an episode of one of his favorites that we'd watched together, called 'Nature's Deadliest Killers.' I pretended I had a pebble in my shoe and let the others go on ahead. Then I used a tissue to pop the mushroom out of the ground and into my purse." She sighed. "Everything else happened pretty much the way Kari said. I made the tincture and slipped it into the beer at Oktoberfest. I knew Charlie loved that kind of thing and he'd drink it before anyone else could. So I walked away and didn't look back."

That was cold. But Kari couldn't really blame her. Not for that, anyway. "Why frame me?" she asked. "I know you thought Charlie was going to get back together with me, but surely by then you didn't still want him, once you'd figured out how cruel he could be."

"Honestly, I thought the police would be certain you were the killer," Tanya said. "You had the most motive, after all, plus you were supposedly married to him. Everyone knows it is almost always the spouse."

Clark nodded. "That's what I said."

Tanya ignored him. "Without any proof, you probably wouldn't have gone to jail, which was okay with me. But you couldn't leave it alone. You kept poking your nose into everything, trying to figure out who had really killed Charlie. Once you'd told the sheriff who I was, and made me go in and talk to him, I knew I would have to make sure they looked somewhere else. Since you were already the prime suspect, and since it was becoming clear you'd never stop unless something happened to stop you, I planted the poison in your henhouse and then made an anonymous call to the sheriff's department."

She sighed. "I thought I'd be home free once you were in jail. I guess I should have known better."

"You really should have," Richardson said, standing up. "Ms. Stuart seems to have a knack for getting to the bottom of murders." He shook his head. "Although she also seems to have a knack for getting involved in them, which is probably less helpful." He gave Kari a meaningful look. "This had better be the last time."

He reached out one long arm and grasped Tanya by the elbow. "I'm afraid you're going to have to come with us, Ms. Baldwin. You're under arrest for the death of Charlie Smith. You have the right to remain silent, although it's a little late for that." He read her rights off a card he pulled from his pocket, and put out one hand for the cuffs Deputy Clark was still holding on to.

"Wait," Kari said. "What about my divorce paperwork?" she asked Tanya.

"I told you," Tanya said with a sigh. "It's long gone. I got rid of it all, just like Charlie asked me to. In the eyes of the law, you were still married."

"But—" Kari said.

"Look on the bright side," Richardson said, walking Tanya toward the doorway. "Now you're a widow instead of a divorcee. Not to mention that you should be able to use the multiple signatures on the paper Ms. Baldwin found to prove to James Torrance that your husband, ex or otherwise, forged your signature on the documents he has." He tipped his hat at Kari. "Plus, you're not going to jail. I suggest you count your blessings."

🐈 Twenty-One

After the sheriff and Deputy Clark left, with Tanya in the back seat behind the bars, Suz and Kari headed over to the shelter to update everyone, Queenie trotting along behind them as usual.

"Oh thank goodness!" Sara said as they came through the front door. She had her cell phone in one hand and the turquoise stripe in her hair was practically standing on end, as if she been pulling on it with the other. "We saw the sheriff drive away with someone in the back and we were sure he had arrested you. I was just calling my lawyer friend to come to the rescue."

Kari slid onto one of the stools behind the front desk, grateful for once that there was no one in the sanctuary looking for a new pet. "Maybe you should finish making that call anyway. I did leave him a message earlier, but Tanya just confessed to murdering Charlie, so I think she's going to need a lawyer more than I will." She thought about it for a minute. "Although there may be some complicated estate issues, since it looks as though I'm actually going to inherit whatever Charlie had left."

Sara's mouth opened and closed without a word coming out—it was one of the few times Kari had actually seen the older woman speechless. And that included the day when Tommy Whitaker had duct taped Karl Furman to the wall of the English classroom in ninth grade when they were reading Poe's "The Cask of Amontillado." "I, what? Wait, *Tanya* confessed?" Sara sat down on the other stool. "I'm confused."

"I'm getting coffee," Bryn said in a firm tone. "Nobody say another word until I get back."

Suz glanced at her watch and said, "I've got about fifteen minutes before I have to leave for my next appointment. I'll help you." The two disappeared into the kitchenette off the main room and returned not too much later, bearing three mugs of coffee and one of tea (for Sara), plus a plate of donuts. Bryn grabbed Kari's desk chair and wheeled it over, the kitten going along for the ride, and Suz hopped up to sit on the top of the counter, her long denim-clad legs dangling down.

Bryn plopped the kitten on the counter beside Suz, sat down, and said, "Ouch," pulled the bottle opener from the brewery out from under her backside, placed it on the counter, and sat back down again.

"Okay," she said. "We're all here. Spill. What do you mean, Tanya said she killed Charlie? Did she really do it?"

"Oh yes," Kari said. "And then she planted the bottle of poison at my place so it would look as though I had done it."

Between them, Kari and Suz managed to relate the entire story to their friends. When they were done, Sara got a grim look on her face and called the lawyer as Kari had suggested, instructing him to head down to the jail as soon as he could.

"Why would you want to help that woman?" Bryn asked, somewhat plaintively. "She killed your ex-husband and framed you for the murder. I'd think you would be happy she was going to spend the rest of her life in prison."

Kari bit her lip, trying to think of the best way to explain where she was coming from. "The way I see it, Tanya was just another victim of Charlie's manipulative and selfish nature. He used her to get what he wanted, and was going to simply discard her when he was done. But when she threatened to get in the way of his plans, he set out to scare her as casually as he'd seduced her in the first place. The fact that he succeeded beyond his wildest dreams was his fault, not hers."

When Bryn started to sputter, Kari held up one hand. "Don't get me wrong. I'm not condoning murder as a solution. I wish Tanya had done something else, anything else. That she'd come to me. Or waited to see if he was bluffing. Anything else. Not to mention that I'm not thrilled she decided to try and pin the whole thing on me."

Kari took a long sip of coffee, suddenly feeling as if the day had already been about sixty hours long. "But she's going to pay for what she did, and I can't help feeling sorry for her. All she wanted was a better life for herself and her son. I know how that feels."

She reached out to pet Queenie, and the kitten licked her nose, then reached out one black paw and knocked the bottle opener onto the floor.

Kari started laughing. "You clever kitten!" she said.

"You were trying to give me a clue all along." When the others looked at her blankly, Kari held up the beer-shaped tool. "The murder took place at Oktoberfest. Although don't ask me how Queenie could know that."

Bryn said in a doubtful tone, "Maybe it is just a coincidence she's been playing with that thing for days."

"Sure it is," Suz said. "And my hair is naturally this color." She sighed and looked at her watch again. "I've got to get back to work. Maybe we can get together tonight and celebrate the fact that this nightmare is finally over and both Kari and the shelter are safe. How about we go out for a beer later?"

"NO!" everyone else shouted. Suz looked taken aback.

"I think I've lost my taste for the stuff," Kari said with a shudder. "How about wine and pizza at my house instead?" She glanced down at the kitten. "And cat treats, of course."

"That's a much better idea," Sara said. "Although I think I'll stick to the pizza."

As Kari gazed around her crowded living room that night, she felt extremely blessed. Not to mention that it felt as though she could take a deep breath for the first time since Charlie had knocked on her door a week ago.

Not only did she not have to worry about going to jail, but she suspected that on some level she had been looking over her shoulder ever since she left him, expecting him to show up and do something to try and ruin the life she'd built without him.

At least she'd never have to worry about that again.

Her eyes fell on Angus, who was sitting on the floor next to a happily panting Fred (who had already stolen a piece of pepperoni from the slice of pizza in the veterinarian's hand and was clearly hoping for another). Angus smiled back at her, the hint of a dimple winking in and out of existence at the corner of his mouth.

His red hair was shaggy and in need of a trim, and his rangy body was clad in jeans and a slightly ratty gray sweatshirt that said *"Trust me, I'm a dogtor,"* instead of a three-piece suit. She'd still rather have him by her side than Charlie any day. Not only was Angus a heck of a lot nicer, but even when she'd been feeling insecure about their relationship, he had never doubted her. She'd given him a big kiss to say thank you when he'd first arrived, and promised him a few more later. She was a very lucky woman.

Suz and Bryn shared the couch with the orange cats Robert and Westley, who had appeared as soon as they'd smelled pizza. The two women clearly didn't mind having to sit close together to make room for their feline companions, and Kari felt her heart contract at how happy her best friend looked. They'd both shown up in matching purple sweaters, although they swore they hadn't planned it, and the usually reserved Bryn was actually giggling at something Suz had just whispered into her ear.

Kari herself was on one of the brown chairs, her own slice of pizza on a plate on her lap and a nearly empty glass of white wine on the low wooden table in front of her. She was absolutely positively *not* feeding Queenie an illicit bit of cheese to reward her for her detective work.

Sara wandered over from the kitchen area where

she'd been fetching another serving and snagging the open bottle of wine. She poured some more into Kari's glass before sliding into the other chair and topping off her own.

"I really don't need this second slice," Sara said, patting her belly. Since she'd retired, she'd taken up yoga and tennis, and was probably in better shape than most women half her age, so Kari didn't take her too seriously. What was an extra ten pounds between friends?

"But it has been a rough week, so I'm going to indulge myself."

"Sounds like a good plan," Kari said, taking a sip of wine. "Don't tell anyone, but I made brownies for dessert. I thought we all deserved a treat. They're just from a box, but I threw in extra dark chocolate chips, so they should be worth eating anyway."

Sara raised an eyebrow. "They're chocolate, right? Have you ever known me to turn down chocolate?" She took a bite of pizza and chewed it, then added. "There is one thing I want from you besides brownies, though."

"What's that?" Kari asked.

The other woman gestured around the room. "Please let me take you shopping for a nice couch and loveseat for this room. If we're going to keep gathering here, you really have to get some better furniture. Look at poor Angus, stuck sitting on the floor."

"I like sitting on the floor," Angus said, hearing his name mentioned. "But I can bring my truck and help you haul whatever you find home." He waggled his slightly bushy eyebrows at Kari. "I wouldn't mind if you got a nice big-screen television for when we watch hockey," he added. "That thing you have now doesn't even deserve the name."

Kari blushed as everyone turned to stare at her battered old TV, which was so ancient it still had a VCR built into it. Angus might have a point. Between movie nights with the girls and her growing relationship with Angus, she really did need to upgrade the entire living room. And probably the kitchen as well.

"Okay, okay," she said. "How about next weekend? Anyone who is free can come with me to the furniture store in Perryville and help me pick out whatever you think we need."

Suz's hand shot up. "I'm in," she said. "And I also vote for a new popcorn maker and better kitchen chairs. Those folding things you're using now are like some kind of torture device."

Kari shook her head. "Hey, I've been a little busy. You know, improving the shelter, trying not to go to jail for murdering my ex-husband. Taking care of this poor helpless kitten." She held up Queenie, who did her best to look pitiful, without much success.

"That kitten is about as helpless as a samurai warrior," Suz said. "I think she helps you at least as much as you help her. But thanks for letting us finally get new comfy places to sit." She smiled to take the sting out of her words. "After all, it's not as though you can't afford it."

"That much is certainly true," Sara said, taking another drink and looking thoughtfully at Kari. "Especially now that it turns out that you'll be inheriting Charlie's money, too. It's a bit ironic that his own actions to destroy all the proof that the two of you were ever divorced meant that in the end, you were his legal heir."

"Really?" Bryn said. "Are you sure?"

"I called our old lawyer late this afternoon. Not the one we used for the divorce. Our old lawyer was more of a family attorney," Kari said. "He always had a soft spot for me, bless him. Anyway, Mr. LaPierre said that in New York State, if someone dies without a will, his or her surviving spouse inherits everything if there are no children. So yes, it looks like once everything goes through probate or whatever, it all comes to me. Not only that, Mr. LaPierre was able to tell me that despite his recent business losses, Charlie's house and retirement savings will still add up to a sizable sum. Probably over a million dollars, once all his debts are paid and the house is sold."

"Wow," Bryn said. "That *is* ironic. Do you know what you're going to do with the money when you finally get it? Are you going to spend it on the shelter?" She was, if anything, more dedicated to the Serenity Sanctuary than even Kari was, since Bryn had started volunteering there when she was still in high school, and had struggled through the lean years before Kari showed up to save the day with her lottery winnings.

"You could give it to Charlie's mother, I suppose," Sara said, making a face. She hadn't been around during the time Kari and Charlie had been married, but she'd heard about Charlie's mother in their discussions this week and knew that the two women had never really gotten along.

"I actually talked to her earlier too," Kari said. "I called her to tell her that the sheriff had arrested the person who had killed Charlie, since she'd begged me to help find out who did it."

"Was she grateful?" Sara asked. "After all, Tanya never would have been found out if it hadn't been for you."

"I don't know about grateful," Kari said. "She did say that now that the police were releasing Charlie's body she would be able to have a funeral that celebrated the great man that he was. And proposed, somewhat reluctantly, that it would be all right for me to attend, as long as, and I quote, 'You can find something presentable to wear for a change.'"

Angus's eyes widened in alarm. "Oh dear. What did you say?"

"I told her that I'd love to, but I was going to be busy that day," Kari said.

"And?" Angus asked.

"And she said, 'But I didn't tell you when it was being held,' and I said, 'I know,' and hung up the phone." Kari said, smothering a laugh behind one hand. "So I probably won't be getting an invitation after all."

"Well, I can't blame you for not wanting to go to his funeral after everything he put you though," Suz said, stoutly defending her friend as usual. "But what *are* you going to do with his money? Use it to buy furniture? Because I really don't want to wait that long to get a more comfortable couch in here. I'm pretty sure this one has a rogue spring that is trying to imbed itself into my thigh." She shifted around, probably trying to find a less problematic spot.

Kari took another sip of wine and shook her head. "No, the furniture can come from the money I already have. Without the threat of Charlie taking half, what I've got left from the lottery should be plenty for my needs, and anything the Sanctuary needs, too. Now that I've done the big improvements, fees and donations and grants should help us keep it running without too much more help from me, although I'm always willing to give it."

"As for Charlie's mother," Kari continued, "She is

already quite wealthy and doesn't need the money either."

She paused, putting the wineglass down with a decisive click. "I gave it a lot of thought after I talked to the lawyer, and I'm going to have him set up a trust for Tanya's son, so he will always be taken care of. It seems only fair, since it is Charlie's fault that Petey's mother will be going to jail."

Sara stared at her with respect. "That's brilliant, Kari. Generous and kind, and very appropriate, under the circumstances. And having it put in a trust for the boy means you won't have to deal with the legal issue of his mother not being allowed to profit from the murder."

And Suz leaned across the table to give her a high five. "Plus, Charlie would have absolutely *hated* it."

Kari grinned. "I know. That's just a bonus."

Then she absolutely positively totally did not give the kitten another piece of cheese. At least, not a very big one.

Acknowledgments

My real-life team may not include a six-foot-tall Amazon with lavender hair, but it does encompass some truly spectacular people. Huge thanks as always go to my wonderful agent, Elaine Spencer, who suggested I write this series in the first place, and to fabulous editor Jenn Snyder, who has been a joy to work with. Thanks too to the entire Berkley/Penguin gang, especially marketing goddess Natalie Sellars and publicity superstar Dache' Rogers, and to Anne Wertheim for another perfect cover. Switching from paranormal romance to cozy mysteries was a big change, and I couldn't have done it without the help and support of my first readers and cheering section, including my favorite mystery author, the brilliant and funny Donna Andrews; super reader and vacation buddy Karen Buys; and Judy Levine (also known as Mom). Thanks also go to my friend Ellen Dwyer for all the help with grooming info and general dog knowledge—you are definitely six feet tall in my eyes. And huge thanks to all the readers who reached out to tell me how much they liked the first book in this series. You kept me buoyed during a time when it was difficult to write, and let me know that maybe, just maybe, I was getting it right. Thank you for taking this journey with me.

Ready to find
your next great read?

Let us help.

Visit prh.com/nextread